PERFECT WEDDING

BOOK YOUR PLACE ON OUR WEBSITE AND MAKE THE ARABESQUE ROMANCE CONNECTION!

We've created a customized website just for our very special Arabesque readers, where you can get the inside scoop on everything that's going on with Arabesque romance novels.

When you come online, you'll have the exciting opportunity to:

- View covers of upcoming books

- Learn about our future publishing schedule (listed by publication month and author)

- Find out when your favorite authors will be visiting a city near you

- Search for and order backlist books

- Check out author bios and background information

- Send e-mail to your favorite authors

- Join us in weekly chats with authors, readers and other guests

- Get writing guidelines

- AND MUCH MORE!

Visit our website at
http://www.arabesquebooks.com

PERFECT WEDDING

ALICE WOOTSON

BET Publications, LLC
http://www.bet.com
http://www.arabesquebooks.com

ARABESQUE BOOKS are published by

BET Publications, LLC
c/o BET BOOKS
One BET Plaza
1900 W Place NE
Washington, DC 20018-1211

Copyright © 2005 by Alice Wootson

All rights reserved. No part of this book may be reproduced, stored in a retrieval system, or transmitted in any form or by any means without the prior written consent of the Publisher.

If you purchased this book without a cover, you should be aware that this book is stolen property. It was reported as "unsold and destroyed" to the Publisher and neither the Author nor the Publisher has received any payment for this "stripped book."

All Kensington Titles, Imprints, and Distributed Lines are available at special quantity discounts for bulk purchases for sales promotions, premiums, fund-raising, and educational or institutional use. Special book excerpts or customized printings can also be created to fit specific needs. For details, write or phone the office of the Kensington special sales manager: Kensington Publishing Corp., 850 Third Avenue, New York, NY 10022, attn: Special Sales Department, Phone: 1-800-221-2647.

BET Books is a trademark of Black Entertainment Television, Inc. ARABESQUE, the ARABESQUE logo, and the BET BOOKS logo are trademarks and registered trademarks.

First Printing: December 2005

10 9 8 7 6 5 4 3 2 1

Printed in the United States of America

Chapter 1

"That was so beautiful." Dana sighed as she stared at the final scene of the latest episode of a new reality show, *Perfect Wedding*. She leaned back and sighed again. "So perfect. So ideal."

On the television screen, the newlyweds were still pressed together in a kiss that promised happily ever after. As if that wasn't perfect enough, Hawaiian music, played sweetly on a steel guitar, swelled in the background. As wonderful as it was, the scenario failed to make Dana forget that she was living in Philadelphia trying to survive another hard, cold winter. She shivered as if Hawaii's warm climate made the Philadelphia temperature drop another fifteen degrees. Her usually vivid imagination was failing her right now. She stared at the television screen as if hoping to find her imagination hiding there.

The camera pulled back a bit and the credits rolled as if the words were overdue for an appointment. Still the couple remained lip-locked.

Dana sighed yet again. A wistful look filled her face.

"Just look at that. They get a beautiful wedding, dresses for the bride and the bridesmaids, all at no cost to them. Best of all, they get an all-expense-paid honeymoon in Hawaii. Two weeks in Hawaii. In the winter, no less, if that's when the winning couple wants to go. Who wouldn't want to go to Hawaii in the winter? Actually, who wouldn't want to go to Hawaii any time?" She pushed the Off button on the remote and turned to Cathy, her best friend. "Why can't I have that? What's wrong with me that I can't have that?"

"You *can* have that," Cathy said. "If you win the contest for the next 'perfect wedding.' " She stared at Dana. "Of course, there's the teensy matter of finding a husband-to-be. I'd say the lack of one is what's wrong with you. At least in this case. We'll deal with your other faults another time."

"The word is *fiancé*, not groom-to-be." Dana glared at her longtime best friend.

"Girlfriend, there's a huge distance between knowing what he's called and having one." Cathy dodged the throw pillow that Dana threw.

"Do you know that I have always wanted to go to Hawaii?"

"No." Cathy feigned surprise. "How could I possibly know that? Let's see, maybe it could be the fact that you have made me watch every single documentary and each and every movie ever made in the history of the movie industry that mentioned our fiftieth state? Or was I supposed to get a clue from the fact that every month or so you bring home a handful of brochures with pictures of pineapples, exotic flowers, and spectacular sunsets over perfect beaches? The last time, you even had a whole pineapple and an honest-to-goodness coconut still in the shell. Each time you start counting your change and checking your bank account. Is that how I should know?"

"Not just sarcasm, but caustic sarcasm. I don't know why I put up with you."

"Well, let's see." Cathy held up her hand and folded one finger down. "A, *I* put up with *you*. B, we've been friends since kindergarten. C, nobody else will understand your craziness. D, nobody else will listen to your lamebrained plans. And E—"

"Okay, okay." Dana held up her hands. "Don't *go teacher* on me. That was a rhetorical statement."

"I can't help but 'go teacher.' Not only is it in my blood, it's also the reason for my paycheck. Besides, I'm good at what I do. Ask my students." With a smug look on her face, Cathy set her nearly empty bowl of popcorn on the coffee table and crossed her arms across her chest.

"They're second graders. They don't know any better. Now, if you had sixth graders like I do, you'd have to prove yourself every period of every day as you try to get through their 'teach me' challenges." Dana ate one final handful of popcorn and placed her bowl beside Cathy's. She sighed. "You think maybe we can get second jobs?"

"What I think is that it takes all of my energy to get through the one job I already have. Those little kids wear me out. I'm sure the big ones do the same to you." Cathy stood. "Hey, look. I like Hawaii too, and I'd love to go there some day, but I'm not obsessing over it the way some people I know are."

"You talking about me?"

"If the shoes fit I hope they match one of my

outfits so I can borrow them." She grinned. "I'd better go. I have those math tests to grade. I want to see how good I am at what I do." She laughed as she took her bowl and glass to the kitchen and rinsed them. Dana followed her. She leaned against the counter and sighed.

"Cathy, when we were young, did you ever think that this would be it when we grew up? Usually in bed every weekday night, including Friday, right after the eleven o'clock news? Did you dream that your big excitement on the weekend would be staying up until after midnight to watch a movie on DVD?"

"Uh-uh." Cathy shook her head. "I expected my own version of Prince Charming to have found me by now, put that beautiful glass slipper on my foot, and carried me off to his castle where we'd live happily ever after. The problem is that there's never a prince around when you need one." She grinned and shook her head. "Ain't that just like a man anyway? He's probably somewhere watching some sports game on television and lost track of time." They walked toward the door.

"Mine must be hanging out with him." Dana put her hand on her hip. "I sure hope their game doesn't go into overtime. They're taking too long as it is." She laughed as she opened the door to let Cathy out. "See you in the morning. My turn to drive."

"Same time, same station as today."

Dana stared at the closed door for a few seconds after Cathy left. Then she turned the television back on to watch the news. She was staring at the screen, but she wasn't watching what was on. The

PERFECT WEDDING 9

image of downtown Philadelphia in January was on the news, but Dana was still seeing Hawaii in all its warm and beautiful tropical glory.

She pulled the knitted throw from the back of the sofa, wrapped it around her, and listened as the weatherman, Dave Roberts, warned of a cold front coming from the north. *Why does he have to be so cheerful about it?* she thought. *Maybe if we all go outside and push up really hard, we can make that weather stay up in Canada.* She sighed. *No matter what we do, nobody could mistake Philadelphia for Hawaii.* She turned off the television and went into the kitchen.

As she made her lunch for the next day, the thought of next week and the week after following the same routine as last week and the week before made her shake her head. She sighed and turned off the light.

"I'm too young to be set in my ways," she mumbled later as she looked through her closet for something to wear. *No matter which of my clothes I look at, it seems as if I just wore it yesterday.* She frowned as she rifled through the clothes, pausing at something a few times, then moving it aside. Then she started over again.

Finally she shook her head and took out a royal blue blouse and a navy blue skirt. She stared at them, then draped them over the chair in the corner as she always did the next day's clothes. She frowned at them. *It looks like a uniform,* she thought. She added a blue and white cardigan sweater to the outfit. She stared at the clothes for a few more seconds, then sat on the edge of the bed.

"I definitely don't want my future to look like

the past." She frowned. "To say my life is boring would be kind. A rut wouldn't describe this. Even a trench is too shallow."

As she got ready for bed, she replayed the conversation she had had with Cathy. They had kidded as they always did, but beneath the lightheartedness was an ache. The television show didn't have anything to do with the way she was feeling. She really wanted a special someone in her future. *And really, really soon.*

"All joking aside," she said aloud. "why shouldn't I have the American woman's dream? I'm a good person. I try to live right. I'm not mean to anybody. Why not me?"

She got ready for bed. By the time she slipped between the sheets, they had been warmed by her electric blanket. When she turned out the light, she still hadn't found an answer.

She sighed and rolled over into the empty space beside her, then rolled back far enough to turn the blanket up another notch.

Maybe this is just my biological clock ticking. She stared into the dark. *I hope it doesn't tick too softly for me to ignore it.*

She pulled the covers up, tucked them around her shoulders, and scrunched down farther. After a slight adjustment of the blankets, only her face was exposed to the cool air. She thought of Hawaii and found sleep.

"Morning, Sunshine," Cathy greeted Dana in the parking lot of their apartment complex early the next morning.

"Yeah. Sure. Whatever."

"My, aren't we chipper this morning?"

"I didn't sleep well."

"Too much popcorn?"

"Uh-uh." Dana shook her head. "Nothing as mundane as that. It was those handsome, bronze, substantial Hawaiian hunks who kept me busy in my dreams." She sighed as she slipped into the driver's seat and looked at the temperature gauge. She tapped it as if it were sleeping and she had to wake it up.

"O-k-a-y." Cathy dragged out the word as she turned to face Dana. "You didn't bring me one back, did you? I thought you knew how to share."

"If I could have, I would have. The guys chickened out and disappeared when I woke up."

"Just like a man. Toy with you, get what they want, then desert you." They laughed. "I'm thinking that maybe we need to cut you off from your Hawaiian habit," Cathy said as she fastened her seat belt.

"Are you kidding? That's the only fun I have." Dana shook her head. "That's so sad, isn't it? The only fun I have is when I'm dreaming." She frowned as she pulled into the street. "You know, if I had just studied harder in high school, maybe I would have had scholarships instead of loans to finance my college education. Then I could afford a vacation to Hawaii. At least two glorious weeks. Maybe three."

"Yeah. And if fate was kind, the men of our dreams would be on their way as we speak." Cathy shifted her purse on her lap.

"Yeah." Dana nodded. "That would most definitely work. Then I could afford Hawaii. Actually, I could handle going alone, if I could afford it. After all, you don't have to have a husband to visit paradise."

"Absolutely not." Cathy grinned. "You could find one over there. After all, brothers vacation alone, too. If nothing else, you could enjoy the male scenery."

"Yeah. Oh yeah. From the pictures I've seen, that view would be better than one of those perfect sunsets."

They rode the rest of the way to school in silence, but Dana's mind was busy trying to figure out a plan to get her to Hawaii.

Chapter 2

Dana dropped Cathy off at Harris Elementary School, then drove over to the middle school parking lot. She shoved the *Perfect Wedding* television show to the back of her mind, took her briefcase from the backseat, and went inside. The old teachers' saying, "another day, another fifty cents," came to mind and made her smile.

After greeting the secretaries and the other staff in the office, she took the papers from her memo box and went to her classroom. She didn't try to block the sigh that rose in her.

It seems as if I have been coming to this same room every school day a whole lot longer than five years.

"Snap out of it," she muttered. "Dana Dillard, this is your life. Deal with it." She set her briefcase on the desk.

"Talking to yourself again, huh?"

Dana looked up at her teaching partner, Steve Rollings, standing in the doorway.

"Hi, Steve." She smiled. "They used to say that

it's okay to talk to yourself as long as you don't answer. Now they say that answering is okay too. Don't you just love progress?"

"Whatever it takes, partner." He followed her into her classroom and sat on the edge of a student's desk. "How was your weekend?"

"Same old, same old."

"That's how it goes sometimes."

"Unfortunately, that's how it goes most of the time." She took a pile of papers from her briefcase and placed it in the middle of her desk. "How about you?" She leaned against the edge. "How was your weekend? Did you have a hot date?"

A frown disappeared from Steve's face almost as soon as it appeared. "A hot date with a basketball and two friends. We're getting ready for the Three-on-Three Tournament."

"Do you think it's fair to those unsuspecting opposing teams for you to play against them?"

"No rule says that a former college player is ineligible."

"Don't be so modest. Making the all-American team four out of four years lifts you out of the ordinary player slush pile."

"My bum knee kind of levels the basketball court." He stared out the window for a few seconds, then smiled at her. "Besides, it's for a good cause. Some kids will be awarded scholarships from the money we raise from sponsors. "Now," he said, as he pushed away from the desk, "to switch subjects. Can we get together at lunchtime? I want to run an idea by you."

"You mean eat together like always?"

"Like always. Today I have a reason."

"You mean I'm not reason enough?"

"Of course you are." Steve stared a few seconds longer. Then his face lightened. "It's just that today I have another reason."

"Okay. You're on. After all, it's not like I have a hot date or anything."

"Hot date?" He frowned and shook his head. "Not possible. Forty-five minutes wouldn't be enough time even for a lukewarm date." He stared at her. "At least not if you do it right." The buzzer sounded for the kids to leave their lockers just as Dana opened her mouth to comment. She laughed instead.

"Saved from responding by the bell," she said. "Okay, see you at—"

"Hey, Steve. I thought I'd find you here." A super-sugary voice from the doorway drew their attention away from the conversation. "I want to talk to you about something. Can we do lunch?"

"Hi, Simone." Steve's tone was serious. "I already have plans." He didn't say sorry.

"I guess *you're* the culprit." Simone glared at Dana. If looks could cause bodily harm, Dana would be a pile of bones and tissue with blood oozing over her floor.

"I do what I can to protect the unsuspecting," Dana said.

"Maybe tomorrow?" Simone's attention was back on Steve. Her smile at him would have made a thousand-watt lightbulb feel dim.

"Sorry," Dana said before Steve could answer. "We have plans for tomorrow, too." An impish gleam appeared in her eyes and she put her hand on Steve's arm. She didn't squeeze it though. *No sense in overkill,* she thought.

Simone glared at Dana again but changed her

expression to a slight grin for Steve. "I have something I think you might be interested in. Really interested in." Her grin, which was more like a smirk, took up her entire face. "I'll talk to you later then," she stared at him then swayed her hips out of the room.

"I'm trying hard not to. But I can imagine what it is that she's talking about that might interest you. Just the thought makes me shudder." Dana shook her shoulders delicately to prove her point.

"What have you got against her?"

"I don't trust her. Not one bit. Whenever I'm around her, my protective instincts roar to life."

"Female intuition, huh?"

"Self-preservation is more like it."

Steve laughed. "Anyway, I think it's so nice for colleagues to get along so well."

"What can I say?" Dana shrugged. "I try."

"You'd better do more than 'try' to watch your back. I don't think she likes you."

"I am so destroyed by that."

"Yeah. You look it, too. 'Your place or mine?' as they say."

"Huh?"

"For our lunch meeting. Stay with me here."

"Oh. I'll come to your room. Knowing you, you have a ton of papers to go with your idea and I wouldn't want you to hurt your dunking arm carrying them all the way here."

Steve shook his head and walked past the sixth graders plodding into Dana's classroom looking as if they would have to spend the rest of their lives in that room.

* * *

The morning passed as it usually did, with the kids groaning at the beginning of the English lesson as if they thought that was what was expected. Then they got involved in the discussion of a book whose setting was just outside Philadelphia. When the bell rang at the end of the period, their groans were because it was time to stop. Dana grinned.

"Hold those thoughts until tomorrow," she said as they gathered around her all talking at once, each trying to make a final point. She smiled as they went slowly to Steve's room next door for math, and his students filed into her room for English. The faces were different, but the attitudes were the same: "Go ahead. Teach me if you can. I dare you."

Dana dumped the grin, stood at the front, stared them into silence, then started the lesson.

For the third period, her own class came back for social studies. They showed a bit more enthusiasm when the discussion of current events began. As the discussion bounced from student to student, Dana longed for the day when the topic would be about dealing with social problems in the United States instead of the latest war somewhere else. Soon it was lunchtime. She grabbed her cup and lunch bag and went next door.

"Okay," she said after pouring water from the electric pot over her tea bag and taking a seat at the table in the back of the room. "What's the latest storm your brain has cooked up?"

"I'd like to field a team for the National Math Olympics for middle school students." He handed her an official-looking form. "The teams compete against other teams from all over the country. I want our city team to blow away, first the other city schools, and then the area suburban schools. Then

I want us to steamroll over other ritzy schools from other parts of the country. I want our kids to show them that brains and money are not glued together."

"You want to shock those poor rich folk?"

"I want us to shake them up so much that they will never look at us the same way again. I also want our kids to realize the same thing. A Philadelphia middle school did that with a chess team. Why can't we do it in math?"

"Yeah. Why not? Why can't we destroy the established mind-set?" She nodded. " 'More power to the people,' as the folks used to say in the sixties." She thrust a fist into the air.

"Right on, right on," Steve said. They stared at each other, then laughed.

"I assume there's a prize?" Dana said after they settled down.

"Oh yeah. You better believe it. The finalists get all-expense-paid trips to the finals in D.C. in May. The winning team gets five thousand dollars for the school to spend on math materials, including computers. Each student wins a five-thousand-dollar college scholarship."

"I can see the scholarships, but five thousand dollars for the school?" Her eyes opened wider and she glanced at the few computers to the side. "Do you know how many computers we can add? How much we can upgrade our equipment with five thousand dollars?"

"I've got the list all made out."

"Sure of ourselves, are we?"

"With the students I have in mind, yeah." He nodded.

"Who's on your list?"

"Kareem and Tamika from your room and Jose, Gary, and Fran from mine."

"Our brain trust." She nodded. "All of them are sure to get offers of full scholarships from more than one university when they graduate from high school. They won't have student loans to pay back to keep them from going to Hawaii."

"What?"

"Never mind." She shook her head. "What's your game plan?"

"I need to have them all in one class. With the help of Gloria, my student teacher, I think we can grab some time during class a couple of days a week. We'll also work during some lunchtimes and after school. After we get things started, they can work a lot on their own."

"Have you talked to them yet?"

"I wanted to run it by you first, since it means shuffling the classes a bit."

"You know I wouldn't say no."

"I know, but I had to talk to you first. Now that I have your approval, I'll go see Mr. Holloway, but I don't expect him to object. He's always supportive of things like this."

"That's true. That man loves his school. Besides, if the kids look good, the principal looks good."

"So true." He took a drink from his bottle of water. "Now that we have that settled, what was that thing about Hawaii?"

"Nothing, really." Dana took a bite of her sandwich.

"That's not how it sounded."

She ate another bite before she said anything else. "Do you watch that new reality show?"

"I would ask which one, but it doesn't matter. I

don't watch any of them. I get more than enough reality in real life and from the news. I don't need more from television. I don't want to get an inside look at private lives. Neither am I into watching people enduring all kinds of pain and discomfort and eating repulsive things for a bunch of money." Steve took a bite of his hoagie.

"It's always a huge bunch of money. What do you watch at night? Sitcoms?" She ate a bit of salad.

"No. When I watch television in the evenings, it's *Law and Order.*"

"Which one?"

"All of them." He looked sheepish.

"What was that you said about not needing reality on television?"

He shrugged. "I watch sci-fi, too."

"Trekkie, huh?"

"Way back to the original. I have them all on tape." He shook his head. "They don't make them like that anymore."

"True. Now let me see that info about the contest. I'm no math whiz, but there must be something I can do for the cause."

"There is. We have to write an essay to go with the application. We have to explain why we want this for our kids." He shrugged. "That won't be the deciding factor, though. I guess they just want to know something about us. Keep that copy," he said as she started to give the application back. "I made it for you."

"That sure of me, huh?"

"Covering the possibility." He grinned. "Besides, I know you have a softer spot for these kids than I do." His grin widened. "And I know that you can go into killer mode when it comes to competition."

"Not killer mode. Highly, extremely assertive mode." She smiled. "I can handle the essay." She chewed at her lip. "I have something I'm working on, too, but not for the kids." She gathered her lunch things.

"Back to Hawaii. You didn't think I forgot about that, did you?"

"No way. I know you could give lessons to pit bulls about perseverance." She frowned. "Forget the 'back' part. I'm wishing for a first trip."

"You know what I mean. What's up?" Steve tossed his trash away, then came back to her.

"Okay." She sat up straight. "Here goes." She took a deep breath. "There's this new reality show, see? They pick a couple, follow them through the whole wedding planning process." She stared at him. "That they pay for, I might add. Then they give them a perfect wedding and a glorious honeymoon to the place of their choice. And did I mention that the show pays for it all?"

"Yeah. I'm not sure there is such a thing as a perfect wedding. Do you know that half of all marriages end in divorce?"

"That leaves half that don't. I see the glass as still having something in it."

"Probably half of the other half should be dissolved."

"Wow. Where did that bitterness come from? Do you have an ex-wife somewhere?"

"Absolutely not. But I do know enough marriages and former marriages that fit into both categories. But we digress. Where does Hawaii come in?"

"The newlyweds go to Hawaii on their honeymoon." She sighed. "I've always wanted to go to Hawaii."

"I know." He patted her hand. "You will one day. Just be patient."

"I will be twenty-seven years old in July. I think I have been more than patient."

"Yes, ma'am. Have you figured out who to complain to about your situation?"

"You don't complain to The One in charge of time allotments." She sighed. "I feel as if life is parading by and I'm sitting on the sidelines watching." The bell rang and she stood to leave.

"The weather probably has something to do with how you feel. You know? What we used to call the doldrums and what scientists now call that seasonal depression or disorder thing?"

"Yeah. Maybe that's it." She stared at him. "But I doubt it." The second bell rang and she hurried from the room.

During her preparation period later, Dana wrote down ideas for two essays: one for the math tournament and one for her dream. Later she'd worry about the little things like needing a fiancé to make hers come true.

Chapter 3

"Going downstairs?" Steve stuck his head into Dana's room. "Our brain team is waiting for me, but I had to check on you."

"Of course I'm going down to our fitness room. I have to. This body won't take care of itself if I leave it alone." She sighed. "Wouldn't it be nice if our bodies thrived on lying around watching television? Or if the medical field learned that being couch potatoes was good for people?"

"Or if the food pyramid was reversed and a high intake of fats was recommended?"

"And French fries and butter were health foods?" They laughed.

"Don't forget chocolate cake."

"Who could ever forget chocolate cake?"

"So. You'll be here for an hour or so? You're doing your whole routine?"

"Since nobody else will do any part of my fitness program for me, I guess I have to do it myself."

"Don't look at me. I have my own program to do."

"Ah, but the difference is that you like what you do." Dana smiled and took her exercise clothes from her closet.

"Find an exercise program that you like."

"Sure. And while I'm at it, I'll find a million dollars, too. That would take care of our computers, my Hawaiian trip, and leave a few dollars for incidentals." She got her purse from the bottom drawer. "Heck, why shouldn't I just buy myself a not-too-little, nongrass shack over there and stay?"

"Because you'd miss me."

"Hey, you could come, too."

"Are you propositioning me?"

"When I find a million dollars I'll make you the offer again." She laughed. "But don't hold your breath," she warned. "Blue wouldn't be a good color for your skin. You'd better go. Your group is waiting. We don't want those kids' brains to vegetate while waiting for you to come back."

"As smart as they are and the way those kids work, by the time I get in there, they might have developed a theory to make Einstein's seem like kindergarten dreaming."

Dana nooded. "Yeah. They are good."

"They are better than good. Man, I can practically see those new computers at the back of our rooms. Just think, the kids in your English classes could do their word processing and write their stories and poetry without having to wait so long for a turn at a computer."

"And we'll get great science software and your kids would have a computer available whenever an idea came to them."

"Oh yeah. Now I have to go so that I can do like Captain Picard says and 'make it so.' " He grinned. "See you in the morning."

"If I survive my workout."

After Steve left, Dana went to the women's bathroom and changed her clothes. All the while she grumbled to herself. *Why do I put myself through this when I don't feel like it?* She frowned. *Because it's good for me and I don't want high blood pressure and diabetes, nor any of their friends, to catch me,* she answered. *Besides, I never feel like doing this.*

She went downstairs. If she hadn't known where the gym area was, she would only have had to follow the noise. Girls were playing what sounded like an exciting game of basketball. *If I wasn't so clumsy, I'd do that.*

She grinned as she remembered the first day of her freshman high school phys-ed class.

She had barely walked into the gym when the teacher, after taking one look at Dana's five-foot-ten-inch height, rushed over. She introduced herself as the girls' basketball coach and told Dana when to report for practice. Dana was glad that she was early and no other girls were there. She and the coach had a long discussion during which the coach refused to believe that Dana could not play basketball. Finally, after Dana proved that she couldn't even dribble properly, the coach was convinced.

That was only the beginning. No matter the sport, Dana had trouble with the basics. Finally, her gym teacher made a deal with her. If Dana agreed to follow the alternate phys-ed program the teacher had designed for her, she would be exempt from basketball as well as the other organized sports. Except for track. Dana learned that she was a natural sprinter. She had found her niche. She wasn't good enough for the team, but she didn't trip over her feet when she ran.

She shook her head at the memories of her high school days. That year her class had won the intramural basketball as well as the field hockey titles and had gone on to win the city title as well. *I couldn't even have hurt feelings,* she thought as she looked back. *Mrs. Bunton was so diplomatic about it and she was so right.*

Dana sighed and went to the small fitness room two doors from the gym and unlocked the door. It was strictly no-frills: two treadmills, two different combination machines, and one complete set of free weights. But it was adequate. If the staff hadn't begged friends and the students' parents for unused equipment, held yard sales and a talent show, and donated money, they wouldn't even have what they had. She set her bags on the table.

Running outside was more fun, but it was harder on the knees, so she settled for the treadmill. *The sooner I start, the sooner I'll finish,* she thought.

"I thought I'd find you here."

Dana turned as Simone strode into the room. "Good for you, although it's no secret that I use this room." *Why is she here? What does she want?*

"I want to talk to you." She stared at Dana for too long.

"So talk. I'm in a hurry." *Like the treadmill is going to take me away from here.*

"You're never in a hurry when you're with Steve."

"And that's your business because . . . ?"

"I want to know what's going on with you and Steve."

PERFECT WEDDING 27

"You're definitely old enough for your wants not to hurt you. Why is that any of your business?"

"I like him. It's no secret. But every time I try to talk to him, you're there."

"Steve and I are friends." *Why am I telling her that? Why am I even having this conversation with this crazy woman?*

"I'm having a hard time accepting that 'just friends' crap."

"That's *your* problem."

"You don't like Steve?"

"Sure I do. I like all of my friends. If I didn't, they wouldn't be my friends."

"Are you gay or something?"

"Get your ideas untangled. Do you think I'm trying to get romantic with Steve, or do you think I'm gay?" Dana stared at Simone. "Or do you think I swing both ways?" She held up her hand. "Never mind. I don't really care what you think. This conversation, such as it is, is over."

Dana walked over to the television set that one of the teachers had donated and turned it on.

"I want you to back off," Simone spat out.

Dana didn't answer. She barely glanced at Simone. Finally the other woman stomped from the room. Dana heard her footsteps fading down the hall. The faint sound of her heels clicking up the concrete stairs reached Dana and finally disappeared. She threw a glance to the doorway.

I'm glad we didn't place this treadmill so my back is to the door. That is one scary, skinny-behind sister. She glanced at the door one last time, then gave the television her full attention.

She turned to the station playing reruns from way back in the day. *One show equals one hour on the treadmill,* she thought as she looked for, then found, the zone.

She stared at the television as she ran, but for once her attention wasn't on it. She wasn't even thinking about Simone and the conversation she had just had. Her mind was busy composing two very important letters.

An hour later she smiled and moved to the free weights. If both letters turned out on paper the way they had in her mind, the competition for both prizes could save their effort, paper, envelopes, and thirty-seven cents each. Harris had the contests in the bag.

She rushed to the parking lot after she finished. If things went as they usually did, Cathy's after-school tutoring group would be leaving for home. Dana smiled. All except for the one child whose mother was always fifteen minutes late. She shook her head. *That woman needs a remedial lesson in telling time.*

Cathy came out the door as soon as Dana pulled up.

"We had a substitute for the gym teacher today," Cathy said as she buckled up.

"Either this was an extremely dull news day, or there's more to the story than that." Dana drove onto the street.

"He'll be there while Jan is on maternity leave." Her eyes sparkled and her dimples showed as she smiled at Dana. "That's about six to eight weeks."

"Okay. So it's a he." Dana nodded. "And? I know there's more or you wouldn't even be telling me."

"Only that the brother looked as if he had stepped from the cover of those romance books that we so love to read."

"Is he married or otherwise taken by another male or a female?"

"I doubt it." Cathy grinned at Dana. "We're having lunch together tomorrow." She widened her eyes and batted them at Dana. "I offered to fill him in on Harris Elementary School."

"I'll just bet you did. Did Prince Charming tell you what took him so long to show up? And did he say whether or not he knew another brother looking for Miss Ample Armful But Fit?"

"We didn't get further than lunch tomorrow."

"Well, what's taking you so long?" Their glances met and they laughed at the same time.

Then Cathy proceeded to tell Dana about Kenny. When a twinge of jealousy tried to surface within her, Dana squashed it. Cathy deserved to find somebody as much as Dana did.

When Cathy was finished, it was Dana's turn. "Steve found information about a contest for the kids."

She told about the contest that she and Steve were going to work on and how they planned to spend the prize money.

"Did you ever think that maybe Steve is your prince?"

"Steve?" Dana laughed. "Please. We're friends. Besides, I've met a couple of the women he was dating. They all looked alike. Skinny, narrow, no-behinds."

"Women? As in plural? He doesn't seem like a player."

"He's only a player on the basketball court. He dates one at a time and for a short while. Eventually they fade away." She stared at Cathy. "Probably from lack of food." They laughed.

Dana pulled into a parking space near their apartment building entrance. "Then," she continued, "after a while, another one drifts into his life and I hear about her."

"He told you the juicy stuff?"

"Steve would never do that. He'd never disrespect somebody like that." She shrugged. "He'd just mention her name and how they met. Then nothing. The next thing I knew, another name was mentioned."

"See? That's what I'm talking about. It's attitudes like that that have us sisters alone. Why can't the brothers follow the rules? Get an education, get a job, find the sister who is his soul mate and waiting for him. Then he settles down. Why do they go against the nature of the universe?"

"Good-bye, Ms. Philosopher." Dana turned off the motor. "When you find the answers, write a book. It's sure to be a best seller if you can tell us how we can break the guys of that bad habit."

They laughed as they got their things and walked into the building.

"I'll pick you up at the usual time tomorrow," Cathy said as she got off the elevator at the third floor.

"As usual," Dana said as she continued to her fifth-floor apartment.

Dana got a bottle of water from the refrigerator and sat at her computer to work.

"I was good at writing in both undergrad and grad school. I hope I've still got it, now that more than an A is at stake."

* * *

Two hours later she reread the second letter she had written and folded it so carefully that it was as if she believed that the neatness of the folds was a deciding factor. That letter was for her. She slid it into an envelope. The other letter went into a folder so she could take it to Steve tomorrow. She stared at her screen saver of a sunset over Maui as if hoping to find a way to enter the picture. Then she turned the computer off and walked to the mailbox on the corner.

She stared at the envelope long enough for her fingers to get cold even inside her gloves. Then she closed her eyes, said a prayer, and dropped her hope through the slot. She peeked at it to make sure it hadn't sneaked out. Then she rushed home.

Once back in her apartment, she took a well-watched tape from a shelf and popped it into the VCR. She sat back, propped her feet onto the footstool, and imagined herself taping the video that she was watching. The word *Hawaii* appeared on the screen and grew until it filled the space. Then it gave way to a shot of Diamondhead. A voice started the narrative. Dana could have provided the narration herself.

When the tape ended, she went into the kitchen to warm up leftovers for her dinner. With the latest romance novel propped against the seasoned-salt shaker on the table, she read as she ate.

Later she followed her usual nightly routine and tried to ignore the fact that it was routine. She drifted to sleep thinking about the letter she had mailed.

* * *

As soon as she saw Steve the next morning, Dana gave him the letter for the kids' contest.

"Wow. This is great," he said after he read it. "If the winner was decided on the application letter alone, we'd be making space for those computers as we speak."

"What can I say? I try." Her thoughts flitted to the other letter. *I hope whoever reads it is as enthusiastic.* Then she pulled her mind back to Steve. "How did the kids take the idea about entering the contest? I didn't write that letter for nothing, did I?"

"You know they were enthusiastic. As Kareem put it, he can't wait to kick some suburban butt. I tried to tell him that the idea was to be gracious whether we win or lose."

"Then you told them that it's easier to be gracious when you win."

"You know me too well." He stared at her. "Or at least you think you do." His stare eased off. "See you at lunch?"

"Did Simone give up?"

"I hope so. She's a great-looking woman and I'm sure she has a lot of brothers waiting for a chance at her." He shrugged. "She just doesn't stir anything in me."

"But you're the brother that she wants."

"I'm the brother she can't have." He turned away. "I'll come to your room for lunch."

"She'll still find you," Dana called after him.

The rest of the day passed for Dana as the weeks before had, except for a couple of things: Steve had put the plans for the math contest in motion and Dana was helping him work out final details. A second difference was Cathy's reporting on her blossoming relationship with Kenny.

"Maybe, if Kenny and I are meant to be, Jan will decide that she doesn't want to leave her precious bundle of joy at the end of her leave."

"Maybe. I hope so since that's what you want."

"I do. I only hope that's what Ken wants too."

Dana smiled as they rode home. She honestly hoped things turned out well for Cathy. She deserved it.

Maybe I'll find a special someone of my own. A football fan would be nice, she thought as she went to her apartment. She tried ignore the loneliness that seemed heavier today. *Get over it,* she told herself. *Appreciate what you have.* She didn't expect that to erase her loneliness. It didn't.

"Are we on for Sunday?" Steve asked at lunch on Friday. They had already discussed the progress of the project and moved on to a subject both of them were near-fanatics about. The Philadelphia Eagles.

"You coming over?"

"You know we have to combine forces so the Eagles can kick serious butt and move on to the Superbowl. I got my Eagles shirt and sweatpants. I even bought some Eagle-green socks with that mean Eagle logo on them." He grinned and handed her a small bag. "I got a pair for you, too. I am seriously ready."

"That makes two of us." She pulled out the socks and held them up. "Hey. Thanks. If our team plays as tough as this eagle looks, the Dallas Cowboys don't stand a chance." She stared at him. "I do draw the line at painting half of my face green and the other half white, though."

"Good. Your brown is much more becoming to you."

"Thank you, kind sir. So is yours."

"Should I stop by for hoagies?"

"Nope. I got everything covered. You can get hoagies for the Superbowl when we play whomever. Tomorrow's menu will be fried chicken, potato salad, and sweet potato pie. Oh. And a green salad to keep us healthy."

"Chicken wings?"

"Uh-uh." Dana shook her head. "Not enough meat. No popcorn, either. The last time, I had to vacuum three times to find all the kernels that we spilled."

"If Donovan hadn't thrown that bomb for a touchdown in the last few seconds, the popcorn would have stayed in the bowl. We were doing okay until then."

"Yeah." She grinned. "It was a mess to clean up, but it was worth every kernel."

"Maybe we'll get a repeat."

"I hope not. My heart can't take too many of those last-minute wins."

"Yeah, but a win is a win."

"You got that right. See you about twelve?"

"You got that right, too."

The bell rang and Steve went back to his room.

During the entire afternoon Dana had trouble keeping her mind on the lessons she was teaching instead of on the upcoming game. *Maybe I'll incorporate the Superbowl into a writing contest,* she thought as once again she had to drag her mind back to the present. *Those not interested in the game can pick an alternative subject.*

With that promise her thoughts stayed on the classwork.

Chapter 4

Early Saturday morning, Dana got her cup of tea and went to her computer. She smiled as she opened the file she was working on.

If someone were to ask me what is the one thing that nobody knows about me, this would be it. She leaned back. She was about to finish the romance novel she was writing. She doubted if she would ever have the nerve to send it out, so no eyes but hers might ever see it, but she was writing it anyway. Just because she didn't have anybody in her real life didn't mean she couldn't have a bronze hunk in her imaginary world.

Three hours later she looked at her watch and hurried to close the file. She didn't wait for the computer to tell her that it was shutting down. She grabbed a folder from the desk and rushed from the room.

Cathy and Steve both knew that she was taking a writing class for adults at the high school nearby, but she let them assume that she was working on something for school. Her romance novel was still a secret that she wasn't ready to share yet, not even with her two best friends. What if they laughed? Or worse yet, what if they tore it apart as a waste of time? She didn't think they would, but she didn't want to take chances.

She grabbed her jacket and ran to her car. She was running late, as usual, but what better excuse could she have except that she had been writing and lost track of time?

Two hours later she was heading back home. A smile stayed in place during the entire fifteen-minute drive. *They liked my last chapter. They really liked it.* Even the instructor had praised it.

Dana had struggled through it, rewriting it more times than she could count, making drastic changes each time. Evidently she had finally gotten it right. *I'm going to miss this class. This was the last session.* She sighed. Then the grin was back. *Maybe I can start another novel and have it ready for the fall session.*

She tried to tone down the sappy grin when she stopped at the supermarket. If she didn't, somebody would think that she had serious problems. She bought the things she needed for the next day. The grin was back before she got to the car.

Dana zipped through her usual Saturday chores, grateful, as she was every Saturday, that she had a washer and dryer and didn't have to use the laundry room.

When the mail came, she couldn't resist rushing to the box and sifting through the letters. "Ridiculous," she muttered as she finished. "How could you expect an answer already? You just mailed it. You're like a kid who plants seeds and then stands over the plot waiting for them to pop up." She went to the phone, shaking her head the whole way.

"Hi, Cathy. I forgot to ask you yesterday. You coming up tomorrow?"

"Tomorrow? What's tomorrow?"

"What's tomorrow? Sunday."

"Duh. I got that. Don't I have my choir robe pressed and hanging on the closet door?"

"Church is of prime importance, but tomorrow is a close second. It's the last play-off game. At this time of year I have one more thing to be grateful for, early morning church service. I don't have to choose between feeling guilty for missing church and deserting my team." She laughed. "So. Are you coming?"

"If you were in the business of converting people to a religion, you'd get a lot of points for persistence. You never give up. Every Sunday during football season it's the same thing."

"So, is that a yes or a no?"

"I'm going to the new exhibit at the art museum. I want to see the work of the Depression-era black artists whose art is dubbed 'primitive.' We'll get into that label at some other time."

"Got a date with Kenny, huh? When do I get a chance to meet Mr. No Longer a Stranger?"

"I'm going to the museum alone, although he did offer to go with me." Cathy sighed. "Wasn't that sweet of him?"

"Yes. Extremely sweet."

"I told him to go on with his friends and watch the game."

"A football fan? You got hooked up with a football fan?"

"Not just a fan, girlfriend. Ken used to play football when he went to Grambling."

"Grambling? You have a guy who played for the famous Grambling Tigers? He must be the only former player who didn't get drafted by the pros."

"He got his shoulder messed up in his junior year and that was that. It's not just football that he's interested in, though. He's crazy about all sports, including hockey."

"Yours will be an interesting relationship. They say that opposites attract. Looks like you're gonna test that theory big time."

"I intend to ace this test."

"Well, you can still come up to my place. I'm making my famous fried chicken and sweet potato pie."

"Steve's coming over, huh?"

"Yep. It wouldn't be a football game if I didn't share it with him."

"Uh-huh."

"What's that supposed to mean?"

"Likes attract too, you know. See you later." Cathy hung up before Dana could respond.

Dana took a critical look around her apartment. Satisfied that it would have passed her mama's clean test, she pulled down the throw that she had crocheted during a short interest in the craft, grabbed the romance book that she was almost finished reading, and settled into a corner of the couch.

A few hours later she closed the book and sighed. "Where can I find a guy like that?" She glanced once more at the cover of the book. "Oh yeah. He wouldn't be hard to take. Easy on the eyes and just far enough from perfect to make him interesting."

Her stomach reminded her that it was tired of waiting for a meal, so she put the book aside.

After dinner, she double-checked to make sure she had everything she needed for the game. Then she put the chicken in a plastic bag to soak in her special blend of milk and herbs. It would be ready to fry when she got home from church tomorrow.

She put the bag into the refrigerator, gave it a final pat, then went to the living room and turned on the television. She had been waiting for this special since it was first advertised.

"Speed dating," the reporter said as soon as he introduced himself, "has become quite popular in this age of instant everything. Let's hear it described by the owner of one of the most popular speed-dating spots in Los Angeles."

Dana grabbed the pen and pad from the coffee table and listened closely as the restaurant owner gave the details of the concept. *I might need to know this,* she thought.

She leaned closer as the picture faded and then the camera showed a huge room full of small tables. At each table were seated a man and a woman. After five minutes, a bell rang and the men moved to the next table.

"It looks like a version of musical chairs, only the players are adults and they are using tables instead of chairs," Dana said after the third time the men moved. The picture faded and the reporter came on again.

"There you have it. The latest trend in dating, speed dating. Two of the participants have agreed to talk with us." He turned to the smiling man and woman beside him.

"I figured this was the best way to meet the most prospects in a short time," the thirty-something woman said. "I mean, I have been fixed up by everybody who knows me and I haven't had any success. I am tired of being alone. I like my own company, but not all of the time. I just know that the man meant for me is out there. I just have to find him and I think this is a good way to do that."

The reporter moved the microphone to the man standing beside her, but who wasn't with her.

"I thought this was better than having somebody fix me up," said the man, who looked as if he was pushing forty—hard. "I mean, for a fee I get to meet all of these women and it doesn't cost me lunch or dinner to do it." He grinned. "This is very cost-effective."

"Yes, and it saves time, too," the woman added. "I'm not getting any younger, as my mother is always ready to point out."

"So you're both pleased with the idea even though you haven't found anybody?"

"Oh yes," they answered together as if they had rehearsed their response. "You mean not yet," the woman added.

"This sort of addresses the 'so many women, so little time' dilemma." The man grinned at the camera.

"I agree, except that I'd change it to 'so many men, so little time.' " The woman's grin was equally wide.

The reporter faced the camera. "This practice is catching on across the country. Only time will tell whether it's here to stay or just another fad." He cued a commercial, and a zero-size model came on talking about the latest sports shoes and how much fun it was running in them.

When the program came back on, a different reporter was talking about nothing that had to do with dating of any kind. Dana stared at the television. *How can I find out if there's a program like that around here?*

She resisted the urge to rush to the computer and start a search on speed dating. Instead she leaned back. *Do I really want to find a husband that way? Won't it make me look like a loser? Like I'm desperate?* She frowned. *If I get selected by the* Perfect Wedding *show, I* will *be desperate.* She frowned. *I have to think this through before I do anything.* She turned to the next program in her Saturday evening lineup.

After watching the eleven o'clock news and learning that tomorrow was going to be sunny, but with the low temperature that was normal in winter, she went to bed. A vision of a long lace-covered wedding dress waltzed around in her mind before it faded away.

After church the next morning, Dana changed clothes and glanced through the newspaper. She got the paper down to a manageable size by discarding the Real Estate, Automotive, and Want Ads sections and what felt like a ream of slick ads. Then she took out the weekly television guide and proceeded to mark the programs that she intended to watch during the coming week. She glanced at her watch and went into the kitchen. It was time to get busy.

PERFECT WEDDING 43

Soon the sweet potato pies and the bread were in the oven and the chicken was sizzling on top of the stove. The aromas from the three seemed to be trying to outdo each other on the "I'm the best" scale.

By 11:45 the pies were cooling, the bread was wrapped to keep it warm, the chicken was waiting on the platter, and Dana was pulling on her Eagles shirt, sweatpants, and socks. She smiled at the eagle glaring from the sides. Then she put on her shoes and went to wait for Steve.

At five minutes to noon she buzzed him in and stood with the door open.

"Hey, partner." Steve hugged her, then stepped back and stared at her. "You look like you are down for a serious game."

"Oh yeah." She stepped aside to let him in. Then she slowly turned around to show her shirt, as if he wasn't wearing an identical one and as if this wasn't her usual game-watching outfit. "I hope our guys want to play one more game after today."

"I would say that makes two of us, but from all of the pennants hanging from just about every car window, I know there are a whole lot more than the two of us sending positive vibes to Donovan McNabb and company."

They laughed as Steve followed her into the kitchen. He looked at the pies. "As my mama would say, 'my, my, my.' I'm changing it to um, um, um." He closed his eyes and shook his head slowly. "I think I should sample a small slice to see if it lives up to your last one."

"Same recipe, same results." Dana laughed again. "I'll bet you were terrible when you were growing up."

"I was a terribly cute little boy. Just ask my mama."

"I'll bet you were."

"Of course, that didn't make her cut me any slack. Her 'no' meant 'no' and I learned early that I couldn't change her mind." He stared at Dana. "But I digress. Just a little slice won't spoil my lunch."

"I've seen you eat. I don't think anything could spoil your lunch. Go ahead. I hate to see a grown man beg."

"That was my next step." Steve cut a fourth of a pie and put it on a plate.

"Wow. I'm glad you took a *small* slice. I'm also glad I made two pies."

"I used restraint since I want to be invited back."

"You know you're always welcome. You have a standing invitation. Now, how about some real food?" She took the bowls of salad from the refrigerator.

"It doesn't get any more real than this." He tasted the pie. "My, my, my, my, my." He licked his lips. "Of course, I know the rest of the food will be equally delicious." He put a piece of chicken on another plate and added salad and bread. He held the plate to his nose and sniffed deeply. "Definitely worth the trip."

"What's my company, cold grits?" She helped herself to more modest portions and led him into the living room.

"Your company is the primary reason that I'm here."

"Sure it is. The food is just an incidental and the game has nothing to do with anything." She put a snack table in front of him and another at her seat beside him.

"Those are just minor attractions, that's all." He grinned and ate another bite of pie. Then they both gave their attention to the pre-pregame show.

The plates were empty and Dana's and Steve's attention was glued to the screen as the Cowboys' kicker came out to attempt what the two of them hoped was an impossible field goal to put them ahead by one. The big Eagle in the middle more than earned his salary when he jumped, shoved up his hand, and blocked the kick. Another Eagle, who also wanted to play the next game, grabbed the ball and lumbered to the Cowboys' end zone. It wasn't a pretty sight to see somebody the size of a hippo running, but it was sweet.

Dana and Steve went as wild as the fans in the stadium. They jumped up, grabbed each other, and danced around the room in their own version of an end zone dance. They hugged again and Steve placed a quick kiss on Dana's lips before holding her around the waist. Then he jumped some more.

The Cowboys received the kickoff, but it was too late. The final second ticking off was an anticlimax. A win was always sweet, but a win to take them into the Superbowl was more so. The only thing sweeter was a Superbowl win itself.

But Dana's mind wasn't focused on the game's aftermath the way it usually was. Steve had kissed her before, but on the cheek. This last was just a casual, buddy-to-buddy kiss, wasn't it? An our-team-won kiss. Right? *Do I want to win that contest so badly that I'm reading something between me and Steve that isn't there?*

She glanced at Steve, who was staring at the television, watching the fans in the stadium still going wild. Then he sat back to watch the post-game show. He seemed to have either forgotten that he had kissed her or given it no importance.

Dana sat beside him and made herself concentrate on the rest of the program.

Later, carrying one plate with enough food for another meal and another with the rest of the pie, Steve left.

Dana stared at the door long after he was gone as if she expected him to come back.

It must be me, she thought as she cleaned up the kitchen. *He probably doesn't even realize that he kissed me.*

Have you lost your mind? Steve asked himself as he drove from the parking lot of Dana's apartment complex. *You're her friend. If you blow it, you won't even be that.* He shook his head. *I hope she thought of it as nothing more than a happy-that-our-team-won kiss. She sees me as a friend. Nothing more. On top of everything else, if I came on to her and she didn't feel the same way, it would make it very awkward for us to work together and I would never have time with her. Why couldn't I leave things as they were? Why did I have to push?*

He shook his head again. He'd have to use a lot more restraint for the Superbowl.

In spite of his dilemma, he grinned. *Oh yeah. The Eagles are going to the Superbowl. Oh yeah.*

Chapter 5

By the time Monday morning came, Dana had accepted the kiss as a way of celebrating a win. *After all, friends kiss each other, right? It didn't mean anything more than being happy together. Celebrating together. Right? Ignore it*, she told herself. *It won't happen again.* She frowned and her frown stayed as she got dressed. Now all she had to do was believe what she was telling herself.

"Hurry over. I have something to show you." Steve poked his head in at the end of the last morning session and was gone before Dana could respond.

At least he forgot all about what happened. She got her lunch from the teachers' room and went to Steve's room.

"You know I'm not giving up," Simone was saying as Dana walked into the room. "I can be very persistent when I decide that I want something." She glanced at Dana as she came in, then gave her attention back to Steve. "All I need is a chance.

Not even a big one." She glanced at Dana again, then back at Steve. "I can make you forget all about every other woman you ever met." Dana stood up to the glare that was thrown her way. "And I do mean every other woman. Present company included." She was wearing slacks, but she still managed to swish past Dana.

"I'm glad I don't have a pet bunny." Dana stared at the door. "I never did like the idea of boiled rabbit." She shook her head. "I'm also glad I don't have a cat or a dog."

"Don't mind her. Come on in."

"Easy for you to say don't pay her any attention. You're not the one who needs a thick piece of armor covering your back." Dana shook her head as she went to the back table. She opened her lunch bag and peeked in. "I think from now on I'll keep my lunch with me." She looked at the door. "All joking aside, that sister scares me. I saw a tiny refrigerator on sale at the superstore. I have just the place in my room for it."

"I don't exactly feel relaxed around her, either."

"Afraid she'll kill you with love, huh?"

"I don't think love has anything to do with it." He pulled out a packet of papers stapled together. "I put this together for the team. Here's your copy. I'll give each of the kids one so that, after I introduce a concept to them, they can practice on their own or together." He opened the booklet and paged through it. "I even built in activities for them to make up problems of their own. Add the time factor and we'll have a team that can't be beat."

"I noticed a fringe benefit. A couple of our other

PERFECT WEDDING

kids asked if there's a contest in writing. They're not even my best. You know I'm looking into it."

"Competition can be a good thing." Steve nodded.

"I especially like the fact that this doesn't center on athletics. I'll be the first to tell you that there's nothing wrong with athletics, but not everybody is good at sports." Dana took a bite of her sandwich.

"Yeah. I also like that the brainy kids aren't worried about being considered nerds."

"I like to think that's partly because we brainwashed them with the idea that the nerds not only make the big bucks, they also have a lot of power."

"Money still talks." Steve took a drink of apple juice.

"When I look at my paycheck, I wish it had a louder voice."

They laughed and finished their lunches. Neither mentioned the kiss. It was as if it had never happened.

Dana and Steve and their students settled into the new routine. The practice sessions fit into the schedule easily. The team was good. The kids might not win, but they'd give the competition a good fight. Win or not, they would have something to be proud of. A bonus was that they'd be comfortable with higher math concepts and operations when they moved on.

Through the week Dana visited various educators' sites searching for writing contests for her classes. The English classes were determined not to be outdone by the math team.

"That makes ten," Dana said on Thursday as the printer spewed out the details of another writing contest. As soon as the printer stopped, she picked up the papers and stapled them together. "Poetry, short stories, and essays. Something for everyone. We'll give them a closer look together and decide which we'll enter." She grinned. "Wait until I show these to Steve." She slipped the papers into a folder and set it aside.

I am not a Simone, she thought as her mind drifted to the kiss and a warm feeling eased over her. *I'm just looking at him in a different light because of the* Perfect Wedding *contest. That's all it is.*

She brushed the feeling away. Then she went to the Perfect Wedding Web site and checked the time line again. She knew it from memory, but still she leaned back and sighed when she looked at it again. The first cut wasn't for another two weeks. She frowned as she read further. The first entries were picked at random. Then those were judged according to whether or not the judges liked the essays. She shook her head. There was a whole lot of chance involved in her quest for Hawaii.

She left the site and focused on the writing contest information she had downloaded. Surely there was at least one that whoever was interested could enter.

"Morning, Glory," Cathy said when Dana got into the car the next morning. "I had a fantastic evening, as usual when I'm with Kenny." They had been seeing each other regularly since soon after they met.

"Morning. Good for you." Dana didn't even manage the hint of a smile.

"It's early. What's pulled you down already?"

"Do you know what the chances are of me making it to the show?"

"Are you talking about that wedding-honeymoon show?"

"What else?" Dana stared out the windshield as Cathy drove onto the street.

"I would say if you spend the same energy and a few dollars on the Powerball Lottery you'd stand a better chance of paying for your own trip."

"Do you know that they don't even *read* all of the entries? That getting to that point is a lottery in itself? Then they still have to judge the handful that they pick."

"You're just finding this out? If I told you once I told you numerous times, you have to read the fine print."

"Yes, Mother." She sighed. "How can I expect to win?"

"Bingo." Cathy glanced at Dana and then back to the road. "Look at it this way. Now you don't have to find a husband."

Dana shook her head and they rode the rest of the way in silence. Cathy's words didn't make her any happier.

"I'm not giving up hope," Dana said as Cathy stopped outside the school. "I still have as much chance as anybody else." She gathered her briefcase and purse from the floor. "See you at the usual time."

"Think lottery tickets." Cathy grinned.

Dana stuck her tongue out at her, then grinned back. She shook off thoughts of the contest and lotteries and went into the school. Whatever would be, would be.

At lunch, after Steve told her about the progress

the math team was making, Dana told him about the writing contests.

"Folks better watch out," Steve said. "Forget charter schools and private schools of any other kind. A path will be carved deep into the sidewalk leading to Harris School's doors by the feet of the many parents trying to get their kids enrolled here."

"You got that right. We might start a new trend, flight *to* public schools instead of *away* from them."

"As a product of public education, I'd love to see that day. I've got some more good news. A few of the other kids asked if there wasn't something special they could do. 'Extra credit' is how Frank put it." Steve grinned. "The kid has a head full of brains gathering dust, but Heaven forbid he should be lumped with the nerds by his 'homies.' He also said he wouldn't mind a trophy with his name on it being on display for the students to see in years to come."

"Watch out, world. Ready or not, here we come."

They got permission to use the auditorium after lunch for a special meeting with both classes.

As Dana and Steve shared the news, the students pretended to be blasé about the contests, but their enthusiasm came through in their questions. After both teachers emphasized that the kids would still be responsible for their regular class assignments and that, although entering a contest didn't guarantee a win, the experience would be good for them, they all discussed and planned the new schedule.

Dana felt a little like a hypocrite when she gave the kids the lecture about not counting on winning, but she gave it anyway. Besides, the discipline and preparation would be useful to the kids in the future.

Meanwhile, she tried not to grab her mail and quickly search for an envelope with the *Perfect Wedding* logo on it. *Will the envelope of the losers be different from the envelope of the chosen few?* She shook her head. *No way to know.* After not finding it, she went on with her day knowing she would go through the whole process the next day. And the next, too, until a letter came.

"Could you make room for two more to watch the Superbowl?" Cathy asked as they were riding to school. "I thought it would be a good time for you to meet Kenny."

"Make room? You know it will only be Steve and me."

"I also know the reason for that is that you said you don't want anybody else to see how crazy you get during a football game. Since this is the Game of Games, I didn't know if you would be embarrassed afterward."

"A little enthusiasm is quite normal under these circumstances."

"From what I know about you, you can push the 'normal' envelope really hard."

"Do you want to come or not?"

"Don't throw an attitude on me, girlfriend, I know where you live." Cathy grinned. "You know I want us to be there when our guys get the trophy and the rings. What you want me to bring?"

"I didn't know you knew rings are involved."

"I will ignore that put-down. I might know a lot more about football than you think."

"I doubt that so very much." Dana let Cathy out. "Of course you can come. I'm anxious to meet the guy who got through to you that a football is not round." She stared at her best friend. "You do finally realize that, don't you?" Dana laughed as Cathy glared. "We'll discuss the food later. Keep in mind, the only health food allowed at a Superbowl party will be a tossed green salad, and that can't be too fancy."

"Yes, Chef Dana." Cathy tapped her arm. "See you after school."

By Friday, Harris Middle School was caught up in the same Eagle fever that gripped the rest of the city. Everybody at school looked as if the school uniform had changed. Light blue tops and khaki or navy blue pants had been replaced by either green Eagle tees or sweatshirts and dark green pants. There was a change in Philadelphia's appearance, also. The city looked as if strange winter plants in the form of huge Eagle signs had sprouted on nearly every lawn.

Mr. Holloway, the principal, not only allowed a pep rally during the last period of the day, but when he strode onto the auditorium stage, not wearing his usual sports coat and tie, but clad instead in an Eagle sweatshirt and pants and with an Eagle hat sitting sideways on his head, the kids went wild.

The auditorium rocked as he led the students and staff in the cheers. Yells of "E—A—G—L—E—S" filled the room and soared to the ceiling. The auditorium wasn't big enough to hold the noise that pushed the boundaries of the entire building.

PERFECT WEDDING

The kids invaded each other's space as they went through the motions that accompanied the cheers. Nobody cared.

Several kids read their own poems dedicated to the team. Three groups did different raps depicting the team's victories so far and predicting the outcome of Sunday's game. Each performance set the students and staff off to new heights of frenzy. When the rally ended, Mr. Holloway came back onstage and led them in the school song. Just before he dismissed them by grade, he admonished them to be on their best behavior as they went home. As always he reminded them that their behavior reflected on Harris Middle School. Every face wore a wide grin as they all left the auditorium and then the building.

It was a hoarse, but fired-up, Dana who drove over to pick up Cathy.

"This whole day was unreal," Cathy said as she buckled her seat belt. "It was like everybody but me has lost their minds. Little kids who can hardly read 'cat' know the words to that Eagles' song." She shook her head. "I think I'm the only sane one left in the entire state of Pennsylvania."

"That should tell you something."

"Yeah. Entire states can lose their minds at the same time. I mean, it's just a game."

"And December twenty-fifth is just the day before the twenty-sixth." Dana shook her head as she drove home. "For your sake, regarding Kenny, I hope that after opposites attract they find enough magnetism to stay together." Dana parked and they left the car at the same time.

"Me too." Cathy smiled.

"See you for church Sunday morning?"

"Aren't you afraid of missing the game?"

"Poor, poor child." Dana shook her head. "I guess I should say poor, poor us, because you will be with us." She released an exaggerated sigh as they walked into the building. "The game doesn't come on until late. We will have plenty of time for church even if it runs long. I'll see you at the usual time."

"You got it. What do you have planned for tomorrow? Want to go to the mall with me? I feel the need for a new pair of shoes and my bank account says that I can afford them."

"Shoes. That is so cliché."

"Some people don't understand the need that we normal women have for shoes."

"I will not debate the 'normal women and shoes' comment. I will be magnanimous and ignore it in order not to send out bad vibes to the stadium. To each her own, but I can't go with you. Tomorrow is Saturday."

"Yeah? That's the day that usually follows Friday."

Dana stopped outside Cathy's door and stared at her. "It's the Saturday before Superbowl Sunday."

"Yeah?"

"I have to get ready."

"Get ready? You're going to watch the game, not play in it."

"I have to decorate."

"Decorate?"

"If you'd taken the time to come to watch a game with me before, you'd know this. I have to make sure to do my part to support Donovan and company. I don't want to send out any bad vibes." She stared at Cathy. "You do know who Donovan McNabb is, don't you?"

"Of course I do. He's the uh . . ." she frowned.

PERFECT WEDDING 57

"The guy who throws the ball. The, uh, the quarterback." She grinned. "That's who he is."

"It is going to be a long game in more ways than one," Dana said, shaking her head. "It will be a mission of mercy to help provide a buffer between a fan like Kenny and a sports-challenged you."

"So. How do you decorate for a football game?"

"Over the top, of course." Dana laughed. "You'll see on Sunday. Have fun at the mall tomorrow." She almost skipped up the flight of stairs to her apartment.

Although she was excited, she forced herself to do the usual Saturday cleaning on Friday evening instead. She needed all of tomorrow to get ready.

After she watched her usual television shows, she went to bed as excited as if the day after tomorrow were Christmas.

Chapter 6

What am I going to do? Steve clicked off the television. He wasn't watching it anyway. He had barely glanced at the news. A problem was growing and he had no idea how to solve it. In college he was "go to Steve with your problems and he'll help you." Now he needed a go-to man himself. He frowned. When had his feelings for her reached this new level?

Dana had arrived at Harris Middle School three years after he had. She had been assigned the classroom next to his. They had become friends and were combining their classes for English and math before the principal asked them to continue officially as part of a new program the school district was piloting. They added the other subjects to their team teaching.

I've had girlfriends, but nothing worked out with any of them. He frowned. Was it because of Dana? She never talked about her social life. To hear her tell it, she *had* no life. He shook his head. *Knowing her, I find that hard to believe.*

He got ready for bed, wondering what had made him kiss her, and even more, why was such a fleeting kiss still prominent in his mind? *What's going on and what can I do about it?* He folded his hands behind his head. *I don't want to scare her off. To her I'm just a friend. I don't want to lose that by pushing.*

By nine o'clock on Saturday morning Dana was up and even more enthusiastic about the game than before. She dressed and ate her usual bowl of oatmeal with raisins.

"Why couldn't they play on Saturday?" she said to nobody. "Why make us suffer?" Dana laughed and shook her head. "I am way too excited about this."

She finished in the kitchen. Then she pulled the three boxes of Eagle paraphernalia from the top shelf of the hall closet and carried them into the living room. Just as she was about to open the first box, the doorbell rang.

I know Cathy didn't forget that I'm not going with her, she thought.

"Are you getting forgetful at such an . . ." The rest of the sentence got lost as she stared at Steve.

"Whatever you were going to say, I'm going to take a chance and answer no."

"I thought you were Cathy."

"I should have called."

"Not necessary. You know I'm always up early." She smiled. "Especially during football season.

Come on in." She stepped aside. "Do you want a cup of coffee?"

"No. I'm good." *It will be hard, but I'd better be.* He tried to ignore the whiff of her signature perfume that nudged him as he stepped past her. "I came to help."

"You know me too well. You're just in time." She pulled the tops off all of the boxes.

"I've never seen your Eagles stuff before you put it out." He stared at the boxes. "You got a lot of it."

"One can never have too much money or too much Eagles stuff." She grabbed his hand. "Come on. Let's get the ladder. Then we can take everything out and you can help me decide what to put where."

"Sounds like a plan."

For the next two hours they made decisions about where each item should go. The last thing to do was to hang the green and white crepe paper twisted together. Steve worked from the ladder and Dana handed him the strip so he could tape it to the crown molding at the top of the walls. Finally, they put the ladder away. They stood in the doorway then took a step back.

"That's it."

"You bought some new stuff."

"I found some really good bargains after last year's season." She touched the lamp with a menacing eagle for the base. "I had faith that they'd be back here this year."

"If you entered the contest for the best-decorated living room, you'd win first prize."

"I wouldn't have a chance." She shook her head. "I've seen the pictures of some of the rooms

PERFECT WEDDING

of other fans. Remember when a local television news program aired a feature on fan loyalty? They would make some national shrines look puny."

Although it wasn't related in any way, the discussion of a contest and a prize made the *Perfect Wedding* contest try to grab Dana's attention. She refused to let it.

"We'll never know unless you try," Steve said.

"What do you have planned for the rest of the day?" she asked him. "Want to hang out?"

"I have basketball practice." *I would love to hang out with you, but I don't think 'hanging out' would be enough.* He frowned. *Get a grip. Find neutral again.*

"Why are you frowning? You love playing round ball."

"I was thinking about something."

"Care to share?"

"It's nothing." *I don't want to scare you off.*

"Okay." She shrugged. "How about my famous grilled cheese sandwich with tomato soup on the side before you go?"

"I'll take a rain check. I'd better go." *I have to put some space between us so I can get myself under control.*

"Okay." She smiled. "See you tomorrow."

"Hoagies or not?"

"If you'll be here for lunch, bring them. If not, we won't need them. I'm doing fried chicken for the game itself."

"My mouth is watering already." Steve resisted the urge to kiss her good-bye. Instead he just stood in the doorway for a few seconds before he left.

What to do with the two hours until practice? He sat in his car until the cold made him turn on the motor and drive away. *I'm acting as if it's springtime and my fancy has turned to where young guys are all year long.*

Dana rushed home from church, changed, and went right into the kitchen to get to work. Forty-five minutes later she placed the last piece of fried chicken on the paper towel to drain. A few minutes later she took the two sweet potato pies from the oven. She had made the potato salad after Steve left the day before and the sodas were in the refrigerator. She was ready. More than ready. She just hoped the Eagles were, too. She dried her hands and left the kitchen.

Exactly at noon, the doorbell rang.

"I come bearing gifts," Steve said when Dana opened the door. He held up a bag with the grease stains to show that hoagies were inside.

"They always taste so good."

"Only if you know where to shop. Fortunately I live two blocks from the shop that knows the secret to making perfect Italian hoagies. If I didn't force myself to use restraint, I'd be eating these every day."

"The pregame show will begin in about twenty minutes."

"You mean the pre-pregame show."

"You probably should put a couple more pre's in front." Dana laughed. "I brought home the essays the kids wrote on Friday. Every one has something to do with this game. We will have some droopy kids on Monday if . . ." She shook her head. "I refuse to voice the possibility of the Eagles' you-know-what."

"Good idea. We don't want to put that possibility out there." He followed her into the living room.

"How did your practice go yesterday? You weren't late, were you?"

"No." *I was two hours early, but I can't tell you.* "It went great." He nodded. "I think we stand a good shot of winning. Even if we only make it into the finals, the sponsors donate to the charities of the final four teams."

"Maybe one day the government will reorder its priorities and causes like yours won't have to go begging."

"Either when dogs sprout wings and fly or when kids get to vote, whichever comes first."

"You got that right," Steve said. "Let's take a look at those papers."

"Some of the kids show great writing skills."

"That's because they have an excellent teacher."

"Why, thank you. I hope the contest judges agree."

They spent the rest of the time reading, smiling at, and commenting on the papers. When the show came on, they focused on it, adding their comments to those of the commentators in between bites of their hoagies.

When Kenny and Cathy arrived about four hours later, they added their comments. At least Kenny did. Cathy just listened. Her intense look made it seem as if she was trying to learn everything about football in the few hours before the game came on.

Finally the preliminaries ended and the game started. Dana, Steve, and Kenny gave the game their full attention.

Cathy tried for a while, but except when the

cheers were loudest, she spent more time reading the magazines in Dana's rack than she did watching the game.

Halftime came and they went to the buffet where Dana had placed the food.

"Halftime isn't just so the players can rest. We fans need it to catch our breath, too," she said.

"I wish they would put the Raiders away and release this tension," Kenny said. "This seesawing back and forth is rough."

"Yeah, they need to quit playing around and get down to business," Steve added. "I hate ties at halftime."

"They look like they're playing as hard as they can." Cathy's words drew glares from the three others. "What?"

"That is a negative comment. No negatives are allowed," Dana said.

"I was just expressing an opinion." Cathy put a piece of chicken on her plate.

"Keep it to yourself." All three spoke at the same time as if they had rehearsed. She stared at each one in turn. Then she shrugged and changed the subject.

"I thought somebody was going to have a heart attack." Cathy stared at Dana.

"That was nothing that my heart can't take." Dana put green salad into her bowl. "In fact, that was nothing so far. When we win the game, now that's the time you'd better get out of the way." She laughed. "Let's go back into the living room and hear the commentators praise our guys and show the highlights."

The second half was almost a duplicate of the first. The score continued to go back and forth, proof that both teams wanted the rings and the trophy.

"Come on, come on." Dana moved to the edge of the sofa and bounced. "Yes!" She and the other two jumped up and punched a fist as McNabb threw the ball to a receiver. "No!" she groaned with the others as a Raider stepped in front of the receiver and stole the ball. He lumbered toward the Eagles' end zone only to be tackled before he ran more than five yards. The ball squirted out and the intended receiver jumped on it. The stadium and Dana's living room filled with cheers. Even Cathy jumped up and yelled with the others.

The announcer's voice rose above the stadium noise.

"The Eagles get a second chance with only a minute left in regulation time. This is the make-it-or-break-it point. They are down by two points. The only sure thing is that there will be no overtime in this game." The announcer stated the obvious. "Let's see if the Birds can capitalize on the opportunity."

Dana, Steve, and Kenny stayed on their feet as if that would help the team. They held their breath as McNabb crouched behind the center, ready to receive the ball. Even Cathy's stare was glued to the television as McNabb faked a handoff before he pedaled backward and drew back his arm. If noise could alter the path of the pass, it would have wobbled. Instead, it flew in a beautiful, perfect spiral and didn't stop until it landed in the hands of Greg Lewis waiting in the far corner of the end zone. He clutched it to himself and held on as he fell inside the lines.

Immediately he stood and went into a dance

more intricate than any of the others that he had performed in the past. It was great, but it was no match for the dances going on in Dana's living room.

Dana grabbed Cathy's hand and pulled her up and led her and the others in a jumping, twirling march around the living room. Then they congratulated each other as if they had had something to do with the win. Still holding each other, dancing around and grinning, they stared at the television.

The stadium crowd was still going wild. Eagles fans wouldn't come down to earth for at least a month.

The local news team highlighted the fans celebrating at several bars and homes. The people all acted as if they were the same fans, only moved into different settings.

Later, still riding a victory high, the other three left. Dana stared at the closed door. Then she danced into her living room and sat on the couch.

"I wished I had taped it," she said. "That was the best game ever played." She sat with a grin on her face. For once she wasn't interested in any other program being aired.

Afraid to go to bed for fear that she would awaken in the morning and find that it had been a dream and that the game was yet to be played, she sat there until midnight staring at whatever happened to come on the channel the television was turned to.

Finally, common sense convinced her that she'd better get some rest so she could face the students the next day and she went to bed.

Chapter 7

Monday morning Dana was still up from the Superbowl win, but that was okay. The kids were the same way all day. Nobody, including herself, could focus on the work at hand. It was like the day before Christmas and the last day of school combined. Today had been a fun day. Tomorrow they would get back to schoolwork.

After she got home, she retrieved her mail and went to her apartment. Once she was there, she carelessly shuffled through the mail, her mind still on the day before.

"Junk," she said as she dropped a letter into the small trash can beside the hall table. "Junk." A second piece followed as did a third. *I wish I had just a portion of the money these folks spend on postage,* she thought. She glanced at the next piece of mail and stopped as her hand started to drop it into the trash.

"It's here! It's here!" She held up the envelope with the pink *Perfect Wedding* logo in the corner and twirled around. "Wait. Calm down," she told herself. "Do they send rejection letters to those they reject?" She turned the envelope over and then back to the front. Then she held it up to the light as if she could read the letter without opening the envelope.

"For Heaven's sake," she muttered as she ripped it open. "The only way to read it, you idiot, is to open it." She opened it as if neatness counted and the judges were watching her. She tore just enough off to allow her to slide the letter out. The letter was short, but Dana spent a long time on it because she read it about a dozen times before she believed what it said.

Dear *Perfect Wedding* Entrant:

Congratulations. Out of the thousands of entries, yours has been selected to continue in our search for the next perfect couple to be featured on a future *Perfect Wedding* show.

Our judges are in the process of reading those entries fortunate enough to have been selected in this first round. In two to three weeks or maybe more a follow-up letter will be mailed to notify you whether or not you were fortunate enough to be selected to advance to the next round.

Please remember, due to the volume of entries, it may take a bit longer. It is not necessary for you to contact us. If this letter reached you, any subsequent letters from us will do so as well.

PERFECT WEDDING

Again, congratulations for advancing to the next level.

The *Perfect Wedding* Team

"Oh yeah. Oh yeah. I made it. I made it." She circled the room twirling as she went. "I gotta tell Cathy." She clutched the letter as if afraid it would run away. She opened the door and started to close it behind her. "Oh no," she said as she shoved it back open just before it could click shut. Then she went inside, grabbed her keys, and went back out the door. It had barely locked when she dashed down the stairs.

"Open up, Cathy. Open up! I know you're in there."

"What's wrong?" Cathy jerked the door open and frowned from the doorway. Dana pushed past her.

"Nothing. Not a thing. Everything is just fine." Dana waved the letter in the air and danced around. "Look. Look at this."

"I would if you'd let me see what it says." Cathy crossed her arms. "Well? Are you going to let me see it, or are you going to keep pretending that piece of paper is covered with stars and stripes?"

"Oh. Sure." Dana stared from Cathy to the letter and then back to Cathy as if trying to decide if her best friend could be trusted with it. "Of course. Here." She thrust the letter into Cathy's face.

If not for her nose, Cathy's eyelashes would have brushed against it. She pushed it back. "That was too close for even a seriously nearsighted person."

"Yeah. Sorry. Here." Dana smoothed out the letter, then held it out to Cathy. "Look. Read this." She shifted from one foot to the other and back.

Cathy took the letter and stared at it. Then she looked at Dana. "You should have bought a lottery ticket the day you mailed your entry. Or maybe you should buy one today."

"Forget all that. Look. I'm going to be on the show."

"Not so fast, Miss Thing. The letter says that your entry was picked from the first batch. They probably selected a thousand."

"Probably not that many."

"Okay then. In the high nine hundreds."

"I don't care. I made the first cut. I have ultra-good feelings about this."

"I will be a true friend, bite my tongue, and not mention all of the other crazy things that you have had good feelings about in the past."

"This is different. Besides, I was younger then."

"You were younger a minute ago. A second ago. In fact you're getting older even as we speak."

"Ms. Philosopher, I presume." Dana tried to look indignant. "Age has nothing to do with this, except for the requirements for the rules of the contest."

"What are you going to do?"

"What do you mean, what am I going to do? I'm going to cross every day off my calendar until I get my letter. We are currently at day one and counting."

"Do you think you can keep your momentum for three weeks? Or more?"

"Three weeks or more? What do you mean three weeks?"

PERFECT WEDDING

"Girlfriend, the way you were waving that letter around, I thought you read it."

"I did. At least I thought I did." She frowned. "I was in a hurry to get to the part about acceptance or rejection." She shrugged. "I may not have read as carefully as I should have." She took the letter back and methodically read it again. "Three weeks? Or more? What are those people? Slow readers? Or did they assign one person to the task?" She frowned. "They probably have one little old lady locked in a room for eight hours every day trying to go through all of the entries."

"Why do the words 'little' and 'old' and 'lady' have to be strung together? Maybe it's a man. Maybe it's a young person."

"Nobody in their right mind would trust a man to decide what's romantic and what's not."

"Bill Shakespeare did okay in the romantic writing department."

"Do you notice how far back you had to go to find an example?" Dana sighed. "Three weeks. That's almost a month. I might have to wait a whole month." She plopped into a chair.

"Maybe you should get permission from Mr. Holloway to come over and sit in on one of my reading lessons. If I know when you're coming, I'll be sure to teach a lesson on comprehension. That, of course, includes reading carefully to make sure you get everything the writer is telling you."

"The last thing I need from you is sarcasm." Dana frowned. "I can't wait that long."

"I don't think you have a choice."

"What am I going to do for a whole month?"

"It might not be that long. Have you given any

thought to what you will do if you make the next cut?"

"You and I will go out to that new upscale soul food restaurant. I'll even treat since I'll be the one with the reason to celebrate."

"Thank you, but you have something to do before that."

"What?"

"I hate to pull you down even further than the waiting period did, but there is that teensy problem of a fiancé."

"Fiancé?"

"Yeah. You know, the other half of a wedding couple? Not only does it take two to tango, it also takes two to get married."

"Married?"

"As in wedding." Cathy shook her head and took hold of Dana's arm.

"Come here, sweetie." She led her to the couch and gave her a gentle push. "Get comfy. Auntie Cathy is going to teach you a lesson." She sat in the chair across from Dana and leaned forward. "Here it goes. Are you listening?" Dana glared and crossed her arms across her chest. "I'll take that as a yes. The show is called *Perfect Wedding* for a reason." Cathy spoke as if she were talking to somebody who spoke English, not as a second language, but as a third. "A couple—that means a man and a woman in this case—are supposed to get married. Before they can do that, they need to find each other. If you win, dear friend, you will be expected to have a man to marry. A f-i-a-n-c-é." She stared at Dana, whose glare intensified. "You do not have a fiancé. In fact, unless you're holding out on me, you don't even have a boyfriend. At this time," she added when Dana started to say something. She switched to her normal voice. "What are you going to do?"

"I—I . . ." The rest of Dana's words got lost. If a clock was ticking loud enough it would have gone through many ticks before Dana spoke again. "I just have to find one. That's all." She sat back and smiled serenely.

"That's all. And how will you do that?"

"I have a very good friend who will help me." She leaned forward and grabbed Cathy's hand. "Please, please. Oh, please. You have to help me."

"I would if I could. When I've tried to fix you up in the past, you chewed me up and down about my choices."

"I'm desperate. I can't be so particular. Besides, I'm looking for a temporary fix, not a lifelong companion."

"Temporary?"

"Just until after the honeymoon in Hawaii."

"Maybe, if you find somebody, he won't want to go to Hawaii."

"Not want to go to Hawaii? Who wouldn't want to go to Hawaii? It's Paradise on earth. Besides, I'll give him some of the prize money they'll give us to spend."

"I hate to break this to you, but there are probably people—normal people, I might add—who might not want to go to Hawaii."

"Then they will be eliminated. Anybody too dumb to accept a free trip to Hawaii and spending money is too stupid to pass the interview phase."

"That's right. There has to be an interview phase. How else could they weed out charlatans?"

"There's that sarcasm again."

"I'm just being realistic." She stared at Dana. "One of us has to be."

"Okay, okay. Let's approach this problem methodically. We'll go through your address book starting with A and pull out the single men."

"You won't find too many there. Not even from A to Z. Actually, there's a Zanders, but it's a woman. I'm not even sure about Y—"

"You do understand the term 'figure of speech,' right?" Dana stared at the address book and frowned. The working of her mind was almost visible. "Okay. How about this? Give me a piece of paper and let's brainstorm ideas. No vetoing any idea until we finish," she called out as Cathy went to her desk in the corner of the dining room. Then Dana followed her.

"I think we should work in here." Dana sat at the table.

"Here we go. Now what?" Cathy asked.

"We make a list of possible sources of eligible men." She grabbed the pen and scribbled on the paper. "Your address book for starters. What next? What next?" She doodled leis in the corner of the almost-blank paper. "How about our high school yearbook? And what about the college alumni directory?"

"It's going to take a long time to go through the directory and yearbook to find out who's still available and who lives nearby."

"Nearby?"

"Close enough for you to date, girlfriend." Cathy said.

"Oh. Yeah. Date. That's right." Dana leaned forward. "But no negatives. Remember?" She stared at the paper. "We'll put that last." She circled it and drew a line to the bottom of the paper. "How about Kenny?"

"Kenny? Kenny for what?" Cathy frowned.

"Relax. I don't mean that he's a potential. I know he's yours." In spite of the situation, she smiled. "I mean, he has to have friends. He plays basketball all the time. It's only logical to go to a man when you want to meet eligible men."

"I'm not sure logic enters into any of this."

"Of course it does. How else am I going to stand a chance of finding somebody? And, I repeat, no negatives, all right?"

"I have one suggestion for you. Ask Steve."

"I can't ask Steve. I have to work with him."

"I meant ask him to hook you up. After all, he's a man, too. He must have friends."

"Oh. Yeah. Ask Steve." She wrote. Then she stared at Cathy. "Only as a last resort, though. I have to see that man five days a week. I don't want him dogging me about this or my opinion about his friends every time I see him. It would be awkward when I have to reject one of them."

"Dana. Have you *really* thought this through? You're talking about going on vacation and sharing a suite with a stranger."

"I'll know some of the people on the alumni list." She ignored Cathy's last comment. "I'll get to know the others as time passes. Once I decide on one, I'll concentrate on him. It can be done. I know it."

"I hope so." Cathy sighed. "For your sake, I hope so." She went to her computer, booted it, and pulled over a second chair. "Your baby, you do the honors," she said as she pointed to the chair in front of the computer.

Dana opened a new database as Cathy got the books.

They spent the next few hours going through first Cathy's address book, then the alumni directory and the yearbook. Pulling the eligible men from Cathy's address book didn't take long. She didn't have many listed. Going through the directory, however, was slow work. First they had to separate the men from the women. Then they had to find those within traveling distance.

Dana insisted that they eliminate any men more than ten years older than she was.

"If necessary, I can go back to them," she said as she entered the phone number for the latest find.

Finally, they reached the last name. Cathy closed the book and leaned back. "I do not want to go through something like that again. That was definitely not fun." She waited until Dana copied the file to a disk and removed it. "I do not envy you." She stood. "You'd better start making those calls tonight."

"I will, but first I think we should celebrate the end of phase one."

"Don't you think that would be a little premature?"

"We'll take this one step at a time. Come on up and help me eat the leftovers from yesterday."

"My stomach says that's a good idea, but I won't stay long. You have a lot of work to do and I don't want to slow you down." She turned off the computer. "Before you ask, I will not, I repeat, I will not make any calls for you from the directory. I will call the guys from my address book, though, when you're ready for that."

"Great. Let's start with them."

"Oh, no, you don't. You start with the directory."

"Oh, okay." Dana wrapped her arm through Cathy's and they went downstairs. "I have a good feeling about this."

"Uh-huh. Take me to your food."

They laughed and walked up to Dana's apartment.

Chapter 8

Dana grimaced when a sleepy voice answered the number she called. She glanced at the clock. Nearly midnight.

"Sorry," she mumbled and hung up. "I hope he doesn't recognize my voice when I call him tomorrow."

She had managed to go through a sizeable number of the names on her list from the directory. Unfortunately, she had also crossed most of them off. *If so many men are getting married, why are there so many single women out here?*

"Three men," she said as she turned off the computer after going through the list once more. She stared at the short list. "All that work and I end up with the names of only three men." She stared a few seconds longer, then set the paper on the desk. "Oh well," she said as she left the room to get ready for bed. "That's more than none and I only need one."

She had made one date for lunch for Saturday

and one for Sunday. *Should I really call the third, Milton what's-his-name, sleepyhead, tomorrow? Maybe I won't need him.* She frowned. *Or should I set things in motion just in case?* She shook her head. *Decisions, decisions.* She sighed. *Yeah, I'd better call him tomorrow and see if he's available for dinner. He might be the one to end my search. Then I wouldn't have to bother with the other two.*

She smiled at her image in the mirror as she brushed her hair. *I've got to stay upbeat. We haven't even touched Cathy's list yet or the high school yearbook. If one of these three doesn't work out, maybe one of those will.*

Thoughts beyond the three men from the directory filled her mind as she turned out the light. By this time next week maybe her search would be over.

The next morning during the ride to school she filled Cathy in on the two calls she had made and the last one she'd make this evening.

"You only got three names from that whole list?"

"Kind of sad, isn't it? Everybody is either married, has a significant other, or has moved away. We seem to be the only two stuck in a rut."

"Speak for yourself, girlfriend. I have climbed out with the help of Kenny."

"Nothing like having a friend rub it in."

"I'm not rubbing it in. I'm giving you hope. Some fine brother will come along and make your time in the rut worth the wait."

"Yeah. Sure. Meanwhile, can we do your list tonight?"

"Why not do the high school yearbook next?"

"That will take longer than your book. Can we? Please?"

"I hate to see a grown woman beg." Cathy sighed. "Only on one condition. We will not touch my book if you're going to call late."

"Okay, so I lost track of time last night. Can we, huh? Can we?"

"Not until you see what happens with those three gems you already found." She glanced at her. "Dana, did you take into consideration that maybe—forgive me for this, girlfriend—but maybe you might be rejected by the man you decide to pick?"

"Aside from the fact that I'm entirely too likeable to be rejected, as I pointed out before, what man in his right mind would turn down a free vacation to Hawaii?"

"You are assuming that these guys are in their right minds."

"Don't try to scare me off."

"They *are* still out there. They might be way out there, if you get my drift."

"Cut it out. I'm on a mission and failure is not in my vocabulary. Besides, we're still out here and we're still okay in the right-mind department."

"All right." Cathy shook her head. "If you're so set on this, we can look at my list, but I'm reminding you, my list is short. Extremely short. And don't get your hopes up, anyway. Remember, you already met these guys and rejected them."

"Rejected is such a cold word. Back then I was looking for a potential candidate for a lifetime commitment. Now I'm just looking for a temporary fix. People are more willing to put up with stuff if the end is in sight." She pointed to herself. "Let me amend that. *I* am more tolerant, et cetera, et cetera."

"I hope I don't have to remind you of those words," Cathy said as she parked.

"Not as much as I do," Dana answered as she left the car.

By the time Dana reached her classroom she had shoved aside the thought of the phone calls she would make later. She had even set Hawaii aside and made herself concentrate on her teaching and on her students' learning.

"So, partner," Steve said as he came into her room for lunch. "How long do you think this Superbowl-win high will last?" He smiled as he sat at the table at the back of the room.

"Until we win another ring next year."

"Greedy, greedy, greedy." Steve shook his head slowly. "Typical Philly fan."

"Uh-uh." She shook her head. "Not so. We are not greedy." Dana opened her salad and took the top off the dressing. "We are just keeping score. They owe us for all of the years they didn't reach the top."

"Why don't we let them savor the victory before we put pressure on them?"

"We have to make sure that they know what's expected of them early so they can be focused." They both laughed.

"Speaking of competition," Steve said, "the math team is doing great. I don't want to jinx them, but I think we just might have another winner for the city."

"*Two* more winners, you mean. I'm getting some high-quality writings from the kids."

"Philadelphia: The City of Champions."

"Oh yeah." She took a fork, dipped it into the dressing and then into the salad.

They finished eating in silence. As they ate, Dana had no idea where Steve's thoughts were, but hers were in Hawaii, smelling plumeria and white ginger trees and pineapple fields.

"So. Why the grin?"

"Huh?" The only smells to reach her now were chalk, paper, and leftover salad.

"You have been sitting there with a wide grin on your face all the while you were eating. Private joke?"

"No, I was in Hawaii. If you hadn't pulled me back, I probably would have raided the pineapple field I was seeing and smelling."

"You got it bad."

"And that ain't good."

Steve stared at her for a few seconds. "I have an idea. On Saturday, let's raid the video store and rent every movie that even hints at Hawaii. We can buy paper leis from the party store, pig out on pineapple, turn the thermostat up to tropical, and pretend."

"I can't. I have a lunch date on Saturday."

"A date? I didn't know you were seeing anybody." He set his sandwich down and frowned at her. "Have you been holding out on me? Huh? Is it anybody I know?"

"No, I haven't and I doubt it." She moved her cup around as if suddenly it was in the wrong place.

PERFECT WEDDING 83

"How about Sunday for our Hawaiian getaway, then?"

"I, uh, I have a date on Sunday, too."

"Wow. Two dates on one weekend. It must be serious. Who is he? Have you ever mentioned him to me?"

Dana sighed. "I'm not seeing anybody, exactly."

"But you said you have a date." He frowned. "I mean *dates*. Plural. Hey, partner. You can't leave me hanging. 'Splain yourself, Lucy."

"That is the worst Desi Arnaz imitation I have ever heard."

"Don't change the subject."

"Okay." She sighed and braced herself. "They're blind dates."

"You made two blinds dates? What if you decide that you don't like him after the first one?"

"My dates are with different men." Her voice had lowered to mumbling volume, but Steve heard anyway.

"No dates for so long and now two in one weekend? What's going on?"

Dana stared at her salad plate as if she expected a refill to appear. *It will be three dates, not two, if my plans work out,* she thought, *but who's counting?* She frowned. Where was the bell when you needed it?

"I decided it's time to get back into circulation."

"That is the lamest reason I have ever heard from you. Actually it tops all of the lame reasons I've heard from my students in my whole teaching career."

"You've been teaching for ten years, so don't try to sound as if it's more."

"You're trying to change the subject again. I'm

not buying that excuse so you have to come up with another one." He crossed his arms and stared at her. "You really have me curious. If you're serious about getting back on the dating scene, don't you know somebody already? Why do you have to go the blind date route?"

"I've exhausted that route. I guess I've been out of the game too long."

"You mean they're all taken? Down to the last man who would have been the last one, boy or girl, picked during choosing sides in gym class? Not one left?"

"Man, you do believe in being thorough, don't you? I haven't gone through my high school yearbook yet. As for those I know, there is not one whom I can think of that even my dream trip would make me call. The government's self-appointed role as boss of the world didn't help. A lot of good guys are probably eating sand way off somewhere instead of kicking back with a plate of soul food here at home."

"Why the rush?"

"I don't have time to mess around. Time is flying." Dana threw her bag of trash at the can. If a net had been attached to the can, the bag would have swished. She didn't get the usual satisfaction from her accomplishment.

"Dream trip?" Steve walked over and dropped his trash on top of hers. He came back to the table, but instead of sitting, he stared at her. Suddenly his eyes widened. "This has something to do with that show you told me about, doesn't it?"

The bell rang just as Dana opened her mouth. *Sure. Ring now, why don't you?*

"Yeah." She walked to her desk at the front of the room without looking at him.

"Dana, are you sure about this?"

"Absolutely." She nodded vigorously. *I hope I sound surer than I feel.*

The second bell sounded and Steve walked slowly to the door. He turned once and looked over at her before he left, but he didn't say anything.

Dana sighed after he left. *At least that's over.*

On the drive home Cathy persuaded Dana to wait until after the three dates before looking anywhere else.

"One of those three might be the one and then you'd have to cancel the others."

"Yeah." She sighed. "I guess you're right."

That night Dana called Milton, the third and last man on her list from the alumni directory. She arranged to meet him for dinner on Friday.

I know that all of the articles say never go to dinner on a first date, she thought as she hung up. *But desperate times call for desperate measures and these are certainly desperate times.* She shrugged. *At least I had sense enough to meet him at the restaurant instead of letting him pick me up.* She hesitated, then made another call. Drastic changes in her life called for drastic changes in her appearance.

She usually did her own hair, but what she had in mind was beyond her capability. She called around until she found a hairdresser with an opening on Friday afternoon. *That gives me a few days to chicken out if I want to,* she thought as she hung up again.

* * *

On Thursday Dana was sitting at the table in Steve's room. She had barely opened her juice when he pounced on her.

"Okay. Why not me?" Steve said before he even opened his lunch bag. He leaned back and stared at her.

Dana coughed before her sip of pineapple juice could go down. "What?"

"Are you okay?" Steve patted her on her back.

"You? For what?" She managed to get the juice to trickle down to where it belonged.

"For this dream trip. Why not me? What's wrong with me?"

"You're my friend."

"Friends can't date? I hear friendship is the best basis for a deeper relationship."

"You're—you're like a brother."

"I am a brother."

"You know what I mean. You're like my brother."

"I thought you were just looking for somebody to go on a honeymoon with you. If you're desperate enough to go the blind date route, why not go with what, or in this case, who, you know?"

"Because." *Girlfriend, you have to come up with something better than that.* She frowned. "If things didn't work out, it would be awkward for us to work together."

"I'm willing to try if you are."

"It's not a good idea."

"Going out with strange men is a better idea?"

"They're not strange men."

"You don't know that. You haven't met them. You haven't even seen them. Haven't you heard

PERFECT WEDDING 87

the saying, 'Better the devil you know than one that you don't'? Why not give me a try?"

Why not? She frowned. *Because I might get used to it and wouldn't be able to let you go when the trip is over.* She shook her head. *Where did that come from?*

"Not a good idea." She stared at her plate. "Tell me about the math team."

"I told you yesterday."

"Tell me again. I might have missed something."

Steve just stared at her. Then he told her the same thing he had told her before.

Dana didn't care. At least it changed the subject. Besides, she wasn't listening to his words. She was listening to his "Why not?" playing over in her mind.

That evening she confirmed her date with Milton, who hadn't recognized her voice. She tried not to think of Steve when she did it.

Friday at lunchtime, blind dates, reality shows, and Hawaii were never mentioned. Both she and Steve acted as if those subjects were on a hands-off list. Instead, all of their conversations centered on safe subjects: school activities and what they had for lunch. Nothing remotely tied to dating surfaced.

Ever since that conversation, though, Dana noticed a strange look on Steve's face several times, but when he spoke, he talked about school or basketball or anything else.

After school on Friday, Dana kept the hairdresser appointment she had made. She reported in and was shown to a chair immediately. *They want to make sure that I don't change my mind,* she thought.

"I'm Nita," the hairdresser said. "I'll take care of you. What can we do for you today?" The young woman's smile eased the tension that had Dana ready to run.

Dana explained what she wanted in a voice that sounded as if she had been planning this for months and had finally been able to fit it into her schedule.

"Are you sure?" Nita asked when Dana finished telling her what she wanted. "You have such a nice grade of hair."

"I'm sure."

How long ago did people start grading hair and what method do they use? The A-B-C system or pass/fail? Maybe they used a satisfactory/unsatisfactory rating system. Dana shrugged. *I'm not going to tick her off. It's like making your dentist mad just before he starts poking around in your mouth with sharp instruments.*

She followed Nita to the shampoo chair. *So far so good. You can do this,* Dana thought as she closed her eyes and let Nita do her thing.

Two hours later she walked out of the shop. She was parked only a few yards away, but she managed to pat her hair half a dozen times before she got to her car. A gust of wind blew and she turned her coat collar up and hunched her shoulders around her ears since she no longer had her hair to shield her ears and neck. *What did I do?*

She ran to the car, turned the heat to the fullest, and kept watching the gauge as if that would make it speed to the hot side.

As she drove home she tried to remember if she had kept any winter scarves when she had purged

PERFECT WEDDING

her closet last spring. *I hope I kept at least one. I don't care which one just so it's heavy.*

After she got home she took off the beige blouse she had worn to school with her chocolate-colored pantsuit and put on a deep pink one. A simple string of pearls completed her outfit. Not too fancy, but not too utilitarian, either.

Date one coming up and counting.

She took a deep breath and walked down to her car. *Nothing to it but to do it.*

Chapter 9

Dana hesitated outside the restaurant and took a deep breath.

"Think live plumeria, leis, and tropical breezes," she muttered as she went inside.

She glanced around. The waiting area was full of people. Had everybody in Philadelphia decided to come here tonight? She frowned. *Note to self: Maybe Thursday would be better the next time?* She closed her eyes. *Please don't let me need a next time.* She opened her eyes. *You can do this.*

Her glance stopped at a man sitting alone in the corner of the bench. He didn't look any more at ease than she felt. *Is he waiting for me?* Another deep breath, a smile fastened on, then shaky legs took her over to him.

"Milton?"

"I'm Milton Jones," he said as he stood. "You must be Dana."

"Got it in one." She looked up into his face. Not handsome, but nice.

PERFECT WEDDING

"It's a pleasure to put a face with the voice." He glanced at her hair and frowned.

Dana's hand automatically patted the top. *What's wrong? I should have gone to the ladies' room to check myself out before I came over to him.*

"I made reservations." She patted her hair again, then looked around. "I guess it's a good thing, huh?"

"Yes." Milton didn't bother to look around. Instead he stared at her and waited for her to lead the way to the reservation desk.

They were seated almost immediately, but there was still enough time for Milton to frown at her hair again.

"Is something the matter?" Dana finally asked after they placed their order.

"Did you cut your hair?"

"Yes." She hesitated. "Do you like it?"

"I'm always one to be frank. 'We can count on Milton for the truth,' my friends say." He stared at her. "One of my friends said that my mother gave me the wrong name. 'It should have been Frank,' he told me after I expressed my opinion on one occasion."

The silence built. Dana stared at him, waiting. The waiter brought the salads and still Dana waited.

"Maybe I should be sorry I asked." She smiled. "I just had it cut this afternoon." She touched the short curls on top. "They usually cut it too short. Not a bad idea, when you think of it. It saves you from having to go back sooner. In a week it will probably look the way I wanted." Dana shrugged and began to eat her salad.

Their entrées came and were almost half eaten before Milton spoke again. At least before he spoke words. His frequent glances at her hair and the sour looks that accompanied the glances practically shouted. Finally he carefully set his fork in the middle of his plate.

"I think that a woman's hair is her crowning glory, just as it says in the Good Book. If God had meant for you to have short hair, he would have given it to you." He placed his napkin beside his plate. "Did you get much cut off?"

"Only about a foot and a half." She shrugged. "Maybe two feet." *Lord, please forgive me for the exaggeration, but he deserves it.*

Dana took deep joy at the way Milton's eyes widened at the amount. She ignored the way his glance marched from the top of her head to her shoulders. She wouldn't have been surprised if he had turned her around, whipped out a tape measure, and marked the spot where her hair had brushed her back before she had committed the terrible sin. "Does the amount make a difference?"

"I suppose not."

"Do you get your hair cut?"

"The Bible makes no reference to men's hair."

Dana stared at him. "Actually, it *does* mention men's hair. It tells us what happened when Samson cut his hair, doesn't it?"

"That is ridiculous." Again his stare fixed on her. "Do you intend to let it grow?"

"It grows on its own. I don't have to give it permission."

"This is too serious for joking. You know what I mean."

"I'm sure that I do."

"One of the problems in this world is the way we have strayed from the Good Book."

PERFECT WEDDING

Dana waited until the waiter had checked to make sure that they didn't need anything else. She started to tell him that she needed to get out of there, but since it wasn't on the menu, she didn't bother.

"That I can agree with. I don't think, however, that the length of my hair contributes to the decline of the human race." She reached for the check.

"I'll take care of this." He snatched the check from under her hand. "I don't think a man should allow a woman to pay for his meal."

"That's very noble of you, but since I invited you and since this woman has the audacity to work for money, I can afford it." She took out her wallet.

"That's a discussion for another day."

"Yes." She nodded. "With somebody else."

She stood and walked toward the door. The only way she knew he was coming was from the sound of his footsteps behind her. She stopped at the cash register with him and waited.

"Thank you," she said as he tucked his credit card away. "It has been very interesting."

"Yes." Milton shook his head slowly. "I'm sorry that we are not on the same page. I could become more interested in you."

"Not only are we not on the same page, we're not even in the same section of the library." She held out her hand. "Good luck in finding somebody who feels as you do."

"The same to you," he said as he shook her hand.

They walked out the door together, but anybody watching them would never believe that they had been on a date.

Day one and still looking, she thought as she drove home.

Dana had barely unlocked the door when the phone rang. She rushed to answer it.

"Okay. What's the story? What was he like? Do you get to put the other two on hold? Did you at least get a base hit your first time at bat?"

"How long were you watching out the window for me to come home?"

"That's got nothing to do with anything. Are you coming down or do I come up?"

"I'm coming down. That way I can leave when I get tired of your interrogation."

"Just gentle, interested questions from your best friend."

"Somebody besides me needs to get a life."

"You could be down here filling me in by now. Hang up and come on down."

Dana's smile stayed as she walked down the stairs.

"Come on, come on. I'm waiting," Cathy called around the corner. "Okay, hurry up. I'm . . ." She stared at Dana. Her open mouth matched the open door.

"Hi, Cathy." Dana slid past her and went into the apartment.

"Girl, what in the world did you do?" She fumbled behind her to shove the door shut as if afraid to take her gaze off Dana. She stared at her as if Dana had sprouted a second head and a third had started to appear.

"It's just a little change."

"Little change? A little change is when you pin it

up instead of back. You . . ." She eased her hand toward Dana's head. It hovered for a few seconds as if conferring a blessing, then drifted back to her side. "You cut your hair off."

"It was just a little haircut."

"Little haircut?" She patted the ends of the spikes that looked as if they belonged on Halle Berry's head when her pixie look was in. "And Philadelphia is just a little country town."

"It was time for a change."

"But you had such a nice head of hair. Such a nice length of such good—"

"Don't you dare add the word 'hair' after the word 'good.' We should be past that. As my science teacher said when he heard one of the other girls use that term, 'Any hair growing on your head is good hair.' I agree."

"Sure. Look what's growing out of *your* head. Or remember what *was* growing up there." She shook her head. "Okay. I need a cup of coffee. I'm speechless."

"Speechless? You just did a fantastic job of imitating a speaker." Dana followed Cathy into the kitchen. "I guess I'll have a cup of hot tea."

"You'll be drinking a lot of hot stuff trying to stay warm until your bout with madness grows out," Cathy said as she got things out for Dana. Then she turned on the burner under the kettle.

"Hurry with your coffee. Maybe a shot of caffeine will blunt your words."

"The truth shall set you free."

"I have been free all of my life. I just decided to allow my head the same privilege."

"Really? Why? Why now? What made you do it? You never mentioned this when we got home from school today. Why?" Cathy dared to pat the curls on top of Dana's head.

"Because I knew you'd try to talk me out of it."

"You know that's not what I meant. Why did you cut it?"

"New approach, new look." She brushed her own hand over her hair. "It will be easy to take care of. Wash and wear."

"But it was a nice length."

"*This* is a nice length." She patted the top of her head.

She was trying to to get used to the hairdo, but she still hadn't convinced herself that the cut was a good idea.

"But doesn't your neck get cold? Doesn't your head get cold?"

"Yeah. Just a little." *And Dalembert is just a little tall.* She shook her head. This was going to be the longest winter of her life.

"Uh-huh." Cathy shook her head slowly. "Oh well." She shrugged. "Talking about it won't make it grow back instantly." She sighed. "Sometimes— and this is one of those times—I just don't understand you."

"It's just that, with all of the changes, I thought a new look was in order."

"Changes? You mean dating with a capital D?"

"Dating, Hawaii." She shrugged. "You know." She stared into her teacup as if hoping to see China on the other side.

"Oh, no, you didn't." Cathy set her cup down. "I know you didn't get your hair cut in anticipation of a trip." She shook her head rapidly. "Scratch that . . . counting on winning that contest?"

"I just wanted something new." She drained her

cup. "Can we please talk about something else? Please? Anything else?"

"Sure. Okay." Cathy stood. "Talking never got anything done except more talking. Let's go into the living room and get comfortable." She pulled Dana up and into the living room. She barely gave her time to sit.

"Okay. Tell me. Is it a go? Did you hit the bull's-eye on the first try? Are wedding bells in your future? Did you even hit the target at all?"

In answer Dana released a sigh and shook her head slowly.

"Uh-oh. This does not look good," Cathy said. "Not good at all. Hit a bump in the road, huh?"

"Hit it, veered off into the woods, and never went back."

"What happened?"

"It would have gone better if I hadn't cut my hair. He agreed with you."

"He didn't drag up that old crowning glory speech, did he?"

"Dragged it out and put it front and center. He did everything but cite the chapter and verse."

"I was speaking from the standpoint of you personally, not women in general. Besides, I'm your friend. Friends are allowed to express such opposing opinions. Strangers are not." She frowned. "Did the brother explain why people can fly without wings and don't have to walk everywhere?"

"We didn't get that far." Dana smiled. "Have I got a story for you? Sit back and settle in."

An hour later, after embellishing her tale and even doing a dynamite imitation of Milton's voice and action, Dana finished her story. They both laughed. Each time the laughter faded they would look at each other, one would repeat a line, and they would be off again. Finally they stopped for good.

"One down and I hope not too many more to go. Actually, I only have two more prospects. I don't hold out much hope from your list or the yearbook, and the deadline is galloping toward me." She stared at Cathy. "A month goes fast when you're not ready for what's at the end of it."

"A month? You have to have somebody in a month? Did you tell me that before?" Cathy shook her head. "No. You didn't. I thought you just had to respond to the next letter in that time frame."

"The letter didn't say so, but I'm sure they'll want some proof of a fiancé at that time."

"Good possibility." Cathy pushed back her shoulders. "But don't panic. We still have my list. We'll go through it again. This time you won't be so particular. We'll find you somebody in time. You got the bad date out of the way. You paid your dues up front." She nodded. "Tomorrow's will be better. It has to be. You'll see."

"Yeah. I hope so," Dana said as they stood.

She left. During the short walk upstairs she kept telling herself, "Tomorrow's will be better." She reached her apartment and still hadn't convinced herself of that.

Chapter 10

It wasn't.

At 11:45 on Saturday Dana left her apartment and drove to Sadie's Down-home Cooking Restaurant. Her destiny was awaiting. She hoped.

She paused outside the door and stared at the logo etched on the glass panel. This was a different restaurant from yesterday, but the quivers in her stomach felt the same. *What if he decides that I'm not right for him before he even hears my suggestion? What if he says "Thanks, but, no thanks" after he hears me out? What if he says he's allergic to wedding bells even if they are phony?*

"Quit with the what-ifs, already. This is your idea," she muttered to herself. "Think white ginger blossoms. Think palm trees and ocean sunsets." She closed her eyes, shook her head, then pushed open the door.

A quick glance around revealed several people waiting at the discreet bar to the side. She hesitated before going to the reservation desk.

"I'm meeting someone. Don Mitchell."

"Oh yes. Just a minute. He just came in. I'll call for him." He leaned toward the mike.

"That's all right. Just point him out." *If I'm going to be dumped, I don't want an audience.*

The man on duty shrugged, then nodded toward a man sitting at the corner of the bar. Dana walked over to him quickly as if afraid she was going to change her mind.

"Don Mitchell?" She forced a smile.

"Yes. Dana?" A smile greeted her as the man stood. A nice smile. "I was a little early." He shrugged and a slight dimple appeared in his cheek. "I don't like to be late."

"On time isn't a fault." Dana's smile was no longer forced. *Nice.*

"Shall we go to the table? I must admit that I'm a little hungry. I was too busy to stop for lunch. Saturday or not, I had work to do." He put his hand under her elbow and escorted her with the proper amount of pressure: not too territorial, not too weak.

"I've had days like that," Dana said. *I can hear that Hawaiian music now,* she thought as they followed the waitress to their table.

"The money business doesn't pay any attention to what day or date it is." Don laughed. "It ignores the clock, too."

The waitress came and took their orders before Dana could respond.

"Money business?" she said after the woman left.

"Yes." Don leaned forward. "I'm am investment broker. I'm also a money manager. You'd be surprised at how many people aren't saving for the future. It's as if they don't expect it to get here. Or

PERFECT WEDDING 101

maybe they don't expect to be there to see it." He laughed as their salads were placed in front of them.

"It might not be that. Maybe they just don't have the money."

"Everybody has some excess expenditure in their budget."

"Not everybody." Dana thought of her monthly bills.

"Sure they do." Don whipped out a small notebook with a built-in calculator. He drew the pen from the side and clicked the point down. "Let's take you."

"Me?" Dana frowned.

"Sure. What does your budget look like?" His pen was poised, ready to swoop down to the paper and make its marks.

"My budget?" She shrugged. "The bills come in, I pay them. If there's anything left, I buy a pralines and cream ice cream cone." She wasn't operating that close, but it wasn't any business of his.

"How many?"

"Huh?"

"How many ice cream cones a week and how many scoops?"

"What? You're kidding, right?"

The waitress brought their food. That should have given Dana time to regroup. It *should* have.

"I'm very serious. Those cones cost . . ." He stared at her. She stared back. "Let's say they cost about two dollars per cone and you get two a week." He scribbled on the pad.

Dana forgot that she found cold smothered pork chops unappetizing. She sat taller so she could see what he was writing. "What are you doing?"

"Showing you how you could save money." He pulled the pen away. "If you buy a half gallon of the same flavor ice cream at the discount supermarket, it would last you several weeks." He stared at her. "Of course, you'd have to limit yourself to eating the same portion and the same number of days." He grinned at her. "At first, it might be difficult to resist the temptation to eat more per cone or to have a cone on more days, but it could be done."

Dana took a taste of the pork chop. "This is delicious." She pointed her fork at his plate. "Your baked chicken is getting cold."

"You're in denial."

"I beg your pardon?" She chewed the bite of pork and washed it down with a sip of her diet soda.

"Don't be concerned. It's quite common for people to avoid facing their frivolous expenditures." He sampled his chicken. "This is quite good." He nodded. "Of course, it could be prepared at home much cheaper. If you read the circulars you can catch a sale at the supermarket. Then you can buy enough chicken to get you through six or even eight meals." He stared at her. "And for the same price as this one." He swallowed. "Dining out is another expense you must examine closely."

"I must?"

"Oh yes." He nodded again. "This can get to be quite expensive. How often do you do this?"

"Not often." *Good thing I didn't suggest the place where Milton and I went.* She ate some more. "This is really delicious."

"Good answer." He laughed. "I mean the fact that you don't eat out often." He tasted the greens.

PERFECT WEDDING   103

"Do you know how cheaply one can cook greens?" He shrugged. "You have to factor in the amount of gas you spend cooking them the proper amount of time, but you would still come out ahead." He nodded yet again. "Would you say you eat out once a week? Or maybe this is how you treat yourself on payday." He pulled the pad to him. "Let's see, you spent . . ." He frowned at her. "What is the cost of your meal?"

Dana shrugged but told him. He probably knew anyway. Often she had used this same tactic with her students.

"Now, this is a prime example." He pointed to his plate. "If you must indulge in such an extravagance as dining out, you should make your choices carefully. For example, chicken is usually cheaper and the portions are larger. You paid two dollars more for your meal than I did for mine." His pen flew across the paper. "If you had opted for water to drink as I did . . ." He paused to take a sip. "You could have saved even more."

"How much would I have saved?" Dana took a bigger bite than usual. She stared at her plate. *Speaking of numbers, how many more bites before I'm finished?*

"You could have purchased a two-liter bottle of the very same thing for a little more than a dollar. Even less if you waited for a sale. You paid more than that for your one drink." He stared at her as if she had added number eight to the deadly sin list.

"They give free refills. Did you factor that in?"

"No, I did not." He moved his stare from her to the paper and then back to her. "But I doubt if you'll drink two liters." He set the pen down and ate another mouthful. "Take care of the pennies and the dollars will take care of themselves, I always say." He held up his water glass and then took a sip.

"I believe you do." Dana held up her soda. The waitress hurried over and topped it off. Dana smiled.

"I didn't say it first, but I find that saying so apropos so many times and in so many ways that I would have said it even if somebody else hadn't coined it first."

"I'll bet you would have."

During the rest of the meal Don cited everyday examples of how people in general and she in particular could become millionaires if they were sincere enough. When he mentioned buying two-ply bathroom tissue and separating it into two one-ply rolls, Dana had decided that not even Hawaii would make her take things further with Don't-Spend-Money Don.

He'd probably want to sell the honeymoon and take the money instead.

They finished eating and, since dessert didn't come with the meal, Don informed the waitress that they were through.

"I'd like to take the rest of my meal with me," he told her. "Tomorrow's dinner."

"Not tonight's?" Dana asked.

"Oh no. This meal was my big meal of the day. I'll probably have a grilled cheese sandwich for dinner. What about you?"

"I'm not sure yet. It's early."

"You could have saved half of your meal, too." He looked at her plate. "The portions were larger than average."

"Yes, they were and yes, I should have. Sometimes I do, but not today. I skipped breakfast."

"That is bad on so many fronts."

"It is?"

"Oh yes. You could have eaten breakfast a lot cheaper at home than what half of your lunch cost you." He held up his hand and folded down one finger. "You should always eat breakfast. It gives you the stamina to make wise choices." Another finger curled next to the first. "Just as you should never go shopping on an empty stomach, you should never go out to eat when you are starving." A third finger dropped down.

"I understand." Dana decided to save the other two fingers. "I'll do better the next time."

"I'm glad I got through to you." Don smiled at her. "Sometimes it only takes a gentle nudge from an observer for somebody to change her ways." His smile widened. Then he pulled his calculator in front of him.

"Let's see. You had the smothered pork chop." This time he didn't ask her the cost. His fingers punched the correct numbers. "And let's not forget the cola." He shook his head as he entered those numbers.

"Yes. Let's not."

Dana stared as Don entered the figures, got totals, and then worked on them. After he finished, he wrote on his notepad.

"Here is what I mean." He held up the paper so she could see it. "Here's your total." He pointed to one. "And here's mine. See the difference a little planning can do? And keep in mind, I get another dinner out of my total." He grinned at her. "I figured in the tip. There was an odd penny, so I'll cover that."

"Thank you so much." Dana took out her wallet. "However, since this was my idea, I'll pay for all of it."

"I wouldn't hear of it. I ate. Therefore, I'll pay for mine. If you're paying cash, I'll put it on my credit card." He smiled again. "The next time we can go somewhere else. I know a very reasonable little place. The neighborhood isn't that great, but we'd be fine for lunch."

"Uh-huh." Dana counted out her share. "I didn't have any pennies, so keep the whole nickel."

"See? That's what I'm talking about." Don pulled out some change. "Here you are." He slid two pennies toward her.

Dana stared at them, then picked them up. "I'm leaving now. It's been . . ." She frowned. "Very interesting."

"I'll call you," Don said as he stood.

"I'm very busy. If I get some free time, I'll call you."

"Well, okay. I hope you learned something." He smiled.

"Oh, I did. I really did."

Dana shook her head as she went to her car. *I learned that I don't want to go to Hawaii bad enough to put up with everything.*

She drove home thinking, *Two down and I don't hold out much hope for number three.*

Chapter 11

"Wow," Cathy said later as Dana finished telling about her lunch. "I'd accuse you of making that up, but not even you could fabricate a story like that." She shook her head. "Down to the last penny, huh?"

"Yes. I mean, not exactly. Remember, he offered to pay the odd penny and he was magnanimous enough not to take the extra two cents." Dana sighed. "After that experience, I'm not getting my hopes up for tomorrow's lunch date with Fred." She shook her head. "I know I'm not perfect." She stared at Cathy. "Milton and Don were very happy to point out some of my flaws. But please . . ." She folded her hands together. "Please, please tell me that I'm not as bad as that."

"You're not as bad as that."

"You're not just saying that because you're my friend?"

"Even your worst enemy would agree with me."

"I think I'll let that one go onto the sidetrack

where it belongs." She shook her head and sighed. "I don't expect success tomorrow. I'm on a strike-out roll. Either that or I discovered the mother lode of losers."

"After the Time Warp Refugee and the Miser, I can understand that." Cathy patted Dana's arm. "On the other hand, look on the bright side."

"Bright side? What? That I've eliminated two out of three? This is like that game show with the three doors. I might not like what's behind door number three, either." She picked up the throw pillow and squeezed it. "I'm not being picky. You know how desperate I am. That deadline is barreling down on me and I'm without a fiancé. What if I get picked and I still don't have somebody?"

"There's always Steve."

"No. Not Steve." She tried not to remember the kiss. "He dates a lot. It wouldn't be fair to take him out of the dating game on a pretense. No, not Steve." She frowned. "I don't know what to do."

Cathy stared at her for a few seconds. "Okay. I have something else to occupy your mind." She leaned forward. "Ken got tickets for the Old School Awards Show next Saturday night. He has a cousin working the event and he snagged tickets." She grinned. "They'll feature all of the groups from back in the day. And there's a dance afterward to the same great music. Is that great or what?"

"That's great *and* what. Overload on fun, but take notes so I can experience it vicariously?"

"Well, okay, if that's what you want." Cathy shrugged and struggled to be casual. "I just thought you'd like to experience it for yourself."

"Huh?"

"We have a ticket for you. You know I can't leave my friend out."

"Really? I get to see the singers we used to listen to in college?"

"Better than a recording."

"Wow. Oh, wow." Dana jumped up and danced around the floor. "Name some names."

Each time Cathy named another singer, Dana jumped and twirled around and sang a few lines from one of their hits. By the time Cathy finished telling the lineup, they were whirling, moving, and grooving to their own singing. Finally, Cathy collapsed on the sofa and pointed to Dana.

"Girl, why don't you show a little enthusiasm?" She laughed. "One thing, though . . ."

"Uh-oh. Here it comes. The catch."

"No problem. No catch. Or maybe a good catch." She frowned. "Can catches be good? I mean besides men?" She shook her head rapidly. "But I digress. We just have to check our wardrobes for something fine to wear. It's a black-tie affair."

"It's been a long time, but I know I have something dressy in the back of my closet just waiting for a chance to see the night lights again. I only hope it's a classic and not outdated." She started dancing around again. Then she pulled Cathy from the couch and led her in one of the fast dances they had loved while in college. They laughed as they moved around the room. Finally they collapsed onto opposite ends of the couch.

"If we do this well now on our own, imagine how well we'll do with music," Cathy said.

"You know, I'm going to get on up next Saturday even though I won't have a partner."

"What do you mean, no partner? Didn't I tell you? Kenny has four tickets. He invited Steve to go, too."

Dana turned to Cathy. "You know Steve's name never parted your lips during this conversation."

"Merely an oversight."

"Still playing matchmaker."

"Come on, girlfriend. Admit it. You'll have more fun with somebody to dance with than you would on the floor by yourself."

"Yeah." Dana nodded slowly. "I guess you're right."

"Good. That's settled. Now let's check our closets. We have to see if we'll have to bite the bullet and go shopping."

"Yeah. Poor us if we do."

"Really, poor us. The look we want will cost big bucks if we don't have something that will work." She stood. "Since we're down here, let's check my closet first."

By dinnertime, they had each found something that would allow them to fit in next Saturday.

"Don would have a cow if he knew, but let's order takeout from Lillie Ann's. After that lunch with him, I have to feed my soul." She went to the phone. "You know," she said as she pushed in the numbers she didn't have to look up, "I'm tempted to call him and tell him what I'm doing." She shook her head. "No. It wouldn't be any fun if I couldn't see his reaction."

The food came and they talked about their favorite songs of the groups they would see. Then they talked about the clothes they would wear and what shoes would be the most comfortable. No matter the topic, though, behind the conversations Dana's thoughts hovered over her being with Steve in a formal setting. *It's not a date*, she told herself for the tenth time. *A mutual friend just happened to offer tickets to something we both would like to attend.*

"What do you think?"

"Huh?"

"Girl, are you already partying without me? We have a week to go. You can't let your mind wander off. If you give it that much time, it might not be able to find its way home."

"What did you say?"

"Out of all of your favorites from back in the day, which one is your all-time-favorite-no-song-could-possibly-top-this?"

"I can't choose. That's like asking a mother to choose her favorite child."

"The songs won't know."

"I'll know and I'll feel guilty every time I hear one of the ones that I don't pick."

"I swear, girlfriend, sometimes your mind goes weird."

"In an artist it would be called creativity."

"In you, it's called weird." Cathy dodged the pillow Dana tossed at her.

They talked a good while longer before Dana went upstairs to her apartment.

Once she got inside, her mind made a straight line to next Saturday as if it had been waiting for the other subjects to get out of the way.

I'm glad to be going, she thought. *I'll see groups I've listened to, but have never seen in person.* She sighed. *I'm glad I'll have somebody to dance with, but Steve?*

She thought of the kiss. The one and only kiss they had shared in all the years they had known each other.

That kiss wasn't spectacular in itself. But sharing it with Steve . . . She was surprised at the heat flowing through her at the memory of Steve's mouth on hers. It had been over almost as soon as it had begun. Still, she remembered it with an intensity that made it feel like a few seconds ago.

As she moved around getting ready for bed, her mind stayed on that kiss as if it had found a groove and had no intention of moving.

Why am I still hung up on it? she asked herself when she tried to think of her lesson plans for Monday, the kids' essays, even the coming dance. *Why won't it work?* She shook her head.

Don't go there. Do not go there. Keep it to a friendship level. If for no other reason than that you know there's no way you could survive working with him if things didn't work out. Move away from there, she ordered her mind. She pulled on her nightshirt, and her mind followed a different tangent.

You're not his type. His girlfriends seem to be little and the cutesy type. The only thing cutesy about you is . . . She frowned. *Nothing. There is nothing cutesy about me.* She sighed. *Where am I going with this? Why am I fixated on Steve?*

She crawled into bed and turned off the light. Her mind took that as permission to run free.

Steve. Steve who would be labeled a hunk by anyone's standards. Steve. Her friend. Steve, the one she had to work with five days a week. Steve, who had never, in all the years he had known her, showed an interest in being anything to her except a friend. Steve.

PERFECT WEDDING 113

She drifted into sleep. As if her internal dialogue had given it permission, her mind created a scenario featuring her and Steve. What they did together in her dream could not be called merely friendship by anyone.

Dana awoke much earlier than her usual time. Shadows had barely begun to lighten in her bedroom. She touched the bed beside her and brushed her hand across the cold sheet.

A dream. It had been a dream. Her face warmed as she recalled her dream. *Dirty young woman,* she called herself as she remembered what she and Steve had done in her dream. They had explored and learned each other's bodies as if a test would be given later and they were determined to ace it.

Dana threw off the quilt as her body warmed even more, but she didn't get up. She shifted slightly. She ached in places that she shouldn't have since she had spent the night alone. She sighed and turned onto her other side.

Steve's hands had worked magic on her that no wizard could achieve. He had touched and stroked and teased every sensitive part of her. Her breathing increased just remembering that part of the dream. His mouth had done things to her breasts that had felt so good they should be illegal. She shifted to her back.

She tried to control her breathing as her hands bunched the sheet. His hands had blazed a slow sinuous trail down her body, circling the tips of her breasts, but, despite their hard anticipation, had refused to touch the tips. His fingers had trailed over her stomach, made a side trip down her hips, before returning to her middle.

She moaned as she remembered vividly how he had found her core, hot and moist and waiting for him. Still, he had used only his fingers, barely touching her, but setting her on fire. She tried to control her moan now as she remembered her moan then.

In her dream, she had begged him for release. An eternity later, he had given it. He had slid into her and she had closed around him, complete. Finally, she was complete.

Now as exhausted as if she had experienced the real act rather than remembered a dream, she lay there and drifted back to sleep. Finally, a long time later she was startled awake.

What had just happened? She frowned. *How could my mind do that to me? I can't get involved with Steve. It would destroy what we have.* When they broke up and she had to see him every day, it would be awkward, embarrassing, humiliating, devastating, and every other word that would make her regret having allowed something to develop with him. She hurried from the bed as if to make sure her mind didn't betray her again.

Cold shower, cold shower, she thought as she went to the bathroom. *Think pure thoughts. Date. Focus on your date. Byron Quimby might be the one.* She turned on the cold water. *That's your problem. You are hearing the contest clock ticking and you are beyond desperate. Chill.* She stuck her hand into the shower, but snatched it out again. *No sense in being ridiculous. Cold showers probably aren't all they're cracked up to be.* She added some hot water, and as soon as the spray adjusted to a comfortable temperature, she stepped inside.

Ten minutes early, Dana stood outside the same restaurant she had been in yesterday. *I'd think déjà vu, if I didn't know this was really happening and that somebody other than Don was waiting for me.* She took a deep breath, then reached for the door. Opening it was hard since her fingers were crossed, but she managed. *Maybe this is the one, maybe, just maybe, just maybe,* her internal voice chanted. She fixed a smile on her face and tried to dump negative thoughts that might jinx her.

She looked around the waiting area. She had beat the church crowd. Good. One man sat alone at the end of the bench talking on a cell phone. *He must be the one.* She was a few inches outside his personal space when he looked up.

"Byron?" she asked.

"Yes." He glanced at her. "Just a minute." He put the phone back against his face. "I'll call you later. Yes." He nodded. "Me too." He flipped it shut, tucked it into his pocket, then stood.

"You must be Dana."

Dana was proud of herself for not saying, "Duh." Who else did he expect to meet? She shook the hand that he held out. "Shall we go in?"

"Yes." Byron waited for her to go first.

Dana's smile relaxed. *Nice voice. Nice smile, too.*

"Good afternoon." The waiter glanced at Byron but stared at Dana. She ignored the puzzled look on his face that changed to a frown and then a smirk when he recognized her.

It was none of his business that she had been here yesterday with a different man, she thought as he led them to a table immediately.

Their orders were taken right away. Then things tumbled downhill from that point.

"My mother always talks about this place. She loves it. In fact, I was talking to her when you came over." Byron frowned. "She hinted strongly that I should bring her with me." He stared at Dana. "I told her that I didn't think it would be appropriate on a first date." His stare grew more intense.

Is he expecting me to tell him it would have been all right?

"So. You stayed in the Philadelphia area after graduation?" *Girl, you have no problem releasing a "duh" of your own, do you?*

"Oh yes." He allowed his stare to release her. "I had to stay close to Mother." He leaned forward, but moved back as the waiter set their salads in front of them. "She's all alone. All of her friends live here. I couldn't expect her to just pick up and move away." He stared at the dressing at the side of his salad.

While his attention was focused there, Dana resisted the urge to see if some long apron strings were fastened to him and she had missed them.

Nothing wrong with being concerned about your mother, she tried to convince herself.

"I do hope this dressing is better than what we use at home." He drizzled a little on a bit of shredded carrot.

"We? You live with your mother?" Dana dipped her fork into her dressing but didn't pick up any salad.

"Of course. I told you. She's all alone."

"Is she well?"

"Oh yes. We just don't think she should be alone."

"Oh." Dana closed her eyes, and not just to say grace. She glanced at her watch. Hawaii was drifting further and further away.

We might be able to pretend to be in love and be convincing about it, but it would strain our credibility to the breaking point if Byron's mother came on the honeymoon, and I can tell that leaving Mommy Dearest at home is beyond his comprehension. No way could I explain that away to the contest people.

"This is good," Byron said after swallowing a mouthful of salad. "The dressing is better than what we use at home. Thank goodness." He poured the rest of the dressing. Then he scraped what was left out of the container.

"You don't like the brand you use at home?" Dana had yet to taste hers.

"It's the worst stuff I've tasted."

"Why don't you switch brands?"

"Mother likes that one. She's used it for years."

"Have you thought of getting a second brand for yourself?" *I can't believe we're having this discussion about salad dressings, of all things.*

"And hurt Mother's feelings?" He signaled to the waiter.

"Oh." *He's acting as if I suggested he set her on an ice floe and shove her out to sea.*

"May I have more dressing, please?" he asked when the man came over.

"Yes, sir." The waiter stared at Byron's plate.

Pieces of salad were barely visible under the thick covering of dressing. He shrugged slightly, then left.

"Do you ever go on vacation?" *Maybe we could make it work out. They'll probably put us up in a suite. They usually have a sofa bed, don't they? It would be unusual, but we could pull it off taking his mother with us.* Hawaii was getting brighter. She could almost hear ukuleles strumming.

"Every summer we go somewhere for a week. We go away again in the fall."

"Where have you gone?" Things were definitely getting brighter.

"We've gone to Canada, the Shore, D.C. Once we went to Williamsburg. I thought Mother would enjoy seeing that part of history." He shrugged. "She didn't. Too much walking, she said."

He took the dressing the waiter brought before it touched the table.

Dana watched Byron dump the new container onto his plate. His salad looked like a very tiny volcano covered with a ton of ranch dressing lava. She continued to stare as he proceeded to clean his plate.

"Have you ever gone to Las Vegas?" Dana ate some of her salad as she waited for Byron to answer. It wasn't until three forkfuls later that he took his attention from his plate to answer.

"It's too far to drive. Mother doesn't like drives that are too long. She gets bored."

"Couldn't you fly?" Dana asked the question, but she was afraid she already knew the answer.

"Mother doesn't fly. She says she has to stay grounded." Byron stopped eating long enough to laugh. "Mother has a great sense of humor."

"You'd never consider going without her, huh?"

PERFECT WEDDING

Byron stared at her as if she had committed the worst sin ever in the history of the world.

"I couldn't leave Mother alone. I thought I made that clear."

"Yes. You did."

Dana ate more of her salad even though she felt Hawaii drifting away and the ukuleles going silent.

Their entrées came and Dana was glad she had ordered baked chicken breast instead of the triple-decker sandwich she had considered. The chicken was less chewy. She'd be finished much quicker.

By the time the meal was over Dana knew more about Byron's mother than she did her own.

"Maybe next time I'll bring her with me." He wiped inside the salad bowl with a piece of bread and popped the dripping piece into his mouth. "You'll like Mother." He glanced at the check and pulled out his wallet. "She's easy to get along with considering that she didn't have an easy life. She—"

"I'm glad things are better for her now." Dana cut off his sentence. Any more about Saint Mother and she would have enough to write a biography.

"I'll call you after I clear a date with Mother." He took out a credit card and picked up the check.

"I'll pay for this. After all, it was my idea."

"Oh, I can't let you do that. Mother raised me to be a gentleman."

"I'm sure she did. Well, thank you." Dana stood.

"She goes to the casinos a lot. I can't expect her to give up a trip just for lunch. That's why I have to check with her first."

"Does she win often?"

"She goes for fun. It's recreation for her. She hasn't had much in her life."

"Oh." *She loses, huh?* Dana thought, but she didn't say it out loud. She walked from the table. Byron followed and stopped at the cash register. "Well," she said, "good-bye. It's been . . . interesting."

"I'm looking forward to seeing you again."

"Uh huh."

Dana could see Hawaii fading away to nothing. She could barely visualize plumeria trees, and they were her favorite.

She walked toward her car.

Byron stayed beside her. "Not everybody is understanding about Mother."

"I'll bet." Dana increased her speed and not just because of the cold.

"You'd think they never had a mother of their own." He shrugged, which was hard to do since Dana was walking so fast and he was trying to keep up. "They probably didn't have the kind of mother that I do. Mothers like her are very rare."

"Uh-huh." Dana stopped beside her car and released the alarm.

"So, I'll call you. Is tomorrow okay?" Byron frowned. "It will have to be late in the evening. I've left Mother alone today. We usually make a day of it on Sunday. Early church service, then a nice buffet brunch afterward. Mother loves buffet brunches." He shrugged. "I can take them or leave them, but . . ." He shrugged again.

"You wouldn't want to disappoint Mother."

"You do understand." He showed his brightest smile yet. "So I'll call you around eight. One of Mother's favorite programs is on then and she won't miss my company."

"Uh, Byron." Dana opened her car door and

scooted inside. "I'm pretty busy. Maybe you should wait awhile."

"Okay. I'll call you next week. Like I said, I have to clear a date with Mother."

"Make it later than that." Dana started her motor. "My schedule is busy for weeks ahead." She fastened her seat belt. "In fact, I'm busy for months into the future. Thank you for lunch," she said before she put the car into gear. "Good-bye."

At least I didn't tell another lie by adding "I'm sorry."

She stopped at Cathy's but remembered that Cathy had talked Kenny into going to Longwood Gardens with her. He agreed and she agreed to let him show her around his alma mater, Lincoln University, while they were out that way.

"Oh well, later will be soon enough. It will give me time to reflect on my date with Byron. Maybe it wasn't as bad as I think." She sighed as she entered her apartment. *But I'm afraid it was. Going over it won't soften the experience. Cathy's list, here we come.*

She tried calling Cathy twice. The last time was after the eleven o'clock news went off. *They must have decided to make a late day of it.* She smiled. *Maybe they made a night of it, too.*

She deserves it, Dana thought as she got ready for bed. *I'll bet Kenny doesn't have apron strings tethering him. Good for them.*

She climbed into bed trying to think of promising options.

Chapter 12

"So. How was your day yesterday?" Dana asked as she got into the passenger seat of Cathy's car.

"Perfect. Just perfect." Cathy's grin was enough to melt six inches of snow if there had been any around.

"You enjoyed Longwood Gardens?"

"Uh-huh." Cathy pulled out of the parking lot and drove to Chester Pike.

"And your tour of Lincoln University?"

"We lucked out there. They had a display in the library mentioning African-American historical sites in the area. A posted brochure gave information about a tour, so we took it." She nodded. "They offer it year-round. You and I have to go this spring. We saw stops on the Underground Railroad in that area. We knew that Cheyney had been a stop, but I wasn't aware of the others."

"So you and Kenny had a good day."

"Oh yeah." She glanced at Dana. "We had an even better time after we got back to my place."

"You didn't."

"If I didn't, my imagination is better than I thought." She laughed.

Dana's thoughts flew to the dream she had had about Steve. It was still so vivid that she was heating up just thinking about it right now. She resisted the urge to open the window. Cathy would think she was running a fever. She sighed. In a way, she was: a more-than-crazy-Steve fever.

"Are you going to tell me about it?" Dana asked.

"Only that it was unbelievably mind-blowing." She glanced at Dana. "All three times." She held up her hand when Dana started to say something. "Uh-uh. No details. I don't want to jinx this thing between us." She stopped for a red light. "Your turn."

"Okay. The short version is that Mother makes three."

"Huh?"

Dana used the rest of the ride to fill her in on the details.

"What are you going to do next?" Cathy asked as she parked.

"At first I thought I'd go to your list, but you were right. I've been there and done that. Even in desperation I can't think of anybody on it that has possibilities." She sighed. "Now I think I'll try speed dating. I told you about that program I saw the other day."

"You told me, but I thought you were just making conversation. You wouldn't really try something like that, would you?"

"Desperate times require desperate measures."

"But those men will be strangers."

"A stranger is merely a fiancé you haven't yet met.

Besides, Milton, Don, and Byron were strangers, too."

"Yeah. And look what happened there."

"Child, don't remind me. I will have nightmares about this past weekend well into my old age." She shook her head. "My never-having-been-to-Hawaii old age." Dana sighed. "See you after school. Have a good one."

"You too."

Dana walked across the lot and entered her building. *When I get home today I'll do a search for speed-dating info. I hope I find something positive. I can feel Hawaii moving out of reach as fast as a surfboard ride on a record-high reverse tidal wave.*

She was frowning as she went to her classroom.

"You cut your hair." Steve was standing in his doorway when Dana reached her classroom. He walked to her slowly. "I like it." He brushed his hands over the curls. "It looks like the look Halle Berry wore a while back." He brushed the short hair at her nape. "Looks every bit as good on you as it did on her." His hand brushed against her neck.

Dana tried to ignore the tingling heat that his hand had caused. She did not want to be aware of how the heat from his hand entered her and started to make its way down and through her body. Just as it was starting to settle into a spot that was not appropriate to think about in the classroom, he stepped back.

"On you it looks even better."

"I—I." *Down, girl.* "Thank you." *What is going on?*

"How was your weekend?"

"Huh?"

"I asked how was your weekend?" He frowned. "Hey. Where were you just now?"

Not only do I not want to talk about that, I don't want to even think about it.

"Here. I'm right here." *Much too close, too.* She frowned. *Focus, girl. Focus.* "My weekend was okay." Her gaze slid away from him when thoughts of her dream came to mind. No doubt about it, the way her imagination had pictured him was right on the money. *He was fine. Is fine. Way fine. Way too fine. Too bad he isn't an option.* She shook her head. No way could she pretend to be in lo . . . Her frown deepened. *Don't you dare go there. You'll break up a good friendship.*

"Just okay?" He followed her into her room. "Your frown doesn't look like it was okay."

"You know." She shrugged and took off her coat.

"No, I don't. Did both of your dates fall in love at first sight? Any wedding bells in the works?" If Dana hadn't been caught up in her own twisted thoughts, she would have noticed that his smile didn't match the serious tone of his voice.

"As Tina said, 'What's love got to do with it?' I'm looking for a business partner, remember?" She stared at him. "How about you? How was your weekend?"

"So-so. No wedding bells."

"Not unless you had more success than I did." She unpacked her briefcase.

"Me?"

"It's time for you to have another hot weekend, isn't it? Way past time."

"We're talking about you."

"No, we're not."

"That bad, huh?"

"You just don't know."

"So are you giving up?" A puzzled look blanketed her face. *Why does he seem so happy at that possibility?*

"I still have a few options open to me." *A very few.* She frowned. She waffled again. *Maybe Cathy's list is worth a second look.*

"Such as?"

"Cathy has a list of possibilities."

"I thought you told me after that last disastrous date with somebody she knows that you'd never touch Cathy's book again."

"This is different. This time I'm not looking for permanent. Just an ideal vacation. Besides, I have another idea to try first."

"Oh yeah? What's that? You're not going to ask me to set you up, are you?"

"Your list is probably made up of players who wouldn't believe that I'm only looking for a platonic business deal."

"I think I've just been insulted."

"How many men do you know who wouldn't take advantage of a situation like that to jump a woman's bones?"

"Dogs do not comprise my entire list of male friends."

"Speed dating." Dana nodded, ignoring his last comment.

"Huh?"

"I'm going to try speed dating. From the little information I have, I know that a group of singles meet and spend a few minutes one-on-one getting to know each other."

"You're going to choose a husband based on what you learn about him in a few minutes?"

"No." She shook her head. "The few minutes are just the introduction. A—a predate, sort of. That's how you decide if you want to see somebody again. I'm not sure of the details. I have to search the Internet when I get home and find out more."

"A few minutes." Steve shook his head. "A few minutes to decide something as important as that. Some people know someone for a long time and still can't make that decision."

"Look. I just wasted an obscene number of hours on three dates that don't hold even a slim chance of going any further. I can meet a lot more potentials in a few hours."

"What if you hook up with a serial rapist? Or a serial killer? What if you find yourself in danger?"

"There has to be a screening. These companies wouldn't open themselves to lawsuits if something like that happened." *Would they?* "Besides, the three dates I just had were with strangers and nothing happened." She sighed. "That is, nothing happened except that I wasted a precious weekend. I don't have much time for this, you know."

"I guess the logic is sound, but the whole concept is crazy." Steve shook his head.

"I don't want to miss a free trip to Hawaii because of a slight technicality."

"I don't think a honeymoon without a husband is a slight anything." Steve pushed off from the door. "Some people never look in the obvious place," he mumbled and stared at her.

"What?"

"I have to go get ready for my class." He stared

at her a second longer. "Oh, I won't be able to have lunch with you."

"Why not?"

"I have something to do."

"Oh." Dana frowned. "Okay."

Dana watched him go. It had been a long time since they had missed lunch together. She sighed. *Maybe after that dream I had about him, it's just as well. I need some cooldown time.*

She was still staring at the empty doorway when the second bell rang and her class started coming in.

The school day ended and Dana rushed home and went directly to the computer. She keyed in *speed dating* and sat back in awe as line after line of information scrolled down her screen.

"Wow," she said as she read that what she was looking at was only ten of more than one thousand entries.

She skimmed the sites on her screen, gleaned out the potentials, and moved on to more.

Finally, after checking about one hundred, she narrowed her choices to a handful in the Philadelphia area that were meeting within a week. In spite of giving Steve the impression that she believed in this concept, she really didn't see how anything could be accomplished in four minutes. Then she reminded herself that this wasn't a date, only a screening process leading to a date. Besides, she didn't have much choice. She needed to meet promising men as quickly as possible, and this was it. She frowned. She also needed a face-to-face. No e-mail preliminaries the way some of the sites offered. She didn't have time. The letter might be arriving any day.

An Important Message From The ARABESQUE Publisher

Dear Arabesque Reader,

I invite you to join the club! The Arabesque book club delivers four novels each month right to your front door! It's easy, and you will never miss a romance by one of our award-winning authors!

With upcoming novels featuring strong, sexy women, and African-American heroes that are charming, loving and true… you won't want to miss a single release. Our authors fill each page with exceptional dialogue, exciting plot twists, and enough sizzling romance to keep you riveted until the satisfying end! To receive novels by bestselling authors such as Gwynne Forster, Janice Sims, Angela Winters and others, I encourage you to join now!

Read about the men we love… in the pages of Arabesque!

Linda Gill
PUBLISHER, ARABESQUE ROMANCE NOVELS

P.S. Watch out for the next Summer Series **"Ports Of Call"** *that will take you to the exotic locales of Venice, Fiji, the Caribbean and Ghana! You won't need a passport to travel, just collect all four novels to enjoy romance around the world! For more details, visit us at www.BET.com.*

SPECIAL OFFER! 4 BOOKS FREE!

ARABESQUE

BET BOOKS

www.BET.com

A SPECIAL "THANK YOU" FROM ARABESQUE JUST FOR YOU!

Send this card back and you'll receive 4 FREE Arabesque Novels—a $25.96 value—absolutely FREE!

The introductory 4 Arabesque Romance books are yours FREE (plus $1.99 shipping & handling). If you wish to continue to receive 4 books every month, do nothing. Each month, we will send you 4 New Arabesque Romance Novels for your free examination. If you wish to keep them, pay just $18* (plus, $1.99 shipping & handling). If you decide not to continue, you owe nothing!

- Send no money now.
- Never an obligation.
- Books delivered to your door!

We hope that after receiving your FREE books you'll want to remain an Arabesque subscriber, but the choice is yours! So why not take advantage of this Arabesque offer, with no risk of any kind. You'll be glad you did!

In fact, we're so sure you will love your Arabesque novels, that we will send you an Arabesque Tote Bag FREE with your first paid shipment.

* PRICES SUBJECT TO CHANGE.

ARABESQUE

Visit us at: www.BET.com

YOU'LL GET 4 SELECT ROMANCES PLUS THIS FABULOUS TOTE BAG!

THE "THANK YOU" GIFT INCLUDES:

- 4 books absolutely FREE (plus $1.99 for shipping and handling).
- A FREE newsletter, *Arabesque Romance News*, filled with author interviews, book previews, special offers, and more!
- No risks or obligations. You're free to cancel whenever you wish with no questions asked.

INTRODUCTORY OFFER CERTIFICATE

Yes! Please send me 4 FREE Arabesque novels (plus $1.99 for shipping & handling). I understand I am under no obligation to purchase any books, as explained on the back of this card. Send my free tote bag after my first regular paid shipment.

NAME _____

ADDRESS _____ APT. _____

CITY _____ STATE _____ ZIP _____

TELEPHONE (____) _____

E-MAIL _____

SIGNATURE _____

ARABESQUE

Offer limited to one per household and not valid to current subscribers. All orders subject to approval. Terms, offer, & price subject to change. Tote bags available while supplies last.

Thank You!

AN125A

Accepting the four introductory books for FREE (plus $1.99 to offset the cost of shipping & handling) places you under no obligation to buy anything. You may keep the books and return the shipping statement marked "cancelled". If you do not cancel, about a month later we will send 4 additional Arabesque novels, and you will be billed the preferred subscriber's price of just $4.50 per title. That's $18.00* for all 4 books for a savings of almost 30% off the cover price (Plus $1.99 for shipping and handling). You may cancel at any time, but if you choose to continue, every month we'll send you 4 more books, which you may either purchase at the preferred discount price. . . or return to us and cancel your subscription.

* PRICES SUBJECT TO CHANGE

THE ARABESQUE ROMANCE BOOK CLUB
P.O. BOX 5214
CLIFTON NJ 07015-5214

THE ARABESQUE ROMANCE CLUB: HERE'S HOW IT WORKS

PLACE STAMP HERE

PERFECT WEDDING

The hurry-up need eliminated some of the choices that she looked at. She liked the questionnaire that was posted on a couple of the sites.

Finally, she selected an organization that required advanced registration. She didn't want to take a chance on wasting a night and finding no potential dates in attendance. The Tuesday session was full so she picked Wednesday. Full was a good sign, wasn't it?

She filled out the form, took a deep breath, and crossed her fingers. Then she gave her credit card info and printed out her ticket.

Tuesday dragged past and Wednesday's school day crawled even slower. The fact that Steve was busy for lunch again made the day pass even slower. *Tomorrow I'm going to ask him what's going on. We are friends. Maybe he has a problem that I can help him with.* She frowned. *I hope he's not mad about that player comment I made about his friends.*

Wednesday evening Dana arrived at the restaurant where the session was being held. She was ten minutes early for the 8:30 session, but a line had formed. Fortunately they were being processed quickly. Soon she was in a reception room mingling with others. The room was large, but so was the group.

Since everybody held a small plate of appetizers in one hand and a glass of whatever in the other, greetings were just words accompanied by smiles rather than handshakes. She threw off the feeling that she was in the meat display case of the supermarket and the men were doing the shopping.

She had lost count of how many people she had spoken to when somebody tastefully rang what sounded like a crystal bell fifteen minutes later.

"Good evening, adventuresome winners. My name is Cheryl and I'm your hostess for this very important evening of your life." She laughed. "It's time to meet your future." She laughed again. "You can just leave your drinks and snacks on one of the trays. More will be available when we break for the short intermission. Right now we have something more important than food for you." Again a laugh. "I just know you'll agree with me when this night is over. But let's not rush things." Please take out the form you were given when you checked in. You'll see space for you to react to fifteen dates." She explained the procedure. "Remember, after your date, circle yes or no for the person you just met."

Fifteen dates? I should have done the math. I should have read the fine print. She shrugged. *Anyway, this could save me time and fifteen gives me better odds than ten.*

Dana forced her attention back to Cheryl, who shook her finger at them as if warning a group of first graders about proper behavior. "Now, make sure you don't let the person see which you mark. We wouldn't want any hurt feelings, would we?" She didn't wait for an answer. Instead she went on. "Please go to the first table number on the form. Remember, no matter how many sparks or how strongly you feel a connection, when I ring this bell . . ." She tinkled it as if they would have to distinguish that particular bell sound from others. "When you hear this, please go to your next table." She held the bell up as if it were a starting pistol. "Okay, here we go."

She rang the bell and some people walked as if they were in a race and a big prize awaited the winner. Others, Dana included, moved as if they were still trying to decide if this was a good idea.

The next thirty-five minutes passed in a blur of eight "predates." Dana felt as if she had barely enough time to say hello and give her name before Cheryl rang the bell. By the time intermission came a little more than half an hour later, Dana felt as if she had run a marathon. She was ready to snatch Cheryl's bell and stomp it flat until the little clapper was strangled to death. And she was only at the halfway point.

She got a diet cola from the bar and drank it down without stopping.

"All that talking makes you thirsty, doesn't it?" A man with a nice smile stood beside her.

"You got that right. I'm a teacher, but I feel as if I have never talked so much in my life."

"Probably the fact that we were so rushed is partly the reason for that."

"Yes, I guess so."

"Is this your first session?"

"Uh-huh."

"Mine too. My friends nagged me to come." He shrugged. "They've been nagging me for months. I agreed to come just to shut them up."

"Oh."

"I came over to you because you look as uncomfortable as I feel."

"This is different from anything I've ever experienced before."

"I don't think it was a good idea for me to come." He stared into his drink. "My wife died a year and a half ago. My friends meant well, but they don't know." He shook his head. "They don't understand. I'm not ready for this. I need more time." He looked at her. "I'll stay for the other half because I don't want to throw their numbers off, but . . ." He shrugged again. "It's still too early for me." He looked at Dana. "I'm sorry. I hope I didn't put a damper on your evening." He walked away before Dana could respond. Suddenly a trip to Hawaii didn't seem that important anymore.

A couple of other men spoke to her and then everybody went to their next tables for their next "dates."

When the final bell rang two hours after she had entered the restaurant, Dana felt the way the people look on the floor of the stock exchange after an extremely busy day.

She tucked her paper away.

"You want to go out for a real drink and really get to know each other?" A man whose smile reminded Dana of the wolf in *Little Red Riding Hood* touched her arm.

"I don't think so."

"We don't need any more connections to Cheryl. We don't need to give them any more of our money." His leer widened. "I'm interested in you and you're interested in me. After all, you've been smiling at me all evening." He looked at her as if he were a beef-lover going through withdrawl and she were prime rib.

"I've been smiling at *everybody* all evening." She eased her arm away from him.

"Yeah, but the smiles you gave me were brighter."

"No, they weren't."

"What you trying to do? Hold out for somebody

PERFECT WEDDING 133

you think is better than me?" The look in his eyes made Dana glad that she wasn't alone with him. "You're no great prize yourself, you know." He glared at her.

"Your opinion of me has marked me for life." Dana's glare met his and held its own. "Why don't you go try your smooth line on somebody who's worthy of you?" Dana glanced at his paunch. If he had buckled his belt *over* his stomach instead of under it, he would have needed pants at least two sizes larger. "Some lucky woman who's a better match for you than I am, Adonis." She stared at him for a few seconds longer, then walked away.

"Hey. Wait a minute." He grabbed her arm. She stared at his face, at his hand on her arm, and then back at his face. He quickly pulled his hand away from her. "You're not worth the trouble."

Dana held his stare until he walked away. Then she took several deep breaths. The first few wobbled in and out, but by the third her breathing was normal. She walked toward the door. Before she left, she looked back. Romeo was deeply in conversation with a woman who didn't look as if she was any more interested in him than Dana had been.

Dana slipped out the door and went to the lot across the street to get her car.

"I can't imagine myself even pretending to be his happy bride," she muttered as she got in and locked the doors. She shuddered. "I hope that image is erased from my mind before I get home."

Once in her apartment, she got a glass of water and went to her desk, hoping her filled-out form held more hope than she remembered. It didn't.

She stared at the six lines with circled yeses. Three of those would have been weak maybes if she wasn't desperate. She sighed. *There's a good chance that none of these men circled yes for me.* She thought of the women who had attended. About half of them were ordinary, but the other half looked like models who didn't need to go through this process. *What next? Do I try again next week if nothing comes of tonight?*

She was still thinking it over when the phone rang.

"Hello, Cathy."

"How did you know it was me? You don't have caller ID."

"I know your ring." They laughed. "Besides, nobody else would call me this late."

"Okay. Guilty. Am I coming up or are you coming down?"

"It's a waste of time, but I'm coming down. That way I can leave when I decide I've had enough of your third degree."

Three hours later, Dana and Cathy had talked out the concept of speed dating in particular and men in general.

"So what are you going to do?"

"They said we should all make the initial contact, but I'm going to hope one of the six contacts me. I'll wait at least a few days. If one does, then I'll hope he goes for the idea. Then I'll hope that he realizes the meaning of the word 'platonic.' "

"That's a lot of hoping."

"Yeah. I don't know what else to do." Dana yawned. "Right now I'm going to bed. I'm exhausted." She glanced at her watch. "Wow. No wonder. It's two o'clock in the morning." She jumped up. "I have school tomorrow."

PERFECT WEDDING

"*We* have school tomorrow." Cathy and stood up.

"See you too soon."

Dana rushed to her apartment and got ready for bed. As soon as she pulled up the covers she was gone.

The next thing she knew her clock was clanging in her ear telling her that it was seven.

She dragged herself up and through her morning routine, yawning every few minutes. A cup of tea later and her yawns had spaced themselves to one every five minutes or so.

"I gotta get another cup as soon as I get to school. Even so, this is gonna be a long day."

She picked up Cathy and they both yawned their way to school.

I'd put my head down at my desk and grab a power nap at lunch if I thought it would help, she thought as she walked to her classroom. She shook her head. *The only power I need is about two hours in my bed.* The image of a tall, handsome hunk who was her friend insinuated itself. *Alone,* the other part of her mind added, and the image disappeared.

"Hi." Steve smiled. He stared at her. "Late night?"

"You could say that." She yawned. "This is going to be a long day." She yawned again. "I guess you're still busy at lunchtime, huh?"

"No." He stared at her. "I'll be over." The bell ringing sent them to their rooms. The next bell brought the kids in.

By lunchtime Dana felt as if she had spent an entire week teaching nonstop. She plugged the pot in, and regardless of the idea that a watched pot doesn't boil, she hovered over it waiting for it to stop groaning. She had just poured the water into her cup when Steve walked in.

"So, fill me in." *Do I really want to hear that a hot date is the reason for her being sleepy?* He shook his head. *Not on a school night. She didn't go on a date last night.* He took a deep breath, then sat in his usual seat.

"I went out last night."

Regret that he might have been right filled Steve. *Get a grip.*

"A date? Another date? You went out three times last weekend. Then you went out again last night?" *Can I accept what she's about to tell me?*

"I can count."

"I'm sure that part of your intelligence is working perfectly." He set his lunch down but didn't sit.

"What do you mean by that?"

"Three dates with three different strangers last weekend and another . . ." He stared at her. "Was this date with one of the three?" *Please don't let her say yes.*

"No." Dana put her lunch in its usual place on the table.

Why doesn't that make me as happy as I thought it would? He refused to explore that question.

"You've started working Cathy's list already?"

"No." Dana busied herself with her lunch bag as if it took great concentration to unzip it.

"Are we playing 20 Questions here?"

"If you must know, I went to a speed-dating session."

"A what?"

PERFECT WEDDING 137

Dana took a bite of her sandwich and chewed as if she had bitten a piece of meat that didn't want to separate. Steve's stare stayed on her as if he didn't have a lunch to eat.

Finally she had to swallow. "I told you about it. Remember? It's a way to get to know a lot of potential dates in a short time."

"Refresh my memory, okay?"

As she explained the details, she managed to look at almost everything in the room except Steve. Finally, almost at the end of the lunch period, she finished explaining. Steve sat still staring at her as if she hadn't told him anything. Or as if she had spoken in some obscure language. His lunch was still unopened.

"Let me get this straight. You spent an evening flirting with a bunch of strangers?"

"I wasn't flirting. I was mingling."

"And you thought you'd find husband material based on talking with him for four minutes?"

"It wasn't the way you make it sound." *It was exactly the way he makes it sound.* "Look. You know how desperate I am. I don't have much time. I expect to hear from the contest people any day now. I probably have to produce a fiancé within a few days of receiving the letter." She leaned forward. "I can't lose out on my dream vacation because I . . ."

"Don't have a fiancé," he finished for her.

"Exactly." She nodded.

"The letter might not be the one you want."

"Bite your tongue."

"Biting my tongue has nothing to do with the content of the letter you receive."

Her brain knew that was true, but deep inside, the part of her that made her cross her fingers and touch wood wasn't so sure. "I don't want to take a chance."

"Speed dating." He shook his head. "What do you think you're doing with these crazy dating schemes?"

"The men have been screened."

"Based solely on what they wrote."

"I hate it when you're so logical." She stared at him. "I need a husband. I can't go on a honeymoon without a husband. It just isn't done. Before then, I need a fiancé. I can't think up any reason why they should consider me for the prize if I'm not even engaged."

"That part is logical. As for the rest..." He shrugged.

"Eat your lunch." Dana glared at him. If his mouth was full of food, he couldn't continue to use reason to poke holes in her plans.

"I've got an idea." He stared at her for too long. "Marry *me*."

"What?" Dana jumped up.

Her can of soda tumbled from her hand to the floor, the brown contents splashed out and escaped toward the last row of desks, and the bell rang all at the same time. If the action had been choreographed, it couldn't have been more synchronized. Dana wasn't aware enough of the activity to appreciate the way it came together. The only thing she was aware of was what Steve had suggested.

"I said—"

"I heard what you said." The soda continued to creep across the floor.

"Then why did you ask me?"

"Why did you ask me?"

Now Steve stared. Then he glanced away. "You're my friend and you need a fiancé. What kind of friend would I be if I didn't offer to help you out?"

"I can't let you do that."

"You're willing to go off with somebody you knew for all of four minutes but not with me?"

"It's not just for four minutes." Her voice rose a few decibels. "Regular dating will follow." *I sound like Cheryl.*

"If somebody calls you, he will expect a normal relationship. Unless he's dating under false pretenses, but I won't even go into that possibility now. You'd waste his time. Is that fair?"

"Logic. Again with the logic," she muttered as the second bell rang.

"Logic prevents chaos."

"Sounds like a fortune cookie slip."

"You want me to clean up that mess?" Sherri, one of the students, was pointing to the floor.

"That looks like something I'd do," Ann said.

Dana looked at the kids standing around as if the entire floor were covered. "I'll get it, thank you."

She stared at Steve, who was moving as if lunchtime had just started.

"I'll talk to you later."

"O-o-o," the students said as if part of a chorus.

"The rest of you go to your seats and take out your papers. I'll only be a minute."

She got a handful of paper towels and mopped up her mess. Every few seconds she glanced at the door as if expecting Steve to come back and say, "Just kidding."

He didn't. All afternoon she had to struggle to keep from replaying lunchtime. She spent the rest of the school day in stunned mode.

Chapter 13

When the bell rang signaling the end of the school day, Dana dashed out of the classroom instead of setting up for the next day as she usually did. She was glad this wasn't the day for the writing group to meet. And that there wasn't a faculty meeting today. *What made him do that?*

She rushed out of the building and hurried away. *Should I be glad about Steve's offer?* Her dream of him came flashing back, so vivid that she was almost ready to take off her winter coat to let her body could cool down. *What's going on?*

She continued moving away from the school as if, if she reached a fast enough speed, she could go back in time and somehow prevent Steve's offer.

"Bye, Miss Dillard."

Dana looked up. She managed to tell Maria, one of her students, good-bye. She even managed a smile. Then she glanced around and shook her head.

What were you going to do, fool? Walk home? She

shook her head again, then turned and walked back in the opposite direction, toward Cathy's school.

Please let Cathy come out before Steve does. He knows I come over here when she drives. She frowned. *I'm not ready for that follow-up conversation with him yet. I might never be.*

During the ride home, she let Cathy talk. Fortunately, Kenny had tickets for Friday evening for a play at Freedom Theater that she had wanted to see, but had never gotten around to. After that they were going to dinner at Zanzibar Blue.

"We decided to work our way through the soul food restaurants in and around Philadelphia," Cathy said and grinned. "My mouth is watering just thinking about eating my fill of down-home cooking." She laughed. "True, Mount Airy is my 'down home,' but I'm looking forward to a meal that will take me back to my roots."

She continued talking about the play they would see. Dana was glad that she didn't have to contribute anything to the conversation. She was still tangled up by Steve's proposal. Regardless of his motivation, it was a real, honest-to-goodness proposal.

"Are you ready for the weekend?" Cathy asked as she parked in her assigned spot in the apartment lot.

"I'll have a lot of free time. I won't have to make many changes in my lesson plan. This is one of those rare weeks when things go according to my plans." *At least academic things. As for that Steve thing...*

"What are you talking about?" Cathy removed her key from the ignition, but she didn't open the car door.

"School. What are you talking about?"

"Since when do I ask you about your lesson plans? I'll tell you since when. Since never." She stared at the blank look on Dana's face. "Girl, where are you? I'm talking about Saturday night. The Old School Awards Show."

"No."

"Child, don't you 'no' me. There are too many people out there who would kill for tickets. Bunches of others have been tying up the lines on WDAS trying to be the tenth caller so they can win tickets. Plus, I have too much time invested in helping you get your outfit together."

"I mean no, I forgot all about it."

"The event of the decade and you forgot about it?"

"I've had other things on my mind, you know." *And Steve dropped a new thing on me a few hours ago and it's still weighing heavily on me.*

"I know." Cathy waved her hand in the air. "The contest, finding a fiancé who will turn into a husband, and Hawaii, but this event is important and it's a definite, not a 'maybe if I'm lucky and the stars are in the right orbit' kind of thing."

"Stars don't have orbits."

"Thank you, Miss Astronomer. I know that. And I sure know you can't possibly think you have the option of backing out."

"I wouldn't back out. I'm definitely going with you."

"Uh-uh." Cathy shook her head. "I'm going with Kenny. You're going with Steve." She got out of the car, but Dana sat as if waiting for another trip.

Steve. Again Steve. The man was definitely alive, but he was haunting her.

"I think maybe I'll drive."

"Not an option. Parking space is limited. What have you got against Steve? Did you two have a falling-out?"

"Nothing like that." *Definitely nothing like that.* She frowned. *Why did I rush out of school like I was being chased?*

"Well then, what are you waiting for? Come on. We can discuss what to do with my hair." She stared at Dana. "Your hair will be easy."

"Don't start on my hair."

"Somebody already beat me to it. Started and finished." She shook her head. "Girl, sometimes I just don't know about you."

"What's to know?" Dana followed her into the building.

Cathy chattered on about her day as she unlocked her door. "Come on. Let's try some dos from that hair magazine I just bought."

"I'll be down later. I—I'm going to take a short nap." She hurried away before Cathy could say anything else.

Once upstairs she leaned against the door as if afraid somebody was going to try to break in.

Why did he do that? I would have found somebody. I was working hard on it. How can I accept his offer and act like it's just business to me? She pushed off from the door and went to her bedroom. *What the heck am I going to do?*

She took off her outer clothes, got in bed, and closed her eyes. The birds outside sounded louder. The hum of the clock radio beside her increased its volume. The heat clicked on. Voices outside her window sounded as if they were leaning against the windowpane and shouting in to her. Dana sighed. Sleep wasn't going to happen.

She opened her eyes but didn't get up. *I gotta analyze this. Why am I so set against marrying Steve? He was right. Why am I so willing to marry some stranger and not him? If I get a hit . . .* She cringed as that word popped into her mind. *If I get a call from one of the men from the speed-dating session, he'll be interested in developing a relationship and all I have in mind is a business deal. If he's not interested in a normal relationship, then he has a hidden agenda, too, and I doubt if celibacy is part of it.* She frowned. *What have I gotten myself into?* She sighed. *That poet was right when he warned of weaving a tangled web. I think I caught myself.*

Dana gave up and went down to Cathy's apartment. They fooled with Cathy's hair but decided on pinning her shoulder-length hair up the way she always did for special occasions.

"I won't put in too many pins and clips this time." She grinned. "I don't want Ken to have much trouble if he decides he wants it down later."

"You are so bad."

"Yeah, but in a good way." They laughed.

For a few minutes Dana was able to forget about the decision she had to make. At ten she yawned, then left.

When she went to bed, she tried not to think of facing Steve the next day, but how could she not think of it? She had to have a reason for her "no" answer. She thought back to her dream. Was that just her hidden feelings showing themselves?

PERFECT WEDDING   145

I can't tell him that my feelings have changed. He's helping me out as a favor to his friend. Me. Friend Dana. I can't make him uncomfortable by revealing my new feelings, but I'm not sure I can hide them from him if I let him close. They're so new, even I don't understand them. I don't want to come off as a pathetic woman who takes advantage of a friendship. That would be so humiliating. Creases formed along her forehead.

I've seen his brown Barbie-doll type of woman. No way could anybody put me in the category with them. She sighed. *Put me in a room with them and nobody would have trouble picking out which one didn't belong. Steve doesn't think of me as anything but a friend. He never could. If I mess up our friendship, I won't have any relationship with him at all, and I'd still have to work with him.* She sighed again.

How could I spend time with him on a personal basis, up close and personal, and not slip and let my feelings show? If I was that good at acting I'd be in the movies instead of a classroom.

Friday morning she left her apartment later than usual. She would have left even later still, but Cathy threatened to drive herself if Dana didn't leave then. She had to face Steve sooner or later. Might as well get it over with sooner.

She walked to her classroom as if a monster waited for her and she knew it. The tension filling her eased away when she saw that Steve wasn't waiting at his door as he usually was.

I never did like cat-and-mouse games, she thought as she went into her room. *But then, do I really know what I like anymore?* She set her briefcase on the desk but didn't open it. *What I want is becoming way too clear,* she thought as an image of Steve emerged slowly.

Steve, with his broad shoulders that needed no help from padding. Steve, with strong arms and a chest meant for snuggling against. Steve, whose mouth looked as if it would fit perfectly to hers. Whose hands could do things to her that would set her on fire. Steve . . .

"Morning."

Dana whirled around to face the object of her daydreams. She felt her face heat as if she were standing too close to a blazing fire. In fact, she was. She snatched her gaze from him as if it had gone to him on its own.

"Morning." She busied herself unpacking her briefcase and laying the papers into piles. *I'll sort them correctly later.*

"No dates last night?"

"No."

"Did you call your other prospects?"

"I—I didn't have time."

"Did you think about . . ." His sentence trailed off. He took a deep breath and started again. "What time do you want me to pick you up tomorrow?"

"Uh . . ." Dana had to chase away the image of him *really* picking her up. "I, uh, I—what do you think?"

"It starts at seven with cocktails. Since neither of us is a drinker, we should plan to get there about seven-thirty. Okay?"

"Yeah. Seven-thirty. Right." She nodded.

"So we need about forty-five minutes to get there. How about six forty-five?"

PERFECT WEDDING

"Yeah. That sounds about right."

"Lunch today?"

"I don't know. I have things to do."

"I need to fill you in on the math contest."

"Okay. Right. Lunch."

"What's wrong with you?"

She thought he was staring at her, but she refused to look to see if she was right. "Nothing. I just have a lot on my mind."

"I know. Hawaii, honeymoon, marrying a stranger. In reverse order, of course."

"Steve, I—"

"See you at lunchtime. My room. I have stuff to show you."

Dana stared at the empty doorway. Then she turned her attention to the papers she had set on the table. She shook her head, but the Steve in her mind was as sharp as, and seemed as real as, the Steve who had just left. What if she *did* marry Steve? Her mind created the scenario. She closed her eyes and let her imagination have its way.

She waited for him to come down the aisle. Her dress fit perfectly, but anything would do. What mattered was that Steve waited for her. Luther Vandross's mellow tones sang her promise to her groom-to-be as Dana glided to her future.

Love filled Steve's face. Desire glowed in his eyes. As Dana placed her hand in his, she knew her eyes held the same emotion. The cameras flashing, the people in the seats, and everything else disappeared as they said their vows. She didn't cringe or stumble over the words. She meant them. Contest or no contest, she was where she wanted to be.

Steve kissed her and proved that the kiss they

shared a lifetime ago wasn't even a preview to this one. This kiss branded and sealed her as his for always. The reception passed in a blur of kisses shared even when glasses weren't tinkled.

Then the traditional dances were over and finally she was in Steve's arms. They were moving as one; she was swaying as if she had been waiting her whole life for this moment. Her fantasies raced on.

The cake was cut, bouquet, garter, and birdseed thrown. Finally she and Steve were on their way to the honeymoon suite in a different hotel, one known by very few to ensure that their wedding night wouldn't be disturbed.

Steve had barely shut the door before she was in his arms. His lips explored her face slowly, finding sensitive spots she didn't even know she had. He reached the place below her ear and kindled a fire hot enough to melt steel.

His hands, although tracing new territory, found her breasts and thoroughly stroked and tugged and brushed. His mouth swallowed her responding moans. He eased the zipper at the back of her wedding dress down and her dress puddled to the floor. She pushed his jacket off to make a puddle of its own. His hands stroked from her waist up her back and brushed under her bra until his fingers . . .

"Miss Dillard? Are you all right? Is something wrong?"

Dana removed her stare from the papers and looked up. Every seat was filled. Thirty pairs of eyes were staring back. She glanced back at the papers, surprised that they weren't at least singed around the edges.

PERFECT WEDDING 149

"Uh, no. I mean yes, Kimeeka." She shook her head and took a deep breath. "I mean, no, nothing is wrong. Yes, I'm all right."

Sure you are. An X-rated fantasy in the middle of the morning, at the front of my classroom. You didn't even see the kids come in. She frowned. *I'm just perfectly all right.*

She glanced at the girl staring at her. Then she looked out at the rest of the class. "I was just thinking about something." She cleared her throat. "Class, please take out your essays."

"We handed them in," Smart Alec was living up to his name.

"You said we were going to do literature first," Perfect Patty reminded her. "I'm starting to get into that book."

"Oh. That's right." She cleared her throat again. "Well then. Let's recap what happened so far."

Dana was glad that her policy was for the discussion to be freewheeling, no raising of hands necessary. No way could she pull that off. She forced her attention to stay on what was happening. The kids' comments flew. Their enthusiasm whirled around the room.

What in the world was I thinking? Even if I marry him, he's offering it as a business deal. There will be no wedding night, as such. No traditional honeymoon. She scowled. *If you accept, you'd better remember that,* she told herself.

"Was my answer wrong, Miss Dillard?"

"Huh?"

"You're frowning. Didn't I get the right idea?"

"Oh. Sure. Sorry. I was thinking about something else."

I'm the one with the wrong idea, she thought and

made herself pay closer attention. Her inattention wasn't fair to the kids.

Dana fumbled through the morning, not really looking forward to lunch. She had barely gotten her thoughts under control, and now she had to face the one who was the star of her fantasy and find a way not to let him know.

Steve walked in and she was hoping he wouldn't bring up the word *marry* at all. She needed time think of somebody else to marry. Anybody else. She had just about ruled out the speed-dating guys. The yearbook and directories hadn't worked, either.

Maybe she should look at blind-date-three again. Byron. Maybe he would work out. His mother could come. After all, it wouldn't be a real honeymoon anyway. Dana shook her head. Nope. The woman didn't fly. *Not even in my wildest imagination can I devise a way to drive to Hawaii. And the woman is probably afraid to go on a ship, too.* Dana's head moved slowly from side to side. *Before all that, though, she doesn't like long drives and scientists are slow at developing that teleportation thing.*

She frowned.

As for Don, he'd have a heart attack at the money being spent even if he wasn't doing the spending. Her frown deepened. *I can't be responsible for somebody dropping dead. And thinking about dead, Milton wouldn't be seen dead with a woman who dared to cut her hair.* She sighed. *Man, oh man, oh man.* She focused back on what Steve was saying. *Did I comment on anything to him? Am I on automatic pilot? Maybe automatic pilot would do a better job than so-called conscious me.*

She stole a glance at him. He wasn't looking at

PERFECT WEDDING 151

her in a funny way. He wasn't looking at her at all. His attention was on the papers in front of him. He didn't even seem aware of the turmoil churning inside her. That was a good thing, right?

She turned her attention back to her lunch and to what Steve was saying about the kids.

Slowly she started to relax. Lunchtime was almost over. She listened as Steve gave an update of the kids' progress with the math project and explained the next step.

"They are really doing great," he said. "At first I figured they would make a decent showing. Now I think they have a real shot at winning the national title."

"That's great. That would be such a boost, not just for them, but for all our kids who have been labeled as poor achievers." She relaxed and gathered her trash. This hadn't been so bad.

"What are your plans for tomorrow? During the day, I mean. I guess you'll be busy on the phone." He stared at her. "Looking for a husband." *He went there. At least partly.*

"Most likely." She stared at the table, wishing she had more stuff to gather or at least something to do with her hands.

Why can't I tell him that I'm seriously considering his offer? Why can't I let go of my fixation with Hawaii? That's why I'm in such a mess. I've never been there, but I've never been to a lot of places and I'm not hung up on them. Why Hawaii?

Steve hadn't brought up his proposal, but nevertheless it hung between them like an elephant sitting in the middle of a crowd and everybody trying to ignore it. *Has he changed his mind? How will I feel about it if he did?*

The afternoon passed routinely and Dana was grateful that something was going smoothly.

As soon as she got home, she stared at the phone. Maybe she should reconsider calling the men from the speed-dating session. She shrugged and walked away from the phone.

At first she left it alone because the men would most likely still be at work. If they had told her the truth. *No.* She shook her head. *I have to accept that they did. If not* . . . She shook her head. *Uh-uh. I can't consider what else about them might not be true.*

Later she went so far as to pick up the phone, but she didn't press any numbers. What if Steve was right? She had no way of knowing how honest the men were. Even if they were harmless, she doubted seriously if they were interested in a celibate relationship when they could be pursuing somebody who held more promise. She frowned. And if they weren't, did she want to take the chance of spending time alone with them as a way of finding out? She thought of the creep who had approached her. How did she know that creeps didn't comprise her list but were just more subtle? *Steve's looking better and better.* She shook her head. *Uh-uh. Impossible. He couldn't look any better.* She resisted the urge to fan herself to cool off.

She spent the rest of the day and Saturday morning cleaning out drawers and closets as if somebody were coming to grade her on her neatness. Saturday afternoon she gave up and drove to the mall.

A little mall walking might work off some of this ten-

sion. Yeah, she quipped as she got into her car. *That will make room for a whole new supply.*

In spite of her looking at the clock too many times, the time finally came for her to get dressed for the show.

She laid the dark red sequined dress on the bed and stared at it. This was the one that she and Cathy had selected. The dress looked small. And short. Were women even wearing sequins anymore? And stretchy fabric? She stared at the dress some more and frowned. No matter. *She* was wearing it. She had no choice. This was all she had that could pass for a black-tie-affair dress.

She slipped it over her head and pulled it into place. It stopped at her knee. No amount of tugging made it any longer.

"I know I haven't gotten taller, but I swear, I don't remember this thing being this short." She tugged again. She stood sideways. "Or this tight. And I know I haven't gained weight." She went to her closet. "I don't know why I'm looking. Cathy and I went through everything in here. I know that no fairy godmothers came in while I was out and left a long, flowing, loose dress." She closed the door and looked in the mirror again.

"At least the neckline isn't too low." Her frown deepened. *Maybe not, but it sure outlines my body from my neck to my waist.* She was still staring in the full-length mirror when the doorbell rang. She glanced at the clock. "Trust Steve to be on time," she muttered as she went to the door. She took in a deep breath, which only made her more aware of the fit of the dress. Then she opened the door.

"Wow." Steve stared at her. "Double and triple wow."

Dana felt as if her skin color matched her dress. "Come on in. I just have to get my purse."

"Okay. Sure. Anything you say." He stepped inside, paused in front of her for a long few seconds, then moved past her.

She stood in place. *How can I turn away without him seeing how this dress clings to my backside? Should I back away? Would that be better?*

Finally she took another deep breath, but not too deep, as she felt the dress tighten across her breasts and saw Steve glance at them, and tried to glide to her bedroom.

She grabbed her purse, took a real deep breath, and went back to Steve. When she took her coat out of the hall closet, she was glad it was long.

By the time they reached his car, she had resigned herself to going with the flow and trying to ignore how she felt in the dress.

The conversation did not contain references to the dress or his marriage proposal. Dana was grateful for about five minutes. Then she brought up the kids' contests.

Steve glanced at her. "Uh-uh. No school talk tonight. We're just a man and a woman out on a date." His voice was nowhere near school mode. "Why haven't we done this before? Go out, I mean. How did we go directly to being buddies?"

"I don't know." She shrugged. "I—I remember what your dates looked like when I first got to Harris School. I don't look anything like them. That's probably why." She managed a weak laugh. "In fact, not only am I not in the same class as they are, I'm not even in the same school."

PERFECT WEDDING

"Times change. People change. Most smarten up. Some later than others." His voice was serious. She stole a glance at him, but he was staring straight ahead. He continued, "Anyway, how did you make out with your phone calls?"

"Phone calls?"

"Your speed-dating Romeos. Find anybody? Make any new dates? Start planning the wedding?"

"I—I didn't call any of them."

"No? Why not?"

She shrugged. "I decided to wait."

"For what?"

"I don't know. I thought about what you said about their agendas." She stared at her lap. "Can we please talk about something else?"

"Sure. Pick a subject."

"That's hard. You already said that school is off-limits."

"Yeah."

"How 'bout them Eagles?"

"No sports, either."

"None?"

"None."

"Well, we don't have anything else to talk about."

"Pretend this is a real date. A blind date. Maybe with one of those guys. Okay?"

"You don't want me to do that."

"Why not?"

"They each had a truckful of baggage."

"Like what?"

"I don't want to go into that right now, okay?"

"Okay by me. What's your favorite color?"

"Huh?"

"First date, remember? Your favorite color. Do you realize how little we know about each other?"

She nodded. "Yeah. Not much."

"Well?"

"Blue. Royal blue."

"Not red? Not dark red?"

"Don't start."

"You already started when you put on that dress."

"Don't make fun of me."

"Making fun of you is not even close to being what's on my mind." He glanced at her. "Do you want to know what is?"

Was she just imagining that his voice was sexier than before? Yeah. That must be it. Desperation distorting her hearing.

"Your turn."

"My turn?"

"Favorite color."

"Dana, Dana, Dana." He shook his head slowly. "Sweetheart. Guys don't have favorite colors. We need a shirt. We go to a rack. We see something, we try it on. If it fits and make us think the women will like us in it, we buy it. Simple as that." He smiled at her.

Did he call me sweetheart? He did, didn't he? What did he mean by that? Nothing. Probably not a thing. Right? She struggled to find a word, any word.

"Oh?"

"That's the truth about men. At least one of the truths." He winked at her. "Stick with me, kid, and, if you're good, I may share others with you."

"Oh." *Wow. If I was wearing any dress other than this one, this coat would be off, the heat off, and the windows down inside the doors. Where did his playful mood come from? And how do I respond?*

"Why Hawaii?"

"Huh?"

"Why are you so crazy about Hawaii?"

"It's just perfect. The weather, the people." She took a deep breath. "I've read about a lot of places." She glanced at him. "You know, if you can't visit them in person, you can at least do so vicariously." She sighed. "That satisfied my curiosity for other places, but not for Hawaii. I have to go there and experience it for myself. For example, everything I've read mentioned the people and how well they get along with one another. I think it's wonderful how people of so many ethnic backgrounds can blend and live in such harmony."

"You make it sound perfect."

"No place is perfect. I know that." She smiled. "I just believe that Hawaii comes closest and that whatever is in second place is way far behind."

She told him about the history of the islands and the people. She filled him in on the foods and plants. Then she told some of the legends she had read.

"I hope I didn't bore you," she said as she finished telling a story.

"No." He glanced at her. "I'm just wondering how a couple in love would have time to tear themselves away from the hotel room long enough to appreciate the surroundings."

Dana was glad that he pulled up to the hotel door right then. How could she respond to that?

Chapter 14

Crowds lining the sidewalk surged closer when Steve drove up to the entrance. One valet opened Dana's door and helped her out while another opened Steve's door. Dana looked around.

She smiled as the people, realizing that these new arrivals weren't famous, moved back to wait for the next car to unload. Steve placed his hand under Dana's elbow and they walked to the door. The line was short and everybody in front had an invitation. Soon they were inside.

"There's Cathy," Dana said as they entered the crowded foyer. She started toward her.

"Don't you want to check your coat?"

Oh man, I forgot about this.

"It's—It's a..."

"Perfect temperature." Steve's gaze challenged her. *Am I imagining a twinkle in his eyes?* She shook her head. *I must be. Santa Claus's eyes twinkled, not Steve's.*

She gulped in the last deep breath she would

take until she got her coat back. Then she exposed her dress to anyone in general who happened to look her way, to Steve in particular, who was staring at her as if he had no idea what he was supposed to do with her coat.

"You made it," Cathy said as she came to stand beside them and broke the spell.

"Did you have any doubts?"

"Not a one." She looked at Steve. "Don't you look gorgeous? The tux is definitely you."

"Thank you, I think." He smiled. "I can't remember ever being called gorgeous before."

"Then it's about time." Cathy wrapped her arm through that of the man standing with her. "You remember Kenny?"

"Hey, man. What's up?" Steve extended his hand. Dana held out her hand, too, but Kenny gave her a quick hug.

"Are you going to carry Dana's coat around or check it?" Cathy's grin was one second from turning into a chuckle.

"Oh." Steve frowned at the coat in his hand as if some wizard had made it materialize there. Then he stared at Cathy. "Sure. I am."

"You look fabulous," Cathy said to Dana. "The dress looks just as good as it did when I talked you into buying it and even more so when we decided that you should wear it tonight."

"You have excellent taste," Steve said. "Dana looks like Cinderella at the ball."

"Cindy didn't wear a dress like this." Dana couldn't resist the urge to tug at the lower part.

"Stop that." Cathy slapped Dana's hand. "Cindy's fairy godmother didn't have a clue. How could she, being stuck wherever fairies hang out when they aren't on duty? Besides, Prince would never have let her go no matter how many gongs that clock sounded if she had worn something that highlighted her charms the way this dress does."

"Thank you for choosing it, Cathy." Steve smiled at Dana. "I know she wouldn't have chosen something like this on her own."

"I am right here. No third person, please." Dana reached for the neckline but didn't pull it away from her body. It wouldn't have helped.

"Okay, folks." Cathy took Kenny's arm and walked into the reception room. "Let's get something to wet our whistles."

As if he had heard her, a waiter appeared carrying a tray.

They each took a glass of sparkling cider and slowly walked around greeting a few people that they knew. Dana was glad to have Cathy as a buffer. She was also glad the room was crowded enough so that the only view Steve had of her was up close. But not too up close.

Dinner was announced and they made their way to their assigned table among those scattered around the front of a stage.

Salads were already in place. As soon as they were settled, they began discussing the songs they hoped to hear. In between bites somebody commented on what they had been doing when they first heard a particular song or told some other memories dragged up by the song.

Dana tried not to look at Steve, but she couldn't help glancing at him from time to time. Several of those times her gaze met his and she forgot all about the meal. Then Cathy or Kenny would say something and the spell was broken until the next

PERFECT WEDDING 161

time. Steve didn't talk any more than she did, at least not with words. His gaze spoke enough to fill a library. It just always said the same thing. It wasn't only friendship showing. It was the gaze of a man looking at a woman and liking what he saw.

Cathy was right, Dana thought after she stole one look at Steve. *Gorgeous is an accurate description of him.* She made herself concentrate on her dinner again. *What am I going to do about this situation? Do I dare do what I want to?*

Dinner was over, the tables were cleared, and the emcee was in front of the mike. Dana still hadn't found an answer.

"Good evening, Old Schoolers." He looked around at the tables. "Some of y'all are either well preserved or masquerading as folks from back in the day." He shook his head. "Y'all know how to make an old man think of younger days."

"Old is just a state of mind," somebody shouted from the audience.

"Yeah," another man yelled. "Speak for yourself. I'm still in my prime." The emcee waited for the laughter and applause to die down. Then he introduced the first act.

Immediately Dana was taken back to college.

Hit songs sung by the original artists kept her and the rest of the audience back there for a while. The award that followed each song made the audience go wild each time. Finally that portion of the show was over and the lead singer of the last group came forward. Dana glanced at her watch and was surprised to see that several hours had passed.

"Enough of the old stuff, even though it was better than good," he said. Applause and whistles showed that the audience agreed with him.

"We appreciate you all for making our careers so successful," the man continued. "Now we got something new for you. We recently cut a new song to show that 'old school' can do new, too. Get up on the floor and let us take you back to the day, but in a new way."

Dana thought she was going to get away with just listening, but when Steve stood and held out his hand to her, what could she do but go?

"Fancy seeing you here. Looking for me? Claxton Jenson? I know you remember me."

An oily voice reached Dana and a hard hand grabbed her shoulder. She turned. The man from speed dating who had thought she had been coming on to him leered at her.

"I didn't think I'd get a second chance at you." Dana shook off his hand, but he didn't seem to notice. "I was hoping for another chance." He reached for her again. "And here you are." He almost grabbed Steve, who was now standing in front of Dana. Claxton's hand jerked back as if it were on elastic and the length had run out. Dana inhaled sharply.

Steve was right. I could have been alone with him, or somebody more subtle but still like him. I would have been in trouble and Steve wouldn't have been there. A slight shiver ran through her at what might have been.

"Can I help you?" Steve eased Dana against him as he spoke to Claxton. His hands brushed up and down her upper arm before he gave it a little squeeze. Then he tightened his hold on her, only enough to reassure her.

"Yeah. You can get out of my way. Foxy Lady and I have unfinished business."

"It's finished."

PERFECT WEDDING

"Who do you think you are?"

"Her fiancé."

A staring match followed.

Neither man looked at Dana, whose eyes were wide with surprise. *Fiancé? Fiancé? Did I say yes? When?*

"What was she doing looking for a date?"

"She was just slumming to make sure nothing better was available. There isn't."

The staring continued as if an award were left over and the people in charge had decided to let this match determine the winner.

Claxton took several steps back. "You might be fine, but there are other women here who look just as good. Some of them will be flattered by my attention."

"You better go find one, then." Steve's voice had dropped to a deadly level.

Claxton threw a final glare at them, then whirled away. Dana was still hearing Steve's word *fiancé*.

"Come on, sweetheart. Let's not waste this music."

Dana's mind left Claxton and came back to Steve. A different kind of tension affected her. *Sweetheart?*

Steve's arm around her had been disturbing enough, but when he put his hand at her waist and gently led her to the dance floor, she could feel her control dropping away. When he turned her into his arms, she didn't care if she ever found it.

At first she listened to the words. It was her story they were telling. It was as if someone had read her thoughts about Steve and put them to music:

"What if we met just yesterday,
And not so long ago?

What if I was a stranger,
Not someone you came to know?
Would a spark appear,
When I was near?
Would my presence make you glow?
What if, when you first met me,
You fell in love with me?

What if we were more than pals,
If you saw me differently?
If I touched something deep inside you,
So unexpectedly?
What if you looked at no one else,
No one else but me?
What if you thought, as I do now,
That love is our destiny?"

Dana frowned as the song was repeated.

What if the words were true? For once she allowed her feelings for Steve to surface. That erotic dream had been closer to her real feelings than the front she had been presenting to Steve for so long. She hadn't wanted to admit her true feelings because she was afraid of looking like a fool. Now they were loose and there was no way to put them back.

As the song continued, Steve eased her body closer against his and she went willingly. All words receded. Everybody and everything disappeared as they moved so close together nothing could come between them.

Her breasts tingled and ached as, during the split second it took for her to respond to his movements from time to time, the already hardened tips

PERFECT WEDDING

brushed against his chest. Her response was to move even closer.

She felt the pressure of his lower body and her body heated in answer. His lips brushed against the side of her face and she was glad she had worn the ridiculously high heels Cathy had talked her into. In fact, she was sorry they weren't even higher. That would have put his mouth even with hers instead of hers a little higher.

The lyrics repeated yet again and Dana didn't think at all, only felt, ached, burned, longed for something she had never had, but had dreamed about even before she understood it.

The band played another song and then another and she and Steve stayed molded together.

"I'd say get a room, but since each of you has an apartment, that would be a waste of money," Cathy said.

Dana came from wherever she had been, but that was all right. She was still with Steve. Cathy was standing beside them. They had the dance floor to themselves. She looked around.

They could have had their pick of tables now. The keyboard player was fastening his case. Some of the lyrics from a song came to her mind: "I got lost in his arms." She had never realized that lost could feel so right.

Steve eased her away a little, but he didn't let her go. Instead he lowered his mouth to hers and brushed his lips across her mouth.

"See you on Monday," Cathy said from somewhere to the side and giggled. Then she left.

"I guess we'd better go too, before they lock us in and we have to spend the night." Steve's smile that accompanied his words told her that he didn't think that would be so bad either.

Still close enough to brush against each other, they got Dana's coat and waited for the car. So the wait time wouldn't be wasted, Steve pressed his lips to hers again, as if to make sure she remembered the taste of him, as if she could ever forget.

Their hands stayed fastened together during the drive. Steve's car wasn't a subcompact, but it still wasn't large enough to contain her feelings and her thoughts. Her feelings won the battle for space. The word *fiancé* didn't seem so wrong anymore.

Chapter 15

"We're here."

"Oh."

As Steve's voice pulled Dana's thoughts away from what had happened, she eased her hand from his.

"Invite me in." He turned off the motor and looked at her. Dana felt as if he was talking about more than just into her home. She meant for her answer to include it all.

"Yes," she released in a whisper.

When he opened the door and reached for her, she was back on the dance floor with him. She placed her hand in his, and the feel of him against her came flooding back, lifting her to a new place.

Holding hands, they walked to the door. Steve held out his other hand and it took a second for Dana to realize that he needed her key to unlock the door.

His soft kiss didn't help unmuddle her thoughts.

It certainly didn't help her separate the outside door key from the rest.

Steve gently lifted the clump of keys from her and held them out in his open palm. "If we don't open the door we can't get in. Right?"

"Right."

The key with the red top should have stood out from the others. She grasped the end and handed the key to Steve. As his fingers brushed against hers, she was back with the kiss. *Focus,* she thought. *I am,* her mind answered. *Just on the wrong thing.* She shook her head. *No. It might not be keys, but it's definitely the right thing.*

Steve opened the front door, then the door to her apartment, all the while Dana was remembering.

"We have to talk," he said as they walked into the living room.

"Yes." Talking was not what was on her mind, and she was a little frightened at the intensity of what was.

"Claxton was one of your blind dates?"

Dana forced her attention away from where it wanted to be.

"No. He was at the speed-dating session." Steve just stared at her. She continued. "You were right."

"About . . ."

"Speed dating. And the possible dangers. I could have actually gone out with somebody just as dangerous as he is and not found out until it was too late. I could have really gotten into a mess." She wrapped her arms around herself and stood beside the mantel. "That is so scary."

"But it didn't happen." He walked over to her, but he didn't touch her. "I thought you were going

PERFECT WEDDING

to say that I was right about the *fiancé* statement that I made."

"Oh." Dana looked at him. His slight grin allowed her to relax. "That."

"Yeah. That."

He brushed his hand against her face before moving it down and slipping her coat off. He dropped it into the wing chair and his coat followed.

"I was thinking about that. At least for a little while. Until we started dancing. Then I couldn't think about it. I couldn't think about anything."

"Uh-huh." His hands found her waist and drew her against him. It didn't take much tugging. "Let's analyze this."

He dropped a quick kiss to her mouth, then stepped away. The last thing Dana felt like doing was analyzing anything. She was too involved with feeling.

"You want to go to Hawaii. Right?" He held up a finger.

"Right." She struggled to concentrate on his words instead of his mouth.

"You didn't win the lottery so you still can't afford to pay your way. Right?" He held up another finger.

"Right." She managed to nod.

"You want to win that contest so you can go. Right?" A third finger joined the other two.

"Yes."

"You're supposed to say 'right.' Follow along with me here."

"Oh. Okay. Right."

"You still need a fiancé. Right?" A fourth finger moved beside the others. She nodded and he continued. "No fiancé, no groom. No groom, no wedding. No wedding, no honeymoon." He let all of that count for one finger.

"Right."

"What have you got against me?"

"Huh?"

"What have you got against marrying me?"

"I just don't want to hurt you. I don't want you to be tied up with me when the next woman comes along who attracts your attention."

"Ah." He nodded. "So you're looking out for me?"

"Yes."

"I'm a big boy. I can look out for myself."

"Right."

"I don't think we need 'right' anymore." He closed the space between them. "I think it's obvious now. Don't you?"

"Yes."

"I'm going to tell you something." He hesitated, then took her hand in his. "I have wanted to move our relationship out of the friendship slot for more than a year, but I was afraid of losing you as a friend." He lifted her chin and looked into her eyes.

"Really?"

"Most definitely really." He smiled and stroked a hand along the side of her face. "I knew you didn't think of me that way."

"But you had all of those girlfriends."

"When's the last time you heard me mention a date?" Dana frowned. "A long time ago. Right?"

"Right." Dana smiled.

"I didn't offer to marry you as a favor. I asked you to marry me because I was afraid you'd find somebody else. When opportunity knocks, you open the door and pull it in."

"Oh."

"I guess I don't fit the profile."

"Profile?"

"You know, the one that says men don't know how to be subtle." He ran a finger down her face and brushed it across her lips. His touch was soft, but it made her feel as if he had used a match to kindle a fire. "Maybe I've been too subtle. Remember the kiss after the Superbowl?"

"Yes." She tried to nod but didn't want to break the contact with his hand.

"I was trying to see if there was a chance that we could take things further." He dropped his hand away and her lips felt cold. He took a step away from her. "You didn't react, so I backed off."

"I reacted," she whispered. "I just didn't show it." She shrugged as she closed the space between them. "You didn't say anything about it later, so I thought you meant it just as a celebration kiss between friends."

"I guess I should have kissed you like this."

His hands framed her face. She closed her eyes, lifted her face, and waited.

His mouth touched hers, visited for a couple of seconds, then lifted away.

"Or like this." His mouth was back on hers. This time he kept it there awhile longer before he pulled away.

Dana opened her eyes and saw the heat in his. She felt the same in her own. Her hands found his hard-muscled upper arms. She raised her mouth to his and he met her halfway. This third kiss was longer, but still not long enough. Then his hands were at her back, exploring, and hers were brushing up and down along his. Their groans met, twined, blended. His tongue found hers and danced with it. Dana felt the length of him against her, his hardness pressing against her.

He kissed the side of her face, then gazed into her eyes.

"I don't want to stop, but if you want me to, I will." His words were barely a husky whisper, but they reached inside her.

"I don't want you to stop." She eased his mouth back to hers and got lost in the kiss that teased, offered, promised, to take her to the place she had dreamed of sharing with him. She didn't question how they had come to this place. What mattered was that they had—that they were on the edge of something wonderful and that they were together.

His hands found the zipper at the back of her dress and she felt the cool room air on her back, but it was okay. Her body was already warm enough to counteract it.

Her hands rubbed against his chest and he moaned. She pushed his jacket down his arms and he released her just long enough to allow it to fall.

Then his hands were at her back, pushing her clinging dress down, forcing it to release her to him, letting it stay at her waist. His hands opened and tightened, stroked fire along her sides, stroking up, but not far enough, before they returned to her waist.

Then he pushed the dress over her hips. It formed a red, shimmery pool around her feet, but neither was looking at it. Their gazes were holding

PERFECT WEDDING 173

together as if outside forces were at work rather than internal ones.

Her hands fumbled with the buttons of his shirt for too long, but her fingers finally managed to free them.

Again he released her, but only long enough for his shirt to join with his jacket on the floor. Then he found the fullness at the side of her breasts as she found his flat nipples hiding in his chest hair. She moaned as he moved his hand to the sensitive front of her breast. She moaned again when he found a hard tip and brushed across it.

Her answer was to flick her tongue over his. His responding groan made her pull it into her mouth and draw on it.

"You know what they say about turnabout." His words sounded as if they had to fight their way out. She knew that no words of hers could manage to do even that.

He pressed a kiss to her forehead. Before she could protest his mouth being too far from where she wanted it, his hands found and released the catch at the back of her bra. For a second, cooling air brushed over her breasts as the filmy red lace drifted down. Then his hands covered them, held their fullness that fit perfectly in his hands. His thumbs brushed across the already hardened, sensitive tips, and Dana leaned her lower body against his hardness.

His hand released one breast and his mouth found it. Dana moaned and rubbed against him as he licked and then tugged. She wrapped her hands around the back of his neck. His mouth tasted hers again and her hands tightened as if her legs no longer had strength to support her. Then, as if that gave him the cue he was waiting for, his hands found the back of knees and he lifted her. Her breasts rubbed against him as he moved, and the heat and ache made them both groan.

His mouth still tasting hers, he carried her to her bedroom.

He let her feet touch the area rug on the floor, but he didn't release her completely. Instead he tasted her breasts again, as if to make sure they were still as sweet as before. Her fingers opened and closed against his head as she urged him closer, as if he wasn't already as close as possible.

Her hands struggled to release the clasp at the waist of his pants, but they managed. She wobbled his zipper down and shoved his pants over his hips, starting a new pile of clothes. His hands stroked along her hips before his fingers found the lace edges of her panties and peeled them away. Her hands pushed his underwear off his lean hips.

"Beautiful," he whispered as he stared at her. Then he took a step away. "Wait a second," he rasped when she protested.

He removed his wallet from his pocket, took out several packets, and smiled at her. "Always prepared." He stepped back to her and his hardness pressed against her. "Or, in this case, always hopeful."

They met in a kiss that held the promise of soon.

Then he sat on the side of the bed and pulled her with him. She opened her legs and his hardness pressed against her thicket as if hungrily seeking its home. He leaned back and took her with him. As their kisses deepened, they shifted until they lay side by side, touching from mouths to toes.

Steve's hand found the swollen nub at the entrance of her. He brushed across, dipped inside, then brushed across again.

"Please," she managed. "Please."

"Yes." He opened a foil packet and quickly rolled the protection into place. Then he covered her with his body.

His hardness impatiently probed her opening. Slowly he entered her, but hesitated when he met a barrier.

"Don't stop. Please, don't stop." She spread her hands across his backside and tried to pull him closer. He remained still for a second longer, then entered her body, which was more than ready for him. Once inside, he paused as she closed around him. Then he withdrew partly before filling her again.

They danced together in the way that was as old as time, coming together and almost separating before coming together again. Their dance continued, growing faster and faster still as they tried to reach the perfect climax.

Dana called out Steve's name as he called out hers. Their hold on each other tightened even more. Then she shattered into little pieces and drifted into nothingness.

Later, she had no idea how much time had passed, but it didn't matter; later, she gradually drifted back together.

"Wow and double wow and triple wow." Steve's arm tightened around her. "That was more wonderful than I had imagined." He tucked her against him. He pressed a kiss to the side of her face. "And you waited for me."

"I never found anybody that I cared enough about to . . ." She shrugged. "You know."

"Yeah. I know." He kissed the side of her face again.

"In high school some of the girls talked about having sex. I remember how a couple of them got pregnant. They dropped out of school and never came back. They said they would, but I don't remember one who did." She shifted. "That wasn't for me. I had dreams that didn't include a baby before I found my way." She brushed her hand along his chest. "I never imagined that it could be like this." Dana sighed and snuggled to him. "No idea." She yawned. "I'm glad I waited." She rubbed her cheek against his before she allowed it to stay.

"So am I." Steve shifted to a more comfortable position, but he didn't let her go. Together they found sleep.

Later, the cold disturbed them and one of them found the covers and pulled them up. Later still, their bodies found each other again and the covers were kicked off. Body heat and their anticipation of what was soon to come kept them from feeling the cold.

"Um, mmm," Dana murmured drowsily and smiled as Steve slipped on a condom and eased her on top of him. She opened her eyes enough to look down at him.

"I want to see you while I'm inside you," he said as he lifted her, then slowly lowered her onto him. Her eyes widened as she felt him swell inside her and her body close around him.

He smiled at her perched on top on him, fastened to him in the best way imaginable. Then he lifted his hand and slowly stroked a sensitive tip to hardness. She gasped as an arrow of heat shot to her core. Then she shifted to accommodate him even more.

"Come here." Steve eased her face down to his and covered her mouth with his.

Their bodies separated a little, met again, left a space, and then closed it. Then they were side by side, moving apart, and coming together as before, but differently. Still, they reached the top of the same mountain again and soared off together.

Chapter 16

Morning came cold. Sleet was rapping at the window and the wind was howling like a house dog forgotten outside. Dana shifted against Steve, then, half asleep, smiled.

"Morning, love." Steve lightly brushed his hand along her hip. "Sleep well?"

"Um-hmm." Her hand found his that was wrapped around her waist. "All four hours."

"Four hours? Why four hours?"

"Because we were both too tired to do anything else during that time." Their laughs mingled.

"Well, we're both well rested now, aren't we?" His hand found a tip and teased it to hardness.

"Yes." Her answer gasped out.

His touch on her breast wasn't heavy. Still, it managed to make her breathing difficult. She leaned back against his chest, closed her eyes, and enjoyed it.

Gently he turned her to him. Her leg slipped between his and she managed to rub back and forth. His hand released the tip to his mouth. He tugged gently, but it was enough to make Dana moan and push to get closer. Her hand found him and rubbed him against the place where she waited for him.

Protection quickly in place, he moved over her. Her hands grasped his hips and pulled him in. Their voyage was different this time, but ended the same way: with both of them coming to a glorious climax. While they slept, the weather rested too. Nature had put away the sleet until another day. What had been used was now just water.

"We should get up." Dana shifted her hands on his chest, but she didn't leave the bed.

"I just did."

"You are so. . ." He kissed her and the rest of her sentence was forgotten.

"Good?"

"Huh?"

"You didn't finish your sentence. I'm so good?"

"There are no words to describe what you are."

"I hope that's good."

"Oh yeah." Dana sighed. "We really have to get up. I'd say we should have breakfast, but it's past lunchtime."

"Time goes fast when you're having fun." His finger toyed with her breast and woke it up.

"Stop that."

"You want me to stop?"

"I am not going to talk about what I want." She rolled out of bed and smiled at him. "I'm taking a shower."

"Is that an invitation?"

"Not this time. Maybe the next." She winked at him, then left the bedroom wondering where her boldness had come from but refusing to question how she and her good friend had reached this new point.

I never imagined this would happen. Steve folded his hands behind his head. *I never dreamed Dana and I would finally get together like this.* He grinned. *Or that the sex . . .* He shook his head as if to erase his last thought. *Uh-uh. What we shared was more than sex. We made love and I never dreamed that lovemaking could be so fantastic.* His body hardened at the memory, but his smile widened. *Dana. All the dreams I had about her have finally come true. Dana. She waited for me.* He blinked hard. *I really never expected that.*

"Okay." Dana came into the bedroom.

Steve tried not to be disappointed that she had covered up with a long red terrycloth robe. The color sent his mind spinning back to the red dress. Then to how he had taken it off her. Then to what had happened next. Then to . . . He shifted in a wasted effort to get comfortable.

"Not right now."

"Huh?"

"The answer is not right now."

"I didn't ask a question."

"Yes, you did." She grinned. "You didn't use words, but your face shouted one."

"That obvious, huh?"

"Oh yeah."

"Is that a new answer to the question?"

She laughed. "It's all yours," she said and giggled again.

"It is? Again?" The redness in Dana's face wasn't from rubbing it with a towel.

PERFECT WEDDING 181

"The shower. You know that I'm talking about the shower. I left a robe on the back of the door for you."

"A man can hope." He got out of bed. "A robe, huh? Am I expected to be part of this cover-up?"

"Are you always like this in the morning?"

"Like what? You mean up?" His slight grin drew her attention. Then she made the mistake of letting her gaze leave his face and slowly move to his body.

She couldn't help noticing how perfect it was. She remembered how his hard chest had pressed against her soft breasts. She swallowed hard at the memory of how his thighs had felt like warm marble when they came against her. How his hardness had probed her. How his hands had worked magic on her body, teasing to life the part that she had only been dimly aware of until then. How his—

"Baby, you keep looking at me like that and the only place I'm going is back to bed with you."

"Oh." Dana pressed her hand to her face, covering her eyes. Her face flushed as if the heat she felt at the sight of him had decided to concentrate there.

"It's too late for that. Not only did you see me, but I saw your reaction to seeing me." He took a step toward her. "What's your favorite dessert?"

"Huh?"

"Dessert. Your favorite dessert. What is it?"

"A toss-up between coconut cream pie and cake with coconut icing. Why?"

"Coconut? Not something chocolate?"

"The only chocolate I like is candy. Why?"

"You looked at me as if you were looking at your favorite dessert. No way could I be considered coconut anything."

"How about chocolate candy?" She grinned.

"That works for me. I'm assuming that it worked for you, too. Notice my use of the past tense." He brushed his lips across hers. "Of course, we can make it the future tense, too." He let a finger rub across her lips. Then he left her before she could say anything else.

"I left a robe on the back of the door for you," she called after him once she could catch her breath. She leaned against the wall, welcoming its coolness.

"So you said." He winked and left.

"Steve and me." She whispered. She grinned and wrapped her hands around her waist. "Me and Steve. Who would have thunk it?" She giggled and made her way to the kitchen.

Once there she hummed the new song from the night before as she got out things for an omelet.

"Hey, sweetness." Steve came up behind her while she was at the stove. "What's cooking?" He rubbed against her slightly. "Besides you and me, I mean." He kissed the side of her face.

"Omelets." She turned her face so that their lips met. The kiss deepened. Then his mouth found her jaw. "Omelets. Omelets are good anytime," she said once she managed to find enough breath for the words.

"I know something else that's good anytime." He kissed her again.

"Stop that." She pulled away but touched the side of his face softly. "At least for now." She backed up a step. "Go sit. Whatever this meal is, it's ready."

She placed their plates on the table, then sat opposite him.

As they ate, an easy silence settled over the room, but it left space for her thoughts to surface. They

PERFECT WEDDING

dragged doubts with them. The quiet was no longer peaceful. Her doubts had made the easy connection she had felt with Steve weaken, then fade. *I should not have let this happen. Now what? This can't be the way a typical morning after goes.*

She pushed her eggs around on her plate. Then she took a small bit into her mouth. She repeated the procedure. Finally she gave up and set the fork down and just stared at the plate.

"Steve to Dana. Come back from wherever you are." He touched her hand.

"Huh? Oh." Her frown was obvious when she looked at him.

"What's wrong?"

"Nothing." She methodically shredded the piece of toast left on her plate.

"That's not a 'nothing' look on your face." He held her hand. His thumb brushed over the back, but it didn't soothe her.

"It's just that . . ." She shrugged.

"Sorry? Having second thoughts about what happened between us?"

Her gaze flew to his face. "Oh no." She shook her head. "Not that. I mean, not really. I just . . ." She shrugged.

"Not really? It's just what?"

"You didn't . . ." She shook her head and stared at the picture on the wall behind him as if expecting it to change. "We didn't . . ." Again she stopped and her frown deepened. "You weren't just trying to convince me to marry you? I mean, I know it's for my benefit, but still . . ." Finally she looked at him. "I might seem like it, but I'm not some pitiful charity case."

"Charity case?"

"I don't have to go to Hawaii. I won't die if I never get there. You don't have to do this for me."

"If I wasn't still high on our lovemaking, I'd be insulted." He let a finger trace a line down the side of her face. "As it is, it would take a whole lot more to bring me down than your second-guessing and getting it all wrong." He removed his hand. "Now, to change the subject a little, we have some unfinished business to attend to."

"We do?"

"Not that, sweet darling, although I'm glad that we have the same goal in mind," Steve said when she glanced toward the bedroom. "At least not that right now." He chuckled as redness gave her face a glow. "No, the business that I have in mind is shopping."

"You want to go shopping?"

"The store I have in mind isn't open today, but after school tomorrow we can go."

"You want to go shopping? I thought men didn't like shopping."

"We usually don't, but this is for a special occasion."

"Yeah?"

"We have to buy a ring."

"Ring?"

"Uh-huh. As in engagement." He held her hand and squeezed.

"I have to work out tomorrow. I can't go."

"I think this weekend's exercise can more than make up for you skipping tomorrow." He rubbed the inside of her wrist. She wished her car heater worked as quickly. "I hope you found our exercise more enjoyable that the treadmill."

"No contest."

PERFECT WEDDING

"Of course not." He chuckled. "I know how you feel about that treadmill."

She laughed, but then her face turned serious and she frowned. "You're still willing to marry me?"

"What kind of a question is that?"

"A simple one. I just told you that you don't have to. I mean, I thought I made it clear that I don't *have* to go to Hawaii."

"And I thought I made it clear that I want to marry you. Not *willing to*, but *want to*. And yes, still." He frowned. "Did you think that after last night I could change my mind? What kind of reasoning is that? I didn't propose to get you into bed." He grinned. "Although, had I known it would be so beyond words to describe, I might have tried to seduce you before." He gently lifted her chin. "I repeat. Yes, I still want to marry you. And not just because of the contest. The contest just gave me a shove in the right direction."

"Oh." She felt more at ease about what had happened.

"That has become a regular part of your vocabulary recently, hasn't it?" He smiled. "So I repeat. Monday, as in tomorrow, we make it official. Of course, I think that what happened between us last night . . ." He leaned over and kissed her. ". . . and again this morning . . ." He kissed her again. ". . . and will most assuredly happen again as soon as we finish here, should make it quite official already." He stared at her. "I never knew you did that."

"What?"

"Blushed."

"I never did before you."

"So I'm a first for more than one thing, huh?"

"Steve." She reddened even more.

"It looks good on you, sweetheart. Of course, everything does." He stood and reached for her. "But you look even better with nothing on."

"What am I going to do with you?" She shook her head slowly, but she went to him.

"I have some ideas I'd like to show you." He held her close. "You can see if they meet your approval." He kissed her. Then, arms around each other, they walked to the bedroom.

Hours later, Steve spoke.

"I hate to do this, but I have to go." His hand brushed along Dana's hip as if it had a mind of its own.

"I know." Dana sighed as she rubbed circles on his chest.

"I can't show up for school tomorrow morning wearing a tuxedo. Not even the most creative writer can come up with anything except the obvious reason."

"That's true." Dana shifted away from him. "Go while you can." She giggled. "The longer you wait, the harder it will be."

"You know, you got that right." He laughed, gave her a pat on the hip, then got out of bed. Twenty minutes later, he kissed her once more, then left.

Reassured once more, she went back to bed. This time her dreams were based on fact rather than fantasy. This would work out okay. It would be fine.

Chapter 17

"Before you ask me about my weekend, I want to hear about yours." Cathy settled into the passenger seat. "And before you part your lips, don't you even think of trying to tell me that nothing happened." She grinned. "I would have bugged you when I got in last night, but who knows what was going on in your place? I'll bet you didn't have to put those fifty blankets that you usually sleep under on you bed. Oh yeah. I'll bet you had something hotter than them to warm you." She laughed again. "If heat didn't rise, I'll bet my apartment below yours would have felt like a hot house." She tapped Dana's arm. "Come on, girl. Open up. Give." She laughed again. "I won't ask you to forgive my choice of words because I bet they are accurate. Well?" She tapped her again. "Talk."

"How can I? Your words are taking up all of the space."

"I thought the weekend would have mellowed you."

"What makes you so sure anything happened?"

"Chile, I saw the way you two were wrapped together on that dance floor. I've seen new braids looser than that." She shook her head. "The music stopped and you didn't even know it. I half-expected to have to come over and bring you two back so you wouldn't get locked in that room all night." She laughed again. "The way you two were gone, you probably wouldn't have noticed where you were." She turned to face her. "Well? Don't keep me waiting."

"How come you weren't too wrapped up in Kenny to notice us?"

"I *knew* what was going to happen between us. You and Steve were the unknown."

"Did you spend the whole weekend wondering?"

"Girlfriend, you know I love you like a sister, but I had more important things to do with my weekend." She leaned her head back and sighed. "I am so in love big time. It's wonderful; it's crazy; it's got me so far off the ground I wouldn't know if ten feet of snow blanketed everything." She sat up. "Guess what? He asked me to marry him. I am engaged." She held out her left hand. "I can just imagine a ring right there." She tapped the spot waiting for a sparkler.

"I guess there's a lot of that going around." Dana purposely kept her voice low and relaxed.

"Huh? What? What did you say?"

"Steve and I are engaged. We'll go shopping for a ring after school today." Doubt poked at her as she spoke. This was such a drastic step.

"You know you have to tell me more than that. It

was that red dress, wasn't it? I knew that would do the job."

"Actually, he offered to marry me before."

"Before? As in before last night? Or was it Friday night? Never mind. That part is not important. When did this 'before' happen?"

"When I was doing the blind date, speed-dating thing." She pulled into the parking lot and turned off the motor. "He offered because of the contest."

"Steve proposed to you that long ago and you're just telling me? What kind of a friend would keep her best friend out of the loop? You knew the very moment I met Kenny." She shrugged. "Well, maybe not the very moment, but you knew the next time I saw you."

"This is different."

"Oh. So nothing happened after you left the dance?" She shook her head. "Uh, uh. No way can you make me believe that. I saw you. I felt the electricity across the room. If I had looked closely, I would have seen the sparks zapping between you. I don't think your feet were even touching the floor."

"I didn't say that nothing happened." Dana sighed. "It was better than I ever imagined."

" 'It' ? Are you talking about what I think you're talking about? You guys really did . . . ?"

"We made love." Dana couldn't help the grin that appeared. "I never dreamed it could be like that. It was perfect." She sighed away the grin. "But I don't know."

"Don't know? What don't you know? What's to know?"

"I don't want him to marry me because of what happened."

"He proposed before."

"Yes, but that was because he knew I wanted Hawaii."

"I still don't get it. What's the problem?"

"I don't want to get married for the wrong reason."

"Trying to win a contest is not the wrong reason?"

"I don't want Steve to be tied down. He might regret it."

"You were willing to go this route with a stranger."

"It would have been for business. Only temporary." A bell sounded in the yard.

"I have to go," Cathy said. "Maybe by the time I see you after school I will have figured out your logic." She shook her head and got out. "I'll catch a ride home with Kenny." She grinned. "Maybe we can manage something else, too."

She laughed as she walked across the yard. Dana watched her, but she wasn't laughing. She was still thinking about her situation.

"Morning, Miss Dillard." Steve stood outside his door. "I hope you slept well."

Dana blushed and shook her head, but it wasn't to answer his question. "Quite well, thank you. For some reason I was very tired." She blinked innocently at him. "How about you? I trust you slept as well as I did?"

Steve laughed. "Probably about the same."

The students coming into the rooms precluded any further conversation between them. The morning classes took Dana's mind off Steve. By lunchtime, he was back in person.

"How did your morning go?" Steve sat at the table in Dana's room.

"Fine. And yours?"

PERFECT WEDDING

"Not as well as yesterday morning, but it went as well as can be expected." He stared at her long enough to see the color rise in her face. "But I digress. Digression will bring nothing but frustration in this case." He opened the folder he had brought with him.

"Hey Steve," Simone said from the doorway. "How was your weekend?"

"It was better than fine." He glanced at Dana, then back at Simone. "I think you should be one of the first to know." He held Dana's hand. "Dana and I got engaged over the weekend."

"Engaged?" If a class had been in session anywhere in the hall, Simone's voice would have disturbed it. "Engaged?" Hatred filled her face as she looked at Dana's hand. "I don't see a ring."

"Check back tomorrow," Dana said. She grinned at the satisfaction she got from the look on the other woman's face. "Same hand, correct finger."

Simone stared at them a few seconds longer, then stalked away.

"That went well, don't you think?" Steve said.

"Just peachy." Dana smiled. "I almost feel sorry for her." She giggled. "Almost."

"Dana, Dana." Steve shook his head slowly.

"How far away do you think she parked her broom?"

"Now, was that nice?"

"No, but it felt good." They laughed.

"On to a more pleasant subject." He held a letter out to her.

"The Math Olympics. This was waiting in my mailbox this morning. Our kids will be competing at the Garvey Middle School a week from Wednesday. They are one of six teams from our cluster."

"Fantastic."

"I'll tell them in front of the whole class when we meet this afternoon."

"Nothing like lighting a spark in the other kids. Some of those who weren't interested could do the same if they'd apply themselves."

"True. Anyway, let's focus on the positive. I know our kids are ready." He tapped the letter. "They'd better be. Things go fast from here. Wednesday after that, the winners from all of the public middle schools meet in the area-wide contest. A week from that is the next step—their first time meeting teams from other than public schools. Two weeks later, on a Saturday, we take on the teams from other districts across the state." He grinned. "Harrisburg, here we come." He shrugged. "I know I'm jumping the gun, but I also know what our team can do. I truly believe they can take it at the state level."

"Congratulations." She squeezed his arm. "You have worked so hard for this."

"We all have. Hey, why don't we bring both classes together and announce the news?"

"Great idea. I'll bring my kids over." She laughed. "Maybe I'll let them use it as a catalyst for a story or an essay."

"We use what we can to get them where they should be."

All of the talk while they were eating was about the math contests. The past weekend never came up. Neither did shopping. At least, not until Steve stood to leave.

"Should we leave from here or do you have to take Cathy home?" He had switched subjects, but Dana knew what he was talking about.

"This is a late day for her. She's catching a ride with Kenny." She stared at him. "He proposed to her over the weekend."

"Just like us."

"See you after school." She watched him leave before she cleared the table. *Despite what he said, it's not just like us at all.*

When Steve told the kids about the letter, high and low fives went around the room as the kids congratulated the team members. It was as if they had won the Superbowl.

"Listen up," Steve said above the noise. Gradually they settled down. "This is just the first competition. We still have a long way to go to win those prizes." The room was subdued. He smiled at them. "By the end of the year, after the awards ceremony, we can celebrate big time."

The room erupted again. Someone started chanting, "HMS. HMS." Soon the whole room rang with the cheer. After a short while, Steve raised his hands and the cheers faded.

"Now let's get back to our regular work." They groaned. "Hey, we might find a social studies or science contest for you guys. We have to be ready, right?"

"Right," came the reluctant answer from them.

Dana's thoughts flew to how the same word had meant something completely different when she had used it with Steve. She smiled. *Completely.*

Through the afternoon she taught her classes, but what little enthusiasm she had had about her situation before, gradually cooled. The class was working on essays and her mind was going over the circumstances.

This is for real; this engagement, she thought. Steve

had suggested it, but, in reality, it had been her idea. She had practically hit him over the head with it by telling him about the contest, the blind and speed dates, and practically whining about Hawaii every time they were together. He had proposed, but what else could he do? He was a friend helping a poor friend reach her dream. He was willing to put his social life on hold for her. She sighed.

He doesn't love me, though, in spite of the way we had connected over the weekend. She blushed. *Connected was exactly the right word.* She felt her face grow hotter.

The weekend had been great. It had been way much better than great, but did that mean anything? Guys don't have to have feelings beyond the basic and the moment, did they? There were lots of females out there who could swear to that. Males didn't have to be emotionally involved to have sex. She shrugged. *I guess it's only right. If I'm going to keep him from other women, I have an obligation to satisfy his needs.* She frowned and shook her head. *There's that tangled web again.*

"Do you want us to do anything when we finish? Should we meet with our critique partners now?" *Bless Mattie for pulling me back to safe ground.*

Dana looked at the class. Twenty-five pairs of eyes were on her waiting for an answer to Mattie's question. She pulled her mind back to the easy part of her life.

"Yes, go ahead and do that."

The students changed seats and began sharing their writing. Dana got up and walked around, pausing at pairs of students from time to time.

She tried not to think ahead, but the end of the school day came anyway. She dismissed the classes at the right time, reminded them of their assignment for the next day, then tried to prepare herself. She wasn't looking forward to what was coming next, but the sooner it was over, the better for her.

"How'd it go?" Steve smiled from her doorway.

"It went."

"Oh. That bad?"

"No. The classes went fine."

He stared at her. "I won't ask you to elaborate. I probably don't want to know. Ready for this?"

"As ready as I'll ever be." Her stare slid from his. She never got close enough for them to touch.

"Not even a little enthusiasm?" Steve said softly when they reached the parking lot.

"I think I should take my car home first. That way we won't have to come back for it." She walked to her car without looking at him.

When they reached her car, he took her keys from her and turned her toward him. Then he took her into his arms and kissed her quickly but thoroughly. He lifted her chin so he could look into her eyes.

"Nothing? I hoped the magic would last longer." His voice was low. He opened her door, then handed her the keys. Without another word, he got into his car and followed her from the lot.

What is going on? Steve frowned. *What happened? After this past weekend, I expected....* His frown deepened. *I don't know what I expected, but it wasn't this. She's colder than the weather, and the temperature is below freezing.*

He was still trying to figure things out when he parked beside her. He got out and went to her car.

"Do you have to go inside first?"

"No." She got out. "Let's get this over with." She

walked to his car. After hesitating a second, he followed and opened the door for her.

"Maybe this will help." He pulled her close for another kiss, a bit longer that the last. Her reaction was the same as before. "Then again, maybe not," he muttered as he closed the door behind her. *Cold.* He kept trying to get her to relax as he drove from the lot.

"I thought we'd go downtown. I know there are jewelry stores at the malls, but I don't want you to be tempted to do other shopping." When she didn't respond, he added quietly, "That was a joke."

If not for the radio that Steve turned on, the only sound would have been from the engine.

Neither spoke as Steve handed the keys to the valet parking attendant. They were still silent as they walked inside the store.

"May I help you?" A salesman, dressed for success, approached them as soon as they entered the store. "I'm Mr. Hastings."

"We need to see engagement rings," Steve told him.

"Congratulations, sir. Best wishes, miss. Please come this way." His grin was wide enough to make up for the lack of one on either Dana's or Steve's face. He had them sit in front of a case. Then he placed a tray in front of them.

"These are small. Don't you have any larger ones?"

"Oh, of course. Just a moment, please." He hurried away as if afraid they would change their minds.

"Those were all right," Dana said after the salesman left them.

"I want more than 'all right' for you."

"I don't know why."

"You don't? I thought I made that clear."

The salesman returned, cutting off any further discussion.

"We have some very nice ones here. Do you know what design you want?"

"No."

"We'll know it when we see it," Steve said when Dana didn't elaborate.

"That's fine. If you don't see something here that strikes you, we have others. I'm sure we can find something to satisfy your taste."

Dana's gaze flew to Steve and his gaze was waiting for her. Her face heated, but she dampened the fire and stared back at the rings.

"How about this one?" Steve lifted a marquise-cut diamond flanked by three smaller diamonds on either side. They were sparkling from a platinum setting.

"Excellent choice, sir. Excellent."

"How do you feel about it, miss? Do you like it?"

"It's okay."

"Okay?" Mr. Hastings frowned. Then he shrugged and looked at Steve. "Your proposal must have come as quite a surprise. She's not as enthusiastic as most newly engaged women." He shrugged as he handed the ring to Dana. "I guess everybody shows it differently."

The ring fit as if it had been made for her, but Dana couldn't find joy at that. She looked at the ring and felt something inside give her an uneasy feeling. Something that didn't have to do with Steve. She poked it down and thought about Steve and what he was doing for her.

I should show something—gratitude toward Steve, hap-

piness at getting closer to Hawaii, something. Her 'shoulds' didn't alter her real feelings.

Things progressed in a blur and soon they were back in the car. The heaviness weighing her down stayed in place, much heavier than the ring on her finger.

"I'd suggest we go out to eat, but I think you'd rather not."

"I am kind of tired. Do you mind?"

"Whatever you want."

"That's what this is about, isn't it?"

"What?"

"This whole charade."

"Does this come under a heavy version of 'no good deed going unpunished' or is something else more appropriate?"

"See? That's what I mean. I'm a good deed."

"What?" He glanced at her. "I'm not getting further into this until I can figure where you're coming from. And, more importantly, where you're going with it." He shook his head. "Until now I wasn't even sure I believed in that Venus/Mars stuff. Now I think they got it wrong. They should have been talking different galaxies." He shook his head. "I'll take you home."

Neither said another word until he parked beside her car.

"I'll see you tomorrow. Thanks, Steve." Dana quickly scrambled from the car.

"Wait." She hesitated and turned back to hear him. "I know you don't believe this, but it's my pleasure." He exhaled sharply. "We have to talk. But first I have to figure out what to say to sort things out."

He watched Dana go inside. She never looked back.

He sat there long enough for her to get to her apartment and hang up her coat. He still hadn't figured out what was wrong, but he went home. He wouldn't get any answers here.

Chapter 18

During the rest of the evening Dana was alone, but her thoughts and second thoughts filled the apartment. For once, she didn't turn on the television. It would have been a waste of time. At eleven, she went into the bedroom. Just staring at the bed flooded back the memories of Steve and how he had made perfect love with her there. She stared a few seconds longer and wiped the few tears that dared to roll down her face. Now it was just a cold, lonely place to sleep. She snatched the sheets from the bed and remade it with the bright yellow ones she had bought on impulse thinking they would help cheer her.

Her eyes filled again as she piled the usual blankets and comforter on top. Then she crawled between the sheets and reached over and turned on the electric blanket. It was going to be a long, lonely night.

* * *

Dana got up before the alarm went off. She got out of bed and never looked back. As she went to take her shower, her gaze stole to the ring. *I should be feeling better than this,* she thought, but the sparkle did nothing to pull her out of the slump she felt trapped in.

Not looking forward to facing Cathy, she went down and knocked on her door.

"Let me see, let me see." Cathy grabbed Dana's hand and held it closer. "Talk about bling-bling. This gives the phrase a whole new meaning." She pulled Dana close in a hug. "Nobody deserves this more than you do, except for me, and mine is coming this weekend." She laughed and pulled her toward the car. "Let's give the folks at school something to talk about, girlfriend."

"I don't think I'll tell them just yet." Dana shrugged. "Steve told Simone yesterday, but I doubt she'll be anxious to let people know that she didn't get what she wanted." She pulled onto the road.

"That may be, but they'll find out even if it's not until the show. May as well let them in on things now." Her voice quieted. "They don't need to know the details." She patted Dana's arm. "I vote for telling them now."

"I guess you're right." Dana shook her head. "I don't think I'm ready for this."

"Ready or not, here it is. I don't mind admitting this, but your plan is working out better than I thought it would. I thought I'd have to dry enough tears from my shoulder to fill that reservoir on Belmont Avenue, but the water will have to come from the old-fashioned source." She laughed. "If you're honest, you'll admit that it's going better than you expected, too."

The word *honest* poked Dana so hard that she cringed. She hadn't thought about that when she had started scheming. She let Cathy go on. She was still stuck on the honest part when she parked.

Cathy got out, still grinning. "I would love to see their faces when you tell them. Unfortunately, I have a date with a roomful of little ones who will start to feel abandoned if I'm not there to greet them with a smile."

Cathy patted Dana's arm, then walked across the parking lot. Dana took a deep breath. *Do I want Steve with me or not?*

It didn't matter. Steve was waiting for her outside the door. He squeezed her hand, then tucked it against his side.

"Showtime," he murmured and placed a quick kiss on her lips. Either he didn't notice her reluctance or he chose to ignore it. He moved his hand to her shoulder and they entered the office.

"Congratulations are in order," he announced to everyone. "Dana has agreed to marry me." He held up her hand and smiled at her. His smile slipped a bit when it didn't find a matching one on her face, but it was back in place as he looked at the staff.

Whistles, shouts, and congratulations tumbled together, filling the small office space.

"I knew something was going on between you two," Mrs. Jones, another seventh grade teacher, said. "There was just something about you together. Like you belonged."

Murmurs of agreement came from several others.

"Best wishes," Janeeka, the secretary, said after the other noises had died down. "You're not sup-

PERFECT WEDDING

posed to congratulate the bride-to-be. It makes her look as if she was desperate to catch a man." She laughed. "I'm giving you fair warning. When I get a ring on this finger"—she held up her hand, wiggled her fingers, and pointed—"y'all can congratulate me all you want." She and the others in the office laughed.

"You got that right," one of the other teachers said. Hugs and handshakes were shared. Best wishes followed them as they left the office.

"What's wrong?" Steve's voice was soft as they walked down the hall. He squeezed her arm, but she didn't move closer.

"I don't feel right about this."

"I'd ask what I can do, but I think the answer is nothing."

"No." She shook her head. "This isn't about you."

"It sure feels like it."

He left her outside her room and didn't look at her again.

Their lunchtime was spent planning schedule changes and working on the mechanics of the contest. A substitute teacher would come on the Wednesdays of the contest. The classes would go back to the procedure from before they restructured for the contest.

Dana listened as well as she could. For a few seconds, she wished she could go back to before she had decided that she wanted Hawaii so desperately. She threw that thought away as soon as it showed itself.

If I did, then Steve never would have happened. We never would have made love. We'd be just friends again and I'd never know what I was missing. She frowned.

If only things had developed between us in a natural way, nothing underhanded involved. If it had, then I would know that he really cares for me that way. If only . . .

"So that sounds okay to you?"

"What? Oh yes."

"So you think it's a good idea for us to build a rocket in the cafeteria and shoot for Mars right through the ceiling?"

"Huh?"

"Have you heard a word I said?"

"I'm sorry, Steve." She sighed. "So much has happened so quickly."

"And not all good, either, huh?"

"I didn't say that."

"You didn't have to. I'm good at making inferences. I'm also good at drawing conclusions." He stared at her, giving her time to comment. When she didn't answer, he turned back to the plan for the math team. *I'm glad something is going according to plans,* he thought. Then he concentrated on something easy: making schedules.

During lunchtime on Wednesday, the kids had asked to practice for the math meet. Dana was glad she didn't have to wonder if Steve would bring up their situation. She had enough trouble wrestling with it by herself.

Steve's puzzled look was there as he greeted her in the morning. It was either still there or back in place when they left for the day.

I never did like unsolved puzzles, he thought. He was glad for the distraction that working with the kids brought. Those problems he could solve. As for the one with Dana, he wasn't even sure what the problem was. His scowl didn't help change the situation, but he wore it anyway. *They say we men are*

PERFECT WEDDING

closedmouthed, but Dana beats all of us where that's concerned. What in the world is bothering her? I don't think it was the lovemaking. Was it?

His body hardened at the memory of her in his arms. He was glad that he was alone in his car. *She acted pleased. She looked pleased. And she sure sounded pleased. Every time.* The image of Dana losing control in his arms flew back as if he were the one keeping it from happening again.

Horns sounded behind him and he pulled through the intersection. He shook his head. *Nothing about her reaction was acting. It was real. It was all for real.* Despite the thirty-degree temperature outside, he opened the window.

I want an explanation. After what happened between us, I think she owes me that much. She let me believe that she was all right with moving our relationship to a new phase. She was even playful the next morning. She didn't put me out. I was the one who said I had to leave. She acted as if she was sorry that I had to go. The least she can do is tell me what's wrong.

He fumed for several hours. Finally he drove to Dana's apartment and parked in the visitors' section. He stared at the building, but he didn't go in. *I can't make her talk if she doesn't want to. I have to wait until she's ready. When will that be?* He stared a few minutes longer, then drove home. *How did this get to be such a mess?*

The next evening was a repeat. As if practicing for something of his own, trying to get it right, Steve repeated the visit to Dana's apartment again on Thursday. *Tomorrow,* he promised himself as he went home. *I've had enough.* He was tired of avoiding the problem. He didn't even know what the problem *was*.

Not even aware that Steve was outside on Thursday, Dana ate her dinner, though she didn't taste a thing. Her mind was churning, blocking out her senses. She was wondering if her common sense had been blocked when she decided to enter the contest.

How much longer can I keep this up? I have to talk with him about this. It's not fair to let him think that it's because of him. He's perfect. Warmth filled her, but immediately regret cooled her. She frowned. *He made me feel so special. He made me feel something I couldn't even imagine. I get hot just remembering it.* She shifted her position in her chair, but it didn't help. *How could I push him away and not even tell him why?* She stared at the wall as if expecting a path to appear. Then she stared back at her almost full plate. *We have to talk.* She frowned. *Not yet, but soon.*

She spent the rest of the evening trying to figure how to go about it. When bedtime came, she was still looking for the solution.

"Guess what, guess what?" Cathy opened her door in the morning before Dana could ring the bell. "Come on. Let's go. We don't want to be late. You can guess on the way." She grabbed Dana's hand and pulled her along as if they were late instead of the usual fifteen minutes early.

In spite of having a heavy mind, Dana smiled.

"Now, let me see. Could this be the day you are getting your ring?"

"Oh. I guess I might have mentioned it."

"A time or two . . . or three . . . or . . ."

"Okay, okay. But I am so happy." She did a little dance beside the car. "Somebody tie a string around my waist so I won't float away." She laughed. "Today is Friday. Glorious, beautiful Friday. Special besides that TGIF thing. What's wrong with shopping on Friday? Why does everyone have to wait until Saturday to go shopping?"

"I see Kenny agreed."

"Chile, if he had his way, we would have taken a quick flight to somewhere that doesn't have a waiting period and I'd be wearing both rings as we speak. If Elkton, Maryland, still had that law, I know I wouldn't have been able to talk him out of it. You know how men are. The less fuss the better." She looked at Dana. "You are so lucky that Steve is willing to go through all of that bother and stuff in public. I'm not so sure that Kenny would."

Then she talked about the styles of rings available, not noticing that Dana didn't look as if she felt lucky.

From there Cathy moved to the wedding itself. "It won't be big like yours, but it will still be perfect."

Dana didn't let Cathy see how her last comment made her cringe. She knew Cathy had no idea how Dana was feeling.

She was still trying to sort it all out herself. She envied Cathy her enthusiasm. *It's your own fault,* she thought. *You set this up, you're getting what you wanted.*

"We want you and Steve to come out with us on Saturday to help us celebrate," Cathy said as Dana stopped the car. "We found this new little restaurant. I was going to cook, but Kenny said that I'm celebrating, too, so I shouldn't work." She sighed. "Isn't he sweet? Isn't he the sweetest man you ever met?" She stared at Dana. "You can put Steve in first place. I won't mind."

"You know the circumstances behind our engagement."

"I know what finally shoved you two out of the rut you have been in for years. There had to have been something between you. No man and woman can be just friends for that long. Neither of you ever had anybody serious in your life." She shook her head. "No, that contest only woke you up. I repeat, you can label Steve the sweetest man you've ever known. Of course, I'm sticking with Kenny." She laughed and walked across the parking lot.

Dana went inside her school, trying to get ready to face Steve, hoping that today wasn't the day that his patience ran out.

The first bell had rung to signal the end of lunch. They had eaten lunch for the first time in a couple of days. He had a feeling that Dana only agreed because they had to make more schedule adjustments. They were clearing the table when he changed the subject.

"We have to talk." He stilled her hand as she was gathering the trash. "Not here and not now," he added. *She looks as if she's a deer in the middle of I-95 with traffic aiming for her,* he thought. *That's not what I want. This has to end.* "I'll be over tonight."

"Not tonight."

"You have something to do, right? Wash you hair, maybe? Look, we can't continue to act as if nothing happened between us." He released a harsh breath. "At least I can't. I'm not that good an actor." He shook his head. "I can't read minds, either, though I've been trying for the past week."

"Okay." She sighed. "Come on over about six."

"I'd offer to bring hoagies, but I don't expect it to be that kind of an occasion."

Without waiting for an answer, he went to his room, glad that they had met in her classroom. The short walk gave him something to do and less time to think. Having to leave her kept him from kissing her and trying to put things back the way they had been.

When she got home, Dana glanced at her mail and barely reacted when the letter she had been waiting for wasn't there. She had other things on her mind. She walked around her apartment, looking for things to do, hoping to find a way to stop the clock that showed a later time when she looked at it every five minutes.

Why can't this be the day of an Eagles game? Then I'd have decorations to put out, food to fix, and special stuff to put on. I'd be waiting for my friend to come over and watch the game with me. Why did I start this?

She picked up the McNabb doll, but the bobble head didn't make her smile this time. It didn't even take her mind back to the Superbowl win. She put it back and looked for something else to do.

At 5:55, Steve parked in Dana's parking lot. He took a deep breath, then went upstairs. He wanted to get this over with, but he wasn't looking forward to what was about to take place. What if Dana decided that she was backing out? Not just the contest, but what they had going? He hesitated, then rang her bell.

She took so long to open the door that he thought she had taken this way to show him that she changed her mind about talking.

"Okay," he said as he stepped inside. "What's going on?"

"Aren't you going to take off your coat?"

"I wasn't sure if you wanted me to." He hesitated, then handed it to her. They had really gone back. Usually he took off his coat, went into the living room, and made himself at home. Today wasn't usually.

"What's the matter. I don't mean right now. And don't say nothing." He took a step closer to her, but he didn't try to touch her. "Are you sorry?"

"Yes." A thousand years passed for Steve before she continued. "But not about what happened between us."

"You mean not because we made love. It's okay to say it. Not saying it won't make the fact that we made love go away."

"I wouldn't want it to." She sighed. "I'm not doing a very good job of this."

She looked at him and it took all of his control not to wrap her in his arms and try to kiss away whatever was troubling her.

"Talk to me. This is your old buddy, Steve. Remember?"

"You're also my fiancé."

"Let me see if I understand. You're acting cold because I'm your fiancé. Friendship was okay. Our engagement ruins it. Have I got it right?"

"No." She shook her head. "I wish we had got-

PERFECT WEDDING   211

ten engaged the conventional way and not because I want to win a contest."

"We went over this before. I thought it was settled."

"You wouldn't have proposed if it hadn't been for the contest. We'd still be just good friends."

"And that's what you want?"

"We were happy."

Happy? Was she really happy with the way things were back then? Doesn't she get it?

"So what are you saying?"

"I think we should go back to the way things were between us." She swallowed hard. "If you want to break the engagement, that will be all right. I'll understand."

"Did you ever try to put spilled milk back into the bottle? I know you know the story of Humpty Dumpty. And even if we could, I wouldn't want to undo what happened between us." He backed up and stuck his hands into his pockets. "If you want to try to pretend that we never happened, I can't stop you. As far as the engagement is concerned, it stands. I'm not pulling out. Too much has happened for it to be for nothing. I'll do what I can to help you win your contest. Outwardly, I'll be your friend, since that's the way you want it."

He turned and got his coat. He left before she could say anything else.

On Saturday Dana rode with Cathy and Ken to the restaurant. Cathy bubbled with happiness and Dana wished she could find just a little for herself.

Steve was waiting for them. Cathy and Kenny

walked to the table as if they were walking down the aisle after the minister had just pronounced them husband and wife. Dana and Steve walked as if they just happened to be going the same way at the same time.

I wish I had just a little of that, Steve thought as he saw Cathy look at Kenny as if she were staring at her whole world and Kenny look back at her in the same way. *I feel my part.* He looked at Dana, who was trying to look happy. *Dana is the one not doing her part.*

During what must have been a delicious meal, Steve glanced at Dana from time to time. Once or twice he managed to catch her gaze. Whenever he did, it slid away from him. Then he looked at the other couple who was showing what love should be like.

The evening ended and Steve took Dana home. He could think of a lot of other places he would rather be. The dentist's office came to mind.

The atmosphere in the car during the ride home was as heavy as rain clouds before they let loose. Steve didn't attempt a conversation and neither did Dana. It was as if they had agreed to let the silence have the space.

When they reached her building, he opened the car door for her and held out his hand for her key.

"You don't have to do this," she said. When his hand stayed out, she dropped her keys into it. Silence was still with them as they went to her apartment. Once there he opened her door and handed the key back to her.

"You don't have to worry about me forcing myself on you. You made it clear how you feel."

"Steve, it's—"

"Please don't tell me again that it's not me. I'm the only other person involved in this." He stared at her. "See you on Monday."

She watched him walk away. He never looked back at her. She stood in the doorway awhile longer, then went inside and softly closed the door.

Chapter 19

An uneasy peace surfaced between them. It didn't grow, but it didn't disappear, either.

It's Dana's move next, Steve decided. *I'll wait, at least for a while, until I can't stand it anymore. Then I'll...* He frowned. *I'll do what? I've almost reached the end of my patience and I still don't know what to do.*

He focused on the math team, on his classes, and on everything else he could think of—anything to try to keep his mind off Dana. She never left it completely, but most of the time he was able to work around her and concentrate on something else besides her, besides the fact that he had lost her and he didn't know why.

During the few lunches when he wasn't meeting with the math team, he and Dana spent the awkward time talking about schoolwork.

I don't know why I bother, he thought as he walked back to his room one day.

Things had been more strained between them now that they had made love, than when he had

PERFECT WEDDING 215

first gotten to know her. She was treating him worse than she would treat a stranger; she was acting as if he was somebody whom she regretted knowing. It was as if she didn't remember how it had been between them that weekend, how perfect they had been together, how it had made him believe that he could have that forever. She must not have felt the same way. If she had, she wouldn't be doing this.

If I had known that it would be the last time I held her, the last time we made love, I would have stayed longer. I would have come to school in my tux if it meant that I had more time to make love with her.

He stared at the sheet of practice problems he was putting together for the team. He crumpled it and tossed it into the basket. Even Einstein couldn't solve impossible equations. That's what he and Dana were: an impossible equation. He didn't need to put any such frustration on the team.

The Harris math team, who had labeled themselves the Mighty Math Nerds, sailed through the first competition as if their opponents were third graders. Steve had to caution them about getting overconfident. He reminded them of how easy it was to make dumb mistakes. For a second his thoughts had gone to his situation with Dana, but he still couldn't see what he did wrong. He brought his attention back to the kids and high-fived all of them.

At the next contest, Harris had no trouble beating the citywide public school teams, and the week after that they met the winning team from the nonpublic schools. The score of that match was closer, but the Mighty Math Nerds won. The school had a celebration rally for them. The assembly rivaled the one the school had for the Eagles before the Superbowl win. This time a team of their own was the champion. Personnel from the district offices attended.

"Miss Dillard and Mr. Rollings, commendations are in order," Mr. Holloway, the principal, said at a staff meeting. Cheers, whistles, and shouts surrounded them. Those sitting close enough patted them on their backs. The principal continued, "I want you to know about some of the fallout from the Math Olympics and the writing contests." He handed them a letter. "District headquarters is taking notice. They want you to speak to the principals in the fall. They intend to encourage other schools to find something similar that the kids can get excited about, something to make them believe in themselves. As for the kids, they want a trophy. They figure, if Harris School can win, they can too."

"You go on," one of the teachers shouted. "We're right with you." Clapping from the others followed.

After it died down, Mr. Holloway continued. "We've had positive reactions from the other kids right here. Some of the other teachers have told me that their kids are showing more interest in, not just math, but their other subjects as well. Mrs. Owens wants to say something."

One of the other teachers stood. "I have a group of boys who used to walk around as if they had a basketball surgically attached to their hands. Now they've been not only carrying their math books, but actually opening them as well." Everybody laughed with her. "Because of you, they are now open to my teaching." She laughed again. "I just might hang around Harris for another twenty years." Everybody laughed as she sat.

"I have some kids who asked if they could work on stories and poems," another teacher said. "Some of the poems are rap, but hey, writing is writing and the lyrics are clean. Who knows? Maybe they can start a new trend. One of the raps is about how cool it is to be a nerd. Maybe they can share it at the next assembly?"

"I guess I can keep from cringing at a rap if it's not too long," Mr. Holloway said. Everybody laughed. He went on, "Competition is great if the kids believe they have a chance of winning if they work hard. You two made the kids believe it could happen."

After the business part of the meeting was over, Mr. Holloway shook their hands again and said, "I'd wish you good luck, but I know luck has nothing to do with this. Nothing but hard work could accomplish this. Even if they go no further, our students have proven to themselves that they can hold their own, and that's the important thing."

The kids asked to meet at lunchtime to work on their weak points. Steve agreed. He would have done so even if things had been right with Dana. As it was, he was certain that she would be glad for the time away from him.

Dana got the letter she had been waiting for, but she opened it as if she didn't care what it said. When she read that they were still working on choosing couples for the next step, she didn't get upset.

She forced herself to focus on school. In addition to the math team victories, two more of her kids got acceptance letters for stories in a magazine that only published kids' writings. She celebrated with all of them.

A group of students asked for a school paper of students' writing. She knew that, even though the students would be working with her, it would be a lot of work on her part. Still, she got approval from the principal.

She and Steve acted as if nothing had ever happened between them. Sorrow moved in on her at that thought and seemed to have settled in permanently. She had no idea what to do. It was true; you can't undo anything. The most you can hope for is to find a way to move on.

Just when she had managed to forget about her situation for a short while, she came home to find another letter waiting for her. The familiar logo glared from the corner. She stared at it. Her enthusiasm from before never surfaced this time. For once she wasn't afraid she would find a rejection letter inside. *That would settle part of this problem,* she thought. *Then Steve and I could put all of this behind us. If not over, we could start at the time before I got that dumb idea.* She took a deep breath, then slowly tore the top off the envelope. She pulled out the letter and read it, almost hoping to see a sentence saying, *We're sorry, but . . .* Instead she read a letter that was supposed to make her happy.

Dear Contestants:

We are pleased to inform you that you are one of five lucky couples in your area chosen to continue our quest to find the perfect couple for our next *Perfect Wedding* program. An invitation is enclosed to a reception. We look forward to meeting you.

The *Perfect Wedding* Committee

Dana stared at the letter. Then she waited for happiness to push away all of the sadness and negative feelings she had. She waited for what seemed forever. Then, still clutching the invitation, she sat beside the telephone. Ten minutes later she was still sitting. Finally she called Steve.

"I got a letter from the *Perfect Wedding* people. They're having a reception for the five finalist couples in this area. We're one of them."

"You sound overjoyed about it. Are we going?"

"If you're still willing."

"Baby, I'm still willing to do anything with you that you have in mind."

"Oh."

Quicker than quick an image of Steve in bed with her came back to her as if it had been waiting for just such an opening. She could almost feel his mouth on hers, his hands on her breasts, him inside her, and her closing tightly around him. Then they . . .

"When and where?"

"What?"

She tried to make the image go away, but it was as stubborn as she was. She had to function with it still as fresh as if it happened a few minutes ago rather than long ago. *Too long ago, if you'll be honest with yourself.* She sighed. *I can't even trust my own body. I try to focus on something innocent and look what happens.*

"Are you doing something else while we have this conversation?"

Nothing but remembering. "Not really."

"The reception. When and where is it?"

"Oh. It's at a hotel in Atlantic City a week from Saturday. Will that interfere with the math competition?"

"No."

"Will it clash with your basketball?"

"No."

"If you have other plans, it's all right if you can't make it."

"If you want out of this, you'll have to make that move outright. No out-by-default or because-of-me on this."

"Okay." She took a deep breath and released it slowly. "It's from four to six, so I figured we can go down and come back the same day."

"No need to spend the night at the hotel. Right? The cost of two rooms would be way too much." He didn't give her time to answer. "We should leave at one o'clock to make sure we won't be late. I have no idea what casino traffic is like."

"Okay. One o'clock sounds good."

"I'll see you at school tomorrow."

After she hung up, Dana sat long enough to make ten phone calls. *I have to go forward on this. Steve isn't going to give me an out and that's only right. I got into this mess and it's my responsibility to make decisions about it.* She stood. *Maybe we won't make the cut.*

Hawaii wasn't as important now as it had been when she watched the first show.

The days passed and neither she nor Steve mentioned the reception that was rushing toward

PERFECT WEDDING

them. It was as if, if they ignored it, it would roll on past them without even pausing.

Meanwhile, the math team won, first the area contest, then the regional, and Harris School kept celebrating. In fact, the celebrating had spread. The district officials had attended the last few contests. The school superintendent and the math supervisor had come forward to congratulate the kids personally.

Steve explained to the team just how big a deal this all was. Their grins widened and they asked him to give them harder problems.

The area stores got in on the celebrating by posting signs in the windows urging them on. Schoolwise, things couldn't be better. That didn't make up for the turmoil inside her.

Finally the Saturday of the reception came and Dana wasn't any more ready than she had expected to be.

How can we pull this off? she wondered as she got out of bed. More questions kept coming through the morning. *How can we make somebody believe that we're a loving couple when we can't even look at each other? How can they not see that? Maybe they will and pick somebody else. Would I feel as bad about that as I would have before I set this in motion?*

She puttered around her apartment, making work where there really was none. She felt as if she had days before the next step came. Cathy was with Kenny, as she was every weekend since their engagement. *At least she's not around to make me more nervous. She'd try to calm me, but I know it wouldn't work. Nothing would.*

At last it was time to get dressed.

Dana stood at her closet trying to decide what to wear. *I should have done this last night,* she thought. She hadn't let Cathy help her, but she could have made a decision herself before now. She thought about Cathy and Kenny. *They should be the ones in the contest. They are for real.*

She shuffled through her clothes trying to decide on an outfit. She knew she had gone too far when her hand reached the red dress that had zoomed them to a new level. She closed her eyes and remembered.

Once more she was back, wearing that red dress and opening the door to Steve. Next she was at the big event. Then in his arms. Hundreds of other people were around them, but she was noticing nobody but him. Despite the pain the memory was inflicting on her, it was relentless.

Since she didn't, couldn't, change the subject in her mind, her memories took her to the time when they had come home that night. It played the scenes of how he had touched her and awakened her body. It was so real, she could feel her body reacting, anticipating, then welcoming him inside where he belonged. That part of the memory was painful and sweet at the same time, but if she had it to do all over, she'd still end up in Steve's arms.

She opened her eyes. *What I would change is how our relationship reached that point. I'd go back to the beginning.*

She frowned into the closet. *Would we have gotten that close if not for the contest? We had been good friends for years. Would we have crossed that line without an outside push? Years. We had been stuck in the same place for years until* Perfect Wedding *came along*. She sighed. She'd never know. Because of her actions, she'd never find out what would have happened if . . . *Go away*, she told her memories and for once they obeyed.

She pulled out three outfits. She looked at the first, a two-piece dress. The magenta top looked a whole lot happier than Dana felt. The saleswoman had told her that the color made her glow. Others who didn't stand to earn a commission had told her the same thing. The skirt was black, but the top provided all the color the outfit needed. The gold buttons on the top kept it from being plain.

Dana held the outfit against her. She always felt upbeat when she wore this dress. She set it aside, although she was sure she'd choose it. She needed all the glow and upbeat she could get.

The second outfit, an emerald-green pantsuit, went beside the first. The third, a silk red dress, went back as soon as Dana looked at it. *No, not red. Any color except red.* Again the other red dress came to her mind, dragging the results with it. *Will I ever be able to wear red without remembering?* She frowned. *Probably not. I'm glad I don't have very many red clothes.* She forced red to stay out of her mind as she got dressed.

She had just finished getting ready when the bell rang. She glanced at her watch. Steve was usually early. Today he was exactly on time.

She folded her coat over her arm. The day wasn't bad for the time of year, but Atlantic City was usually cooler and she didn't know how far they would have to walk. She got her purse, took a deep breath, and opened the door.

"Hi." Steve smiled slightly. "Nice dress."

"Hi."

That's a big difference from the three "wows'" he gave the red dress. This is a good thing. Right? She frowned. *Why doesn't it feel like it?*

They walked to the car and it was as if they were strangers who had been forced into this. *It's my fault that things are awkward between us,* she thought as she got into the car. *I engineered every last bit of this. It's all on me.*

They had wound their way down Lincoln Drive, fought their way down the Schuylkill Expressway against the usual drivers who drove as if they were trying to get somewhere yesterday. Still, neither made a sound. They reached the Walt Whitman Bridge before either of them spoke.

"Want to put in a CD?" he asked.

"Okay." *He's as tired of the silence as I am.*

She shuffled through the choices, then shuffled again. All of them were about love: past love, present love, love gone bad, anticipated love. She paused at the Nina Simone collection she had given him for his birthday several years ago. She loved Nina Simone. She sighed. *No way can I take Nina's sultry soulful voice today.* She looked through the CDs again and pulled out an old Arethea Franklin collection. It wasn't all about love, but there was enough to make her wish she had picked James Brown or at least Ray Charles.

By the time they were parking, Dionne Warrick, Patti LaBelle, and even Smokey Robinson had shared their views of love.

I wouldn't mind feeling a little of that, Dana thought as she tuned off the controls. *Of course, it wouldn't help if I was feeling it all by myself. I don't care what*

Steve says. If it wasn't for the contest, we'd still be just football-game-watching buddies. She sighed. *You made your bed. Now, no matter how uncomfortable it is, you have to lie in it.*

Chapter 20

At the hotel, the valet rushed up to the car as if he expected somebody famous to get out rather than a woman who was a cheat and a man who, out of sympathy, was helping her. They got out of the car and watched as the occupants of the next car received the same VIP treatment. The couple who got out looked as though they hated to part even for the short time it took for them to meet on the sidewalk. They grabbed each other's hands as if afraid one of them would disappear if they did not touch. They kissed as if one was just returning from a trip that had separated them for at least a year. When they got to the door, they leaned together in another kiss.

Dana and Steve walked toward the same door as if they were going into divorce court and each one blamed the other for the breakup.

If part of the decision-making for the contest involves judging on how we look together as we enter the hotel, we've lost points big time, Dana thought as they

PERFECT WEDDING

walked into the building. She didn't bother trying to fake a smile.

Once inside the building they followed the signs giving directions to the room. Too soon they were at the door.

"Welcome, I'm Lewis." A man with teeth to make a dentist ache to use his mouth in an "after" portion of an ad stood guard at the door. Dana didn't think it possible, but his smile widened when she handed him the invitation. "Good luck. Please help yourself to refreshments. And mingle," he added. "Have fun." He beckoned them in and stepped aside.

Near the door of the small room, a table was piled with food. Another table next to that held beverages tastefully arranged. A bartender stood behind it as if to make sure nobody took more than their share. To the side of him was a linen-covered table holding a tabletop fountain bubbling champagne.

Steve squeezed Dana's hand, then led her to the food table. After they had assorted cheeses and crackers and raw vegetables on their small plates, they stopped at the bartender and each of them got a soft drink. Then they walked a few steps farther into the room and stopped.

"No tables. I guess we're really expected to mingle," Dana said. "Or maybe they want to see how long women can stand in ridiculous shoes and pretend not to mind." She glanced at a woman standing nearby. "Look at that. Three-inch heels. At the least. Look at her face. She's trying to look comfortable, but I know she's fussing at herself for not wearing flats." Dana stuck out her own foot. "Fashionable I hope, and comfortable I know.

Actually, I wouldn't care if they were fashionable or not. In situations like this, comfort comes first."

"Hi. We're Barb and Bud," a woman said as she came over to them. "Barb as in the doll." She laughed. "Isn't this exciting?" She grabbed the hand of the man beside her as if afraid he'd leave. "I had to twist Bud's arm real hard to get him to agree to this, but when I pointed out that he won't have to pay a cent for either the wedding or the honeymoon if we win, he was all for it." She laughed. "I don't know why men are so closemouthed, you know what I mean? I say if you got it, flaunt it. Right? Love is to be flaunted. It's kind of an in-your-face thing, you know what I mean?" She smiled at Dana and kept her smile there. Finally Dana realized that she expected an answer.

"Oh. Right. Yes." She peeled the red rind from a wedge of cheese and took a bite.

"And you are . . . ?"

Dana swallowed. "Dana and Steve." She looked at Barb's hand and held up her glass and her plate. "Sorry. I guess they don't expect us to shake."

"That's okay," Barb said. "I only have a free hand because Bud and I decided not to drink tonight." She stared at Dana's drink as if she were a narc and had caught Dana with an illegal substance.

"I don't think there is anything wrong with soft drinks, do you?"

"Oh. No. Not a thing. We don't sell many of those straight-up where I work, though. I drink those myself." She grinned. She looked like Bud's twin. "Most people do. Sodas rule." Barb's grin got even wider. "Pleased to meet you, but you'll forgive

PERFECT WEDDING 229

me if I don't wish you good luck, you know what I mean?" She laughed at her own humor.

"I can understand that," Steve said.

"I like Hawaii," Barb continued, "but I would have entered no matter where the honeymoon prize took us. At least it's farther than here. I like Atlantic City, but I want something a little farther away from the Northeast and a little more exotic. You know what I mean?"

"Yes." Dana nodded politely.

"I wonder how long this will be. I have to work tonight." Barb looked at her watch. "Not everybody had Saturday off. I'm a waitress and Saturday is my biggest tip day." She grinned. "It's hard work, but I can walk to the restaurant from home and the tips are okay." She laughed again. "They could be better, but they could always be better, you know what I mean?"

"Yes."

"Hi, I'm Noreen." An early-twenty-something woman came over to them. "I'm on the selection committee."

She looks as if she could have been one of my students last year, Dana thought. *She's making the decision? Based on what?* Dana forced her attention back to Noreen.

"Congratulations on being chosen as finalists in the *Perfect Wedding* contest." She smiled wide enough for dimples to appear and to include both couples. "We are always so excited about our search for the perfect couple. Today you are one of three groups. Committee members are meeting with other finalists in the Midwest and on the West Coast. By the end of the day we will have narrowed the field to one couple each." To make sure everybody understood, she added, "That's a total of only three couples left nationwide." She scanned the group as if making the decision right away. "You've made it this far, good luck. Those of you not chosen this time will receive a gift certificate with your letter. The certificate will be good at any store you wish. You can use it to help with your wedding expenses." She spread her arms. "So you see, you are all winners." She clapped. The other committee members joined. The contestants finally added their applause to the mix. "Now mingle and have fun." She shouted her last word as if sheer volume would make them obey the order. Then she moved to the couple standing a little way off. Dana watched her smile at them and begin talking.

"I guess we should move on," Barb said. "She said for us to mingle. They might be judging on how well we mingle with others. You know what I mean?"

"I know," Dana answered, but Barb had moved toward the next group and had dragged Bud with her. Dana watched as they kissed. She glanced around.

Her gaze found a couple a few feet away. They looked as if they had decided to feed on each other instead of the food. *This is where somebody would usually tell them to get a room.* She frowned. *They probably already did. No rushing home for them.* She shook her head slightly. *I know Steve and I would have used more restraint even if things were okay between us.* She sighed. *Still, I wouldn't mind having a little of that.*

Steve glanced at Dana and then followed her

PERFECT WEDDING

gaze. *It must be nice to be at the same point as your fiancée,* he thought.

"Hello, hello." A woman stood at the front of the room with Noreen. She didn't look a minute older than the other teenybopper. "I'm Seleema. We're going to have a little fun as we find out a little more about you. Let's go into the other room."

One of the sections between their room and the next was open. Everybody followed her as if she were a modern-day Noah filling an ark.

If the floods come, will frauds be left to drown? Dana wondered as she followed with the others. *And will I have company?* She glanced quickly at the others. *Did anybody else enter the contest just for the trip?*

"Okay. We need the women up here." Seleema led the way to a row of chairs facing the room. "Ladies first."

If this is a game of truth or dare, I'm telling the truth and getting it over with, Dana thought.

"Okay," Seleema said as the five women sat. "Ladies, tell us why your fiancé deserves to win."

"I'll go first." A woman wiggled her hand in the air as if she were in a classroom and had the answer to the question that would exempt her from a big test.

"I want to go first," Barb said. Her glare at the other woman was heated enough to raise the temperature of the ocean five degrees.

"Ladies, ladies," Seleema said as she held up her hands. "Just be patient. Everybody will get a turn. The order doesn't matter. Your hand was up first." She pointed to a woman who looked tempted to stick her tongue out at Barb. "You go first. Tell us your name."

"Hi, my name is Ruth." She paused as if waiting for the others to greet her as they do in support groups. When they didn't, she continued. "My honey, Ted, deserves the trip more than anybody. He is so nice to me. He is so cuddly that I call him my teddy bear." She giggled.

No points for originality, Dana thought as Ruth continued.

"Ted is so considerate. Every morning he brings me my coffee in bed even though he doesn't have to get up as early as I do." *Will she lose points for admitting that they live together?* Dana wondered. *Probably not. Big-time television stars do the same and nobody seems to care.*

Ruth continued to give examples of Ted's goodness to her.

"Thank you, Ruth." Seleema looked at Barb. "I guess we all know who's next, don't we?"

Barb smiled, then cleared her throat as if she intended to give a long speech.

"Bud is just the sweetest man." She paused to glare at Ruth. "We both work hard, but we don't live together. We believe that we should wait until after we get married." Ruth received a smug look this time. "Bud deserves to go some place far away, and this is the only way we can afford it."

The other two women had similar reasons. Finally it was Dana's turn. She had no idea what she would say until she started. She didn't even glance at Steve. While the others had been talking, she had spent the time going over what she knew about Steve and trying to figure out how to use it to give a picture of him. She took a deep breath and started.

"Steve is a good, caring person. In his senior

year of college he messed up his knee during his final basketball game. That killed his chance at the pros, but he didn't let bitterness take over. He added education courses to his roster and earned his certification in education. We teach at the same school. I teach English and social studies and he teaches science and math." Her glance flitted to him but left right away. She continued.

"Steve is strict, but fair. The kids love him. He's always participating in some sports event to raise funds for charity. He does more than teach academics. He's giving them lessons that will take them through life." She smiled. "This school year he started a math team. He said the inner-city kids need to believe in their abilities. He has worked so hard on this." Again she glanced at him. His intense stare almost made her forget where she was. "He gives up his lunchtime working on schoolwork. If a kid needs it, he's there after school." Her gaze found him. This time it stayed. "He works so hard and gives so much and never asks for anything in return. Steve has more than paid his dues. He deserves to win."

Seleema thanked the women, dismissed them, and then called the men up. "Okay, gentlemen. Your turn. We'll go in the same order as the women so it will be easier for us to see which two of you are together."

Ted squirmed and frowned. "Man, this is hard. I wish Ruthie had let somebody else go first." The others laughed. "Okay. Here goes." He took one deep breath and then another. He still didn't look ready. "Ruth told what I do for her, but she does for me, too. When I was laid off for a few months, she never nagged me or put pressure on me. She picked up the slack and she still fixed dinner for me every night." He smiled at Ruth. "I love her." He shook his head. "If I didn't, I sure wouldn't be going through this torture." Again everyone laughed. "She deserves more than I can give her. She deserves this."

When it looked as if he was through, Seleema thanked him and turned to Bud.

"You've all met my Barbie doll." He looked at her as if she were prime rib and he were a meat lover coming off a vegetarian diet. "Barb works hard as a waitress. She's on her feet during her whole shift and she's expected to smile the whole time. Still, she never complains. We have dinner together every night." Bud glanced at Ted. "As Barb said, we don't live together, so we take turns cooking and the other one comes over. We'll get a place together after the wedding." He gazed at Barb again. "Because she works so hard, she deserves this."

Dana listened to the others. She was wondering what Steve would say. *Will he tell about how I entered the contest fraudulently? Will he tell that I didn't even have a boyfriend when I entered and he took pity on me and offered to marry me?*

Then it was Steve's turn. Dana knew he wouldn't say any of the things she had been thinking, but she didn't think there was anything he could say to show that she deserved to win. Not even she believed he could find words that would do that.

"Dana and I were friends before we became engaged. Actually, we hit it off when we first met five years ago. From the time we learned how crazy we both are about the Eagles, we have watched every Eagles football game together." He smiled. "If this contest were about who is the craziest about the Eagles, she'd win. However, that's not all she's about." He leaned forward. "She's a great and caring teacher. When she calls her class 'her kids,' she means it like that. She pushes them when they need it and comforts them when they need that, too. If the kids go to her with an idea that will help them, she'll go along with it no matter how much extra work it makes for her." He glanced at Dana. The tenderness in his eyes made her own eyes fill.

Steve thinks that I do have good qualities. I'm not sure they are enough to deserve this win and certainly not enough to deserve him. He thinks I do, though, and he's willing to sacrifice for me in order to prove it. She smiled at him as he continued.

"Recently she started a school newspaper after the kids asked for a way to share their writings. It takes a lot of her own time as she knew it would. Still she didn't hesitate to agree." He looked at her again and smiled. Only Dana saw the sadness in his eyes. "She has dreamed of going to Hawaii since she first learned about it. She would have gone before now if not for the student loans that she has to repay." He slowly looked at the group. "She got a small scholarship, but basically she had loans and had to work her way through college." He looked back at Dana. "It's time for something for her." He blinked hard. "She deserves Hawaii even if she goes without me."

Dana felt pinned in place by Steve's words. A few slow tears made a path down her face. She smiled at Steve through her tears as she wiped her face. *Is it possible that he could really feel more than friendship toward me?*

"Thank you, gentlemen," Seleema said quietly

after a long pause. She shook her head slightly, then grinned. "Let's move on," she said as she stood. "Ladies, please come with me to the other room. Gentlemen, you'll stay here with Lewis."

Barb and Ruth followed Seleema and Noreen as if the first one in line got extra points. Dana walked as if the points would be awarded to the last woman to enter the room.

"Okay," Seleema said after they were seated. "Let's talk wedding. I want to hear what you have in mind."

"I'm going first since Ruth went first before." Barb looked as if she dared anybody to rule against that idea.

"I don't think anybody would dare disagree," Noreen said.

"I didn't mean it that way," Barb said quickly. It sounded as if she suddenly realized that this might be part of the judging, too. "I know you decide who goes in what order."

"You can go first," Ruth said. "I don't have any objection. I'm easy to get along with."

"Well, so am I." Barb glared at her.

Seleema looked at Barb. "Why don't you go first? Ruth, you can go second." She looked at the others. "I assume there are no objections?"

"No," the answers came from the other women at the same time. Noreen looked back at Barb.

"My sister, Gloria, will be my maid of honor. My two best friends will be bridesmaids." She stared at Seleema. "I would have liked a bigger wedding, but . . ." She shrugged. "You know how expensive it can be." She shrugged again. Then she told of her color scheme and where the wedding would be held.

"Of course, if we win, we're more than willing to change anything you want."

After Barb finished, Ruth told her plans. The others followed. Dana's turn came too soon.

"We really haven't made plans yet. We haven't been engaged very long." She shrugged and looked at Seleema and Noreen. "Sorry." She shrugged again. "This came unexpectedly."

"Okay," Noreen said. "Let us tell you a little about what goes into producing the show. It's a long, involved process, but if we do our job right, it doesn't look like it to the viewers."

She began to explain each step. All of the women were listening as if they expected to be chosen. All except one. Dana was wondering what the men were doing and if Steve was sorry he had ever gotten into this.

Chapter 21

"Okay, gentlemen. I know how enthusiastic all of you are to have this public attention surround you," Lewis said. He waited while they laughed. A few groans, Bud's the loudest, mixed with the laughter. "If you had you way, I know you'd take your fiancée and meet in the judge's office with his secretary as the only witness to the wedding. Then you'd complain as you wondered why even *she* had to be there." They laughed again and he continued. "Then after the ten-minute ceremony you'd wonder why it took so long. Right? Tell the truth and shame the devil."

The other men nodded. One muttered, "That's the truth."

If they're so reluctant to do this for the women they claim to love, how much can they love their fiancées? Steve wondered. *I wouldn't mind if the whole world watched me promise to love and cherish Dana for the rest of my life.* He shook his head slightly. *She probably still wouldn't believe it. After years, I finally admit to my-*

PERFECT WEDDING   239

self that I love Dana. I took an opportunity to do something about it, yet she won't believe me. She thinks I'm doing it just for her. I don't know how to convince her.

"I see you shaking your head," Lewis said to Steve. "Do you disagree?"

"I just don't see what the big deal is. I'm glad for the opportunity to show that I love Dana in front of the whole world. I want every other man to know that she's off-limits."

"Trying to win points, huh?" Bud glared at him. Then he stared at Lewis, waiting for a reaction to Steve's answer.

"I'll bet you were a suck-up to your teachers all through school, huh?" Ted asked, but he acted as if he already knew the answer.

"Is this part of the process? It isn't, is it?" Bud asked. "I thought we were just making man talk."

"You know, everything is part of the process," Lewis reminded the group. Bud frowned. He stared at Lewis again. "I should have thought of that before I reacted to your question. I don't guess we can start over, huh? I'd do better with another chance."

"Chill, gentlemen, relax. Don't stress." Lewis held up his hands. "This is nothing compared to what being on the show is like." He smiled his dentist-pride smile. "I doubt if any of the men who went through the process were happy about it. The only thing they were glad about was that they didn't have to pay for the wedding." Easy laughter sounded around him again. "Each man did it for the same reason you are doing it—the woman he loved wanted it and he wanted to give her what she wanted. There's nothing wrong with that." He leaned back. "Now, let's go on. What kind of food would you pick if your fiancée let you choose?" He stared at them. "Which you know she won't, but fantasize, okay?" He grinned again. "Don't be shy. Shout it out. I'm not keeping a record here." He leaned forward as if afraid of being overheard. "We're just doing this for something to do while the women are busy with Seleema and Noreen." He gestured to them. "Come on. Don't be shy. Maybe we can have a special plate prepared for the groom and you can slip away and eat the real food. Let's hear your food fantasies."

Steak and lobster and prime rib were shouted out, with steak being the favorite.

"I'd be nice and agree to baked potato, but I'd really want mashed potatoes so I could get all of the juices, you know what I mean?" Ted added.

"Yeah," Bud said. "And forget the salad. In fact, forget the veggies altogether. After all, it's my wedding, too, and I don't like vegetables."

"Yeah," the others agreed.

"I want chocolate cake," Bud said, "but Ruthie said it's devil's food and she doesn't want the devil at her wedding."

"I like chocolate, too," Tim agreed. "Who, back in history, decided that chocolate cake should be called devil's-food cake instead of pinning that label on white cake? And why are we still stuck with that label?"

"Give me a big scoop of chocolate ice cream on the side, too," Bud added.

"Can you imagine a bride, dressed in all of that white, eating all of that chocolate? Barb has a fit when she drops a crumb on her everyday clothes. Imagine dropping chocolate on the wedding gown, even if she doesn't intend to wear it again."

"I prefer vanilla cake," Jason said, voicing his

PERFECT WEDDING

first opinion of the day. The other men glared at him. "I really do. I'm not sucking up." He frowned. "How can choosing vanilla over chocolate be sucking up, anyway?"

"Okay, guys. Let's change the subject. How many of you think you have enough closet space? Rhetorical question," he added quickly. "No answer needed. You know about closets and women, don't you, Bud? You've already found out since you and Barb live together."

Bud stared as if trying to figure out if he should be worried that Lewis brought that fact up. Finally he shrugged. "Yeah, I know."

"To the rest of you guys, you know all of those shoes your ladies wear? They have to go somewhere when they aren't on her feet. They usually have matching purses. And those clothes that you like to see on her? Those don't disappear when she doesn't have them on. Guess whose closet a lot of them will end up in."

"Ours," the men agreed.

"Absolutely," Lewis said. "The ratio will probably be at least three to one. She gets three times the space you do."

The men nodded.

"No more wedding stuff. You guys tell us about yourselves. What kind of things do you do when you have a choice? Where do you see yourselves ten years from now?"

They relaxed and started to talk about their hobbies and their plans. Steve listened and thought about his own.

Hobbies are easy. The dreams will be the hard part. I'm afraid Dana doesn't share mine, but mine are all about her. I would love to wake up each morning with her in my arms and know she will be there the next morning, too. He frowned. *If the women cover the same questions, what will her answer be? Will it include me?*

"You're quiet. No dreams?" Lewis asked. The other contestants stared at Steve as if they were waiting for him to give a wrong answer.

"I haven't thought about my future beyond wanting Dana to be a part of it."

"Did somebody give you these questions ahead of time?"

"Man, I'm just telling how I feel." Steve frowned at Ted. "You need to lighten up."

"We're back." Noreen peeked into the room. "Come on, ladies." The women followed her. "We're almost finished. You can feel free to help yourselves to more food. It's probably more than a short ride home. Besides, playing 'questions and answers' probably made you work up an appetite."

Most of the men and women found their partners right away. Only Dana seemed to be trying to decide if she wanted to claim Steve. Finally she walked over to where he was standing. "I guess he put you through the mill, huh?"

"Nothing I couldn't handle." He put his hands into his pockets so he wouldn't put one around her waist. "How about you?"

"No problem. Some of the other women didn't do a good job of hiding their agendas. A couple of them admitted that they entered because they want a big wedding."

"That's the reason anybody would enter this contest. That and the ideal honeymoon."

"Yes, but I'm the only one who got engaged for that reason."

"You don't know that. Besides, you are engaged

and we're getting married. That's what matters. That follows their rules. Was there a rule that stipulated that you had to be engaged a certain amount of time before you entered the contest?"

"No, but—"

"Dana, you followed their rules." Steve stared at her. Then he took a chance and put his hands around her shoulders. "Let's go see what's left. I'm sure you don't want to stop for dinner on the way home."

Dana's only answer was to go with him.

"Okay, people," Noreen said after everybody left the food tables and drifted back. "We have just a few more items to cover. If you'll have a seat, we can go over some important things."

Chairs were repositioned as if they weren't already placed correctly. Finally everybody gave her their full attention.

"First, let me thank you again for coming. I know some of you had quite a way to travel. Now for some specifics. We know this will be your one and only wedding and you want it to be perfect. We want that, too." She chuckled. "It would be bad for our ratings if we botched it. After all, our show is named *Perfect Wedding*. Not *We Tried to Do a Perfect Wedding.*" She laughed at her own joke. "We also know that you have definite ideas about what your special day should be like. We'll honor those ideas as much as possible, but we must have a say. We are paying the bills, you know. That means you have to be open to possible changes. Any questions?"

"Do you make big changes?" Barb asked.

"We never have so far."

"Good, because I have been thinking and plan-

244 *Alice Wootson*

ning since I got this ring on my finger." She glanced at the other women. "I'll bet they have, too. They just don't want to say anything. They're afraid of blowing it."

"Who named you group psychic?" Ruth asked.

"You know you've been planning, too."

"I sure have. It's only normal. That still doesn't mean you know what's in my mind."

"Ladies, ladies," Noreen interrupted before they could come to blows. "We want you to have the wedding that you want. We're on the same page as you. We'll work with you to try to see that you get it. Any more questions?" When nobody else said anything, she went on. "Okay. Seleema will go over the next part."

"Here's the reality." Seleema said, "No matter how much we want to help all of you, we can only pick one couple for the show, but the rest of you won't go away empty-handed. We think we'll make it worth your while. Each couple will receive a very generous gift card today. You can use it as cash at most places. Even if you aren't the couple chosen as the final winner, you can buy something nice to use for your lives together. We also have a form for each couple to sign. We want you to attest to the fact that, should you win and your marriage doesn't last for at least two years and a day, then all prize money spent on you must be repaid." She smiled wider. "Noreen is distributing the forms now. Please read them carefully before signing, but I'll read them aloud also, so there can be no misunderstanding. Please don't sign them until I tell you to." She waited while everybody got a form. Dana was stuck on the words Seleema had used already.

Two years? We have to stay married for two years?

PERFECT WEDDING

Steve had to nudge Dana to take the paper from Noreen. *Where did that rule come from?* She blinked.

"Did we know about this?" she asked.

"About what? The form? It's just a standard agreement."

"No." Dana shook her head. "The two years."

"It was plainly stated on the entry form. Is there a problem?" Seleema asked.

"No problem," Steve answered. "None at all." He squeezed Dana's hand.

"Good. Two years isn't long. Even most bad marriages last longer than that, and all of you will have good marriages. The best ever. Right?"

A chorus of "right" sounded. Nobody noticed that Dana didn't add one.

Seleema read the form as if the contestants had to hear the words read slowly or else they wouldn't understand them. Dana wished she had heard them aloud before she got Steve into this trap. *Cathy always tells me that I don't read the fine print,* she thought. *I guess this proves that she's right.*

"Are there any questions?"

Steve tightened his hold on Dana's hand. When she opened her mouth as if to say something, he covered it with his, blocking any words she had planned to use.

When he moved away from her, she could barely breathe, let alone remember how to put together the words she had been planning to say. At Steve's urging, she signed the paper. He whisked it away and added his signature as if afraid she would hold on to it and not hand it in.

"Okay," Noreen said when the signed forms were back in her hands. "Now we have goodie bags for you." She and Seleema gave each woman an iridescent gift bag with the glittery *Perfect Wedding* pink logo on both sides. "Again, thank you for coming. And good luck, everybody."

The soft sounds of chairs sliding, people standing and murmuring reached the air. Some of the couples said good-bye to each other. Most did not.

In a daze, Dana left with Steve. If not for his arm around her shoulders, she might have turned to the right out of the room instead of turning left. She was dimly aware of stopping for their coats and putting hers on. Too much else was going on in her head to pay attention to something as ordinary as that.

She let Steve lead her out of the hotel. She stood while the valet brought the car; then she got in. Still she hadn't said a word since hearing about the two-year clause.

Chapter 22

Thoughts raced and tripped through Steve's mind as he drove the White Horse Pike, heading home. Each time he thought he had an idea to help Dana, he found a flaw in it. He glanced at her.

She was sitting stiffly beside him. Her only movement was the twisting and untwisting of her hands in her lap.

What can I say to her to help? She is so stressed about this. Steve glanced at Dana. *And she looks so fragile. How can I help? I could tell her that I love her.* He shook his head. *This is definitely not the situation for that. She'd never believe me. It's true, but I don't think truth has anything to do with this.* He frowned. *I have to do something. But what?*

"You're very quiet," Steve said after they had been riding for twenty minutes. "I would offer a penny for your thoughts, but I think I'd be throwing my money away. I think I know what's bothering you."

"I swear I didn't know about the two years. Honest."

"I believe you."

"That's what I get for rushing into this without thinking things through. Cathy's always telling me about how I do that and I did it again." She frowned. "Actually, this time it's not that I didn't think this through. It's worse than that. I didn't *read* the directions through." She twisted her hands again.

"Hey, it's okay." Steve reached over, freed one of her hands, and held it.

She gripped it as if that was the only way she could keep from falling apart. "I teach kids about reading directions. Cathy teaches her little ones that skill." She shook her head. "Two years. Two years. I've obligated you for two whole years."

"And a day. Don't forget the day," Steve added and smiled.

She didn't smile back. "I don't know." She shook her head again.

"What's to know? I don't have a problem with the time frame."

"You're just being nice."

"Being nice is offering somebody a short ride home."

"You're right. This is way beyond being nice."

"That's not what I meant." He glanced at her. "And you know it."

"I could drop out of the contest."

"Is that what you want?"

"You know it's not."

"Then why do it?"

"Steve, I've got you twisted up in my little scheme." She shook her head. "There's nothing little about this. My *big* scheme. It was bad enough

PERFECT WEDDING 249

when I was the only one affected. It was even worse when I involved you."

"You didn't involve me. I'm a big boy. I asked to be in on your dream."

"But not for two years."

"What did you expect?"

"I'm not sure." She shrugged. "I guess I thought that, after the show airs, they forget about that couple and move on to the next. I never thought there would be a time stipulation." She frowned. "If I could afford to pay to go to Hawaii, I wouldn't have entered the contest."

"What are you going to do?"

"I don't know. I have to think."

Steve left her alone with her thoughts for the rest of the ride. After he pulled into her parking lot, he turned off the motor and turned to her.

"I'm coming up with you. We have to talk." He got out.

She didn't wait for him to open her door. "I don't know how that would do any good." She looked at him. "Thank you for coming with me. Thank you for everything. I really appreciate it."

"You can't get rid of me that easily. I'm coming up. I'm in this too, remember?" He stared at her. "I have something to say to you."

"Two hours in the car wasn't enough time?" She shook her head. "There's that 'two' again."

"What I have to say requires all of my attention."

"Okay." She led the way up the stairs and unlocked the door. He followed her in. "Do you want a cup of coffee?"

"No."

"Tea? A Pepsi?"

"Uh-uh." He shook his head.

"Something to eat? I can fix something."

"There's only one thing I want. You."

"What?"

"I want you. Is that such a shock?"

"Look, Steve, I really appreciate what you're doing for me."

"I'm not doing this for you. I have a selfish motive. I'm doing it for myself."

"Yourself? I don't understand."

"No, I guess not. And I'm not sure I can make you understand. But I sure hope I can." He paced a few steps away, then came back.

Dana's gaze stayed on him the whole time. "You have to explain. Please."

"How long have we known each other?"

"Five years. Since I came to Harris Middle School. What's that got to do with anything?"

"That's almost how long I have felt an attraction to you."

"But we were friends. We've had a happy, satisfying friendship from the beginning. We're football-watching buddies."

"Most of that is true."

"We were satisfied with things the way they were."

"The happy part is right and the satisfied part is right on your part. As for me, satisfied is definitely wrong."

"What?"

"My feelings for you reached a new level long ago. I was afraid to tell you. I could tell that you didn't feel the attraction, the chemistry, that I felt." His stare intensified. "Do you know how hard it was to see you five days a week and keep my feelings a secret?" He smiled.

"Make that six during football season," she added.

"Yeah. An extra day to go through the pain of not having the one I wanted mixed with the joy of being close to you. Each day I wrestled with whether or not to tell you how I felt, and each day I chickened out." He shook his head. "You weren't interested in me in that way and I didn't want to lose what little I had with you. The contest gave me a way to move things off center." He stared at her. "I knew I couldn't stand for you to marry somebody else, even if it was just pretend. I didn't want to take a chance on something permanently developing and my losing you forever. So I proposed. If I had thought that you would accept, I'd have done it about four and a half years ago."

"The kiss was real? It wasn't just a Superbowl celebration kiss?"

"You remember it?"

"Of course I do. I had trouble sleeping that night."

"Good. I've had a lot of sleepless nights because of you."

"Really?" She smiled at him.

"You'd better believe really."

"I never knew you felt that way."

"I guess I'm a better actor than I thought."

"I guess." She closed the space between them until only a few inches separated them.

"I didn't plan to seduce you." He frowned. "I meant to leave it at the pretend that you wanted. The next time I kissed you, I just wanted you to see me in a different way. I never meant for it to go further." He exhaled sharply. "But there you were that night in that red dress, and there the music was, and you finally seemed as ready to move forward as I was."

As much as he wanted to, and even though it was small, he wouldn't let himself close the gap between them. He still wasn't sure she would believe him, that she wouldn't reject him. He was finally able to be honest with her, to put his emotions out for her to see. He wasn't sure she would accept him.

"Oh, Steve." She put her hand on his arm. "I'm so sorry."

Steve tensed, trying to find strength to accept that she was going to let him down and he'd have nothing. He stared at the floor. She was happy just being his friend. Just because he felt differently and finally told her didn't mean that her feelings for him had changed. *Can I just walk away?*

"I'm sorry I put you through this." She touched the side of his face and then lifted his chin. She saw the anguish in his eyes. "I'm sorry I didn't realize how you felt sooner."

She took his hand and led him to the sofa. He went gladly. At least she hadn't thrown him out. Not yet.

"To me you were a friend. Then you kissed me and I felt something change. I—I wasn't sure what to make of it." She shrugged. "You acted as if it wasn't any big deal. The next day you never brought it up, so I figured that I was mistaken. That the contest was clouding my sense of reason. I concluded that it was just a celebration kiss and you didn't mean anything by it."

"I didn't bring it up because I didn't want to risk losing what little I had with you."

She stared at him. "I didn't want to read something into the kiss that you didn't mean." She shrugged again. "You always had a glamorous girlfriend. One right after the other. I could see that I wasn't your type."

"When was the last time you heard me mention a girlfriend?"

"I don't know." She frowned.

"I tried to find somebody to take my mind off you. I didn't use them, though," he added quickly. "It didn't get that far. Each time I found somebody else I thought maybe she would be the one, but in a short time, things ended. She wasn't you." He held her hand. "Just now when you said 'I'm sorry' I was terrified that you were getting ready to dump me." He rubbed the back of her hand. "As for my type, baby, you are the only one who *is* my type." He leaned over and kissed her. Then he brushed his thumb across her bottom lip. "I want you more than I wanted you that first time. At the time, I didn't think that was possible. Now that I have tasted your love, I know what's in store."

He covered her mouth with his. His tongue touched hers. The kiss deepened and the memories flooded back. Slowly, as if fighting the biggest battle of his life, he leaned away from her. He brushed his hand down her arm, then stood as if something were trying to hold him back.

"I hate myself for saying this, but I think we should stop here. We've covered a lot. I think you should think this over." He took her hand and drew her up beside him. "I don't want you to regret it if we make love again. I couldn't stand that kind of strain again." He leaned in and brushed his lips across hers. Then, before she could react, he moved away.

"I'll see you on Monday."

He left Dana standing as if trying to figure out

where she was. *What am I going to do?* she asked herself. She didn't expect an answer.

Was I a fool to stop us? Steve thought as he closed the door behind him. *I could be making love with her right now. I could be inside her. We could be losing ourselves in our own magic.* He frowned as he drove away. *What if that was my last chance to hold her? What if she never lets me make love with her again? What if I have to spend the rest of my life without her? Can I be satisfied just to see her at school? Work with her, be so close, but never allowed to touch her?* His hands ached at the thought.

Two blocks away, he pulled over. *If I don't clear my mind before I go on and concentrate on my driving, somebody might get hurt.*

Chapter 23

Why didn't I see that coming? She stared at the door after Steve left. Then she moved to the living room, sat on the couch, and stared some more.

Why not? Didn't you think sleeping together took the term "friends" a little too far? Her mind went back to the night they had spent together. The memory still made her warm, but now it was tinged with regret. *It didn't feel as if he was acting out of pity for a friend. It didn't feel like anything except fantastic lovemaking.* She stood. *I have to be honest. I wouldn't have made love with him if all I felt toward him was friendship. Why can't I give him credit for the same thing? Why can't I admit that I'm afraid to . . .* She sat in the armchair. *I'm afraid to let myself love him? Afraid that he's doing all of this because of the contest? All because of how much he likes me?* Again she stood. *How do I know that what he said this evening isn't because of my situation? How could a woman marry a man because she was pregnant? How could she spend the rest of her married life knowing a man married her because he had to? How could she wonder if he would ever have proposed otherwise?*

She straightened the pile of magazines on the coffee table. *What I have to do has nothing to do with magazines.*

Sunday passed in a confused blur for Dana. She begged off from church, knowing she wouldn't do the sermon justice.

Heavy thoughts kept her company. They even made her do other stupid things. Things like putting a meal into the microwave oven and waiting for it to cook. It took too long for her to realize that her food would never cook if she didn't turn the oven on.

Monday passed almost as badly as Sunday. She did manage to separate her personal life from her professional one. In fact, she was grateful that she had something else to occupy her attention. She and Steve acted as if they were polite strangers.

He reminded her that Saturday was the day the math team was going to D.C., as if she could have forgotten. He quietly came to her room at lunchtime. No smiles. No light conversation. All business. Dana knew she had pulled him down with her. That made her feel even worse.

They set up final team practice sessions for Tuesday and Thursday. That meant no strained lunchtimes together. *Will we ever be back the way we were?* she wondered. *Maybe Simone would have stood a chance if her timing hadn't been bad,* Dana thought.

She thought about the bus ride and was glad she had given her seat on the bus to a parent who had been able to get off from work at the last

PERFECT WEDDING

minute. She knew it was cowardly, but she had not been looking forward to a long trip with Steve, even if they did have five kids and a bunch of parents as chaperones. *I never thought I'd be glad for an excuse not to spend time with Steve, but I'd hate to spread my sad mood to everybody.*

Friday wasn't any better. As if by silent agreement she and Steve both had lunch in their own rooms.

When she got home, the now-dreaded pink logo stared at her from an envelope. She knew before she opened it that she and Steve were one of the final three couples. The show would fly them to Los Angeles for the final phase. She stared at the letter as if trying to make it change into a sorry-but-we-chose-somebody-else letter. That would have made things easier for her.

At 8:30 on Saturday morning, Dana joined the crowd of students, staff, and parents in the school yard. Not only were the other students from her and Steve's classes there, but it looked as if every student from every other class was there as well.

Mr. Holloway spoke. Then final wishes of good luck and encouragement were voiced. Hugs were given all around.

At one point Dana found herself off to the side and face-to-face with Steve. They stood staring at each other, and then she smiled at him.

"I'd wish you good luck, but I know luck doesn't have anything to do with this. You worked so hard on this. Our kids are ready."

"Yes, they are, but you worked hard too. We make a good team ourselves. Don't you think?" Still, he didn't touch her.

"Hey, Miss Dillard? Ain't you gonna give Mr.

Rollings a good luck kiss? Or at least a good-bye kiss?" Tamika asked.

"Yeah. You don't act like you're engaged," Fran said.

Steve stared at Dana as if to say, "It's your move."

Dana swallowed hard, then closed the space between them. She lifted her face, ready for a token kiss. What she got was a this-is-how-it-should-be-between-us kiss. A promise that what they had wasn't close to being over. That what was between them now was only a simple glitch in an equation and they would correct it real soon.

Then he stepped away, touched the side of her face, and, promise still burning in his eyes, walked toward the bus.

Dana stood with the rest of the crowd until the bus was no longer in sight.

"You're coming back this evening, aren't you?" Mrs. Wilson, Gary's mother, asked.

"I don't know."

"We're putting on this big party for the kids. Whether or not they win, they fought a good battle and we want them to know how proud we are of them. You had a big part in this." She grinned. "We'll have another get-together to celebrate the kids' writing successes." She shook her head. "I can't believe the positive things going on here at Harris School. I am so thankful that my kids go here. I knew it was a good school. I just didn't expect anything except the basics. How blessed we are." She shrugged. "Sorry. I do go on. So, can we count on you being here? I know the kids will be disappointed if you're not here to share with them, win or lose."

PERFECT WEDDING

"All right." She managed a smile. "I'll come back. Can I help with anything?"

"No way. You're being honored too. We just want you to enjoy yourself, Miss Dillard." She winked. "This might be the last time I see you that I can call you Miss Dillard. Next school year you'll be Mrs. Rollings."

"I'll see you this evening."

Mrs. Wilson told Dana what time to be back, then walked into the school, unaware of the new tension she had caused.

Once back home, Dana made work for herself, but still the time wouldn't rush past. Several times she stared at the phone. Finally she got a business card and placed it on the hall table.

I know what I have to do. I guess I've known it all along. Too bad I have to wait until Monday.

At eight o'clock that night Dana was back in the school yard with a larger crowd. Steve had made a call to let them know that the bus was on its way home. He refused to tell whether they won, and the others went along with him. Dana shoved her personal concerns aside and put herself into the celebration.

In spite of herself, she searched the faces of the people getting off the bus, even though she knew that Steve would be the last one off.

Her heart felt as if it leaped in her chest when he stepped off, and it wasn't because of the trophy he was holding high. Happy noises filled the school yard and spilled beyond the fence and onto the street. Somebody blew a whistle. Others were just as loud with their mouths. The noise reached an even higher level when Steve put the trophy into the hands of the team.

Reporters and parents flashed so many cameras that the kids would probably be seeing spots for days. Their faces said that they didn't care.

Steve and the kids were surrounded by people, but his gaze found hers and held it.

The team, followed by the parents from the bus, led the crowd into the school. Steve found Dana standing to the side.

Their gazes held. Then Dana blinked the spell loose. "Congratulations. You did it."

"Uh-uh." He shook his head. "The kids did it. They just took me along for the ride." He took her hand. "Let's go inside. They're probably waiting for us."

"Okay."

Having him hold my hand feels so right. So awfully right. How can I give this up?

Steve had all of the kids give their own versions of the victory. The crowd roared its approval after each child spoke. Then he told why he was proud of the kids.

"All of our students have talent in something. We have to work together to help them discover what it is. These kids have worked so hard. That in and of itself is enough for them to be proud. The victory makes it even sweeter." The crowd sent their agreement to the ceiling. "I want to thank Mr. Holloway and the staff for their help and encouragement. And you parents for your support." He looked at Dana trying to blend in with the wall at the side. "There's somebody else involved. Miss

Dillard was instrumental in this from the beginning. She has done so much. I can't leave her out."

The crowd focused on Dana. Their applause and shouts didn't let up.

"Go on up there," somebody shouted from the audience. "We're not quitting until you do." The noises got louder.

Slowly Dana walked to Steve. He hesitated, then put his arm around her shoulders.

"Thank you for everything. You wouldn't believe how much you mean to me." He brushed his lips across hers in the kind of kiss she had expected before. Then why was she disappointed?

"Let's eat," Mrs. Wilson said. "I know everybody must be starving."

It was ten o'clock before Dana and Steve walked outside.

"I know it's late, but I have to talk to you." Dana stared at him. "Or it can wait until tomorrow."

"I'll follow you home."

Steve watched her get into her car and drive away. *I know what she's going to tell me. Why didn't I hang on to her as long as I could?*

"I've been thinking all day." She shook her head. "No. I've been thinking about this for a lot longer than that," Dana said as soon as Steve got there. She stared at him, then let her gaze slide away. "I got a letter on Friday saying that we're one of the three final couples."

"Congratulations. You're almost there. Can you hear that Hawaiian music?"

"I want to drop out of the contest." She swallowed the lump that had tried to block her words.

"Why?"

"I entered the contest fraudulently."

"You didn't break their rules. You reached this point fair and square."

"Then why doesn't it feel like it?" She hesitated, then pulled the ring from her finger and held it out. "I can't keep this." She ignored how lonely her hand felt without it.

Steve stared at her, but he knew the ring was still waiting for him. Finally he opened his hand and let her drop the ring into it. "This is what you want? After what we had, you're doing this? The ring had nothing to do with the contest."

"It has everything to do with it. You wouldn't have given it to me if it wasn't for the contest. "

"No." He moved his head slowly from side to side. "It doesn't. My feelings for you are not related to the contest, although you refuse to believe me. I'd like to think that we would have reached this point anyway, but you don't believe that either. Maybe it was a mistake for me to think that you could love me." He dropped the ring into his pocket and left.

Chapter 24

During the drive into school on Monday, Dana told Cathy about the letter and what she intended to do.

"Are you out of your mind? Have you forgotten how much you want this? You are so close you can smell the plumeria blossoms, and you're quitting?"

"I can't take it this way."

"But you didn't do anything wrong."

"That's what Steve said." She held up her bare hand. "I gave him back his ring."

Cathy shook her head. "You must have a full lighter, because, girl, you are burning a lot of big bridges. So you told Steve about what you're going to do. What else did he say?"

"That what I do about the contest is my decision." She stared at her bare hand. "I withdrew for another reason. I felt as if I was cheating Steve, too. I don't care what he said, I still believe that he only proposed to me because of the contest. I'll always believe that. I couldn't let him make that kind of sacrifice for me."

"And you're so sure that's all it was on his part."

"We never even had a date until I got that crazy idea. I don't see how it could be anything more."

"At least think about it some more. Spring break is next week. Why not take the time to think things over?"

"I don't need to."

"What can it hurt? If you still want to quit after next week, you can still do it. Okay?"

"I guess."

"Uh-uh, sister girl. That's not the same as okay."

"Okay." Dana sighed. "See you after school."

I'm glad nobody in the office noticed that my ring is missing, she thought as she walked to her classroom. *No, not mine anymore. I know I'll have to deal with that, but later is better than soon. Maybe I have until after next week.*

She and Steve met at lunchtime to make the changes necessary to return to the old schedule. It was close to the end of the school year, but they did it anyway. Both found the idea of continuing to work any more closely than necessary painful, and for the same reason. Neither would admit it. Steve went back to his room as soon as they finished with the plan. Both spent more time mulling things over instead of eating.

Dana struggled through the afternoon, glad when it was over. She got through the rest of the week the same way. *Next week should be easier. I won't have to see him every day and fight the memories of us together.*

The next week was lonely and made lonelier by the fact that Cathy and Ken had gone away together. Dana didn't hear from Steve, but she hadn't expected to. Still, he held a big part of her attention. The *Perfect Wedding* squatted in place in her mind and didn't budge. Her mind was made up, but Dana still kept her promise to wait until next week to withdraw.

The Monday after spring break came as expected and it brought beautiful almost-May weather with it. It was wasted on her.

At least the kids would be anxious to share what happened during their week off. She'd have them write essays about it and let them share. Maybe she could catch some of their enthusiasm. Probably not. She went to Cathy's apartment.

"You didn't change your mind, did you?" was how Cathy greeted her.

"No. Please. I don't want to talk about it. Tell me about your week. I need to hear some good news."

"Okay." Cathy began to talk and continued during the ride.

Dana was happy for Cathy, but she couldn't help wishing that she could find a bit of happiness for herself. *I didn't throw away my only chance, did I?* She walked into her school wondering.

She and Steve spoke, but that was it. Neither mentioned lunch. Dana got through the day, more determined than ever to act on her decision.

She wasn't looking forward to the phone call she had to make, but she wanted to get it over with. She practiced deep breathing while she waited for her call to be put through to Noreen.

"I have to withdraw from the contest," Dana blurted as soon as Noreen said hello. "I'll send back the gift card if you'll give me the address."

"Wait a minute. Back up. Withdraw? Why?"

"I wasn't engaged when I entered the contest."

"There's no rule that said you had to be."

"I feel as if I was cheating. Where should I send the gift card?"

"Not so fast. Were you engaged when you and Steve came to the reception?"

"Yes."

"Dana, you were the most charismatic couple there. Your love for each other was so obvious in your words when you each answered our questions."

"I gave Steve back his ring."

"You two had a fight. That's it, isn't it?"

"No. That's not it. I can't let him tie up two years of his life for me."

"According to Lewis, he didn't sound like he was only marrying you because of the contest."

"We've . . ." she swallowed hard. "We've been friends for years."

"I've heard of friendships developing into love."

"Not in this case. He was doing me a favor."

"That's a big favor."

"Yes. That's what I thought. Too big. That's why I can't let him do it. Where should I send the gift card?"

"You're certainly anxious to get rid of it, aren't you? Don't you want to think this over?"

"I have done nothing but think it over each time I get a letter from you. I won't change my mind."

"Dana, I hate for us to lose you." She hesitated. "The card is yours to keep. I'm sorry you decided to drop out. You would have made a beautiful bride and I know it would have been a highly rated episode. I wish you good luck."

PERFECT WEDDING

Dana hung up the phone. She felt as if a heavy weight had been lifted. The small regret at losing Hawaii was nothing compared to the load of guilt that had been weighing her down. In time, she'd get over the hurt. *I'll get there someday,* she promised herself. *I've done without it this long.*

She sighed and went into the living room. She had just sat down when the doorbell rang. *It's probably Cathy coming to sympathize.* She tried to smile as she opened it.

"Steve?"

"I thought we should go out." He hesitated, then stepped inside. Dana stepped back to let him in.

She doesn't want me close. It wasn't so long ago that she was willing to . . . He forced himself to stay relaxed. *I've started this. I have too much to lose if I give up now.*

"Out?"

"Sure. Dinner. To celebrate."

"Celebrate?"

"People celebrate when they get engaged. Why not when they get unengaged? We can celebrate your freedom from me."

"I don't think—"

"Did you call the contest people?"

"Yes."

"Did you withdraw from the competition?"

"Yes."

"See, that's a second reason to celebrate." He hesitated, then took her hand. "Come on. I know you didn't fix your dinner yet. This is on me, not me mooching a dinner from you."

"You never mooched. I invited you."

"So, is that a yes?" *I need that or I'm finished before I get started.*

"Okay. I'll go with you."

At least this would use up some more of the long evening ahead of her.

She followed Steve out to his car. *I'm not sorry that he didn't hold my hand, am I? Why don't I feel happy that he's obviously glad that he's not shackled to me anymore?*

She wrestled with those questions during the ride, but no answers came. She was still waiting for them when she and Steve walked into the restaurant. The questions hadn't receded even after they were seated.

Steve tried to pull her away from her thoughts to get her to order. *Maybe this wasn't such a good idea after all, but what else could I do?*

"Do you want me to order for you?"

"Okay."

Ordering for her was the easy part. He knew what she liked almost as well as she did. Or at least he thought he did.

This is not a good thing, he thought as the waiter left. *She never lets me decide for her. Too bad she didn't let me decide about our engagement. Then I wouldn't be going through this.* He glanced at her. *She looks as if she's some place else. I don't want to think that she wishes she were. She looks like she's beyond pain and into numbness. Man, what a mess.*

They ate with silence as their only companion. Neither acted as if they were celebrating anything.

Finally the waiter was offering them dessert. Dana declined. She just wanted the evening, the whole day, over.

Steve gave the waiter his credit card, then stood.

"Wait a minute," he said to Dana. "Just stay right there."

PERFECT WEDDING

Dana watched as he took a deep breath and reached into his pocket. Then he got down on one knee.

"Dana, I love you with all my heart. Please do me the honor of being my wife."

"Huh?" Dana stared at him as if he had lost his mind. Or as if she had.

"Well? You going to leave me looking stupid?"

"No. I mean yes. I . . ." Dana joined him on the floor. "I . . ." She frowned. "Are you sure you want this?"

"I've never been more sure of anything in my life." He started to touch her but pulled his hand back. "Was that no, you won't marry me?"

"No." She laughed. "It's no, I won't leave you looking stupid. I mean you could never look stupid to me. I mean . . ." She stared at him. "Oh, just kiss me. Please kiss me."

She had barely finished asking when Steve pulled her to him. He pressed his mouth to hers. Then she opened her mouth to him. They made promises to each other with their kiss. Gradually they were aware of the restaurant filling with cheers.

They looked up. It looked as if every patron as well as the wait staff was surrounding them. Dana reddened as Steve helped her up, but she didn't mind the attention. *Steve really wants to marry me. No contest involved. He really loves me.* She grinned as he lifted her hand and slid the ring back into place.

"I think you lost this. Think you can hang on to it this time?"

"I'll never take it off again." She pulled him close and kissed him. Then she wrapped her arm through his. He picked up his card. Amid cheers they walked to the car, but Dana felt as if she were floating.

"Big wedding or not?" Steve asked as they stopped at the car. "You call it and I'll go along with it. Whatever you want as long as you end up as my wife." He lowered his mouth to hers, pulled back, but stood holding her within the circle of his arms.

"I don't care. Just as long as you end up as my husband." She brushed her hands up and down his back. "I love you so much it scares me."

"Baby, you've got nothing to be afraid of. I love you more."

"I doubt that. We could debate this forever. Why don't we settle on showing each other?"

"That we can agree on."

They held hands during the ride to Dana's apartment. They had barely gotten inside when they reached for each other.

"I have missed you." Steve's hands brushed up her back. His mouth found the spot below her ear, the spot that had been aching for his kiss. His hands kneaded the sides of her breasts.

She pushed closer to him as her own hands were busy trying to find a way under his shirt. She felt his hard muscles ripple beneath her hands. She freed a button of his shirt and pressed her lips to his warm skin. His hands on her bare skin told her that he had done the same with her blouse.

"I wish we had worn T-shirts," he rumbled against the side of her mouth. "No buttons." He kissed his way around her mouth, then ended with his lips covering hers. Both sets of hands were busy opening buttons. His shirt dropped to the floor a second before her blouse joined it.

PERFECT WEDDING

"No fair," he said as he undid the clasp of her bra. "But I'll fix it." His mouth found a waiting peak before her bra reached her blouse.

Dana gasped as heat shot from her breast to the place that was waiting for him, had been waiting for him since the last time.

"Please," she whispered.

"Yes," he answered. They grabbed each other's hands and went to the bedroom as if a prize were waiting for them when they got there. In a way, one was.

Both of them thought it had taken too long. They were side by side. Then Steve was on top. Then, after way too much time had passed, he was inside her and she closed around him, welcoming him home.

They spent the too-short night trying to make up for the time they had foolishly lost.

Chapter 25

"Good morning, beautiful." Steve pressed a kiss to Dana's cheek, then pulled her close. "I was afraid I'd never get to say that again."

"And I was afraid I'd never hear it again." She pressed her lips to his chest. "I hate to say this, but don't you have to go home and change?"

"Nope. If I wear what I had on last night, we can show each other our love one more time."

"You are insatiable, but that's all right with me." Dana smiled as she brushed her hand to his waist and lower. "So am I."

Once more they found their secret place together. Too soon, Dana stirred. "We have to get up."

"Speak for yourself. I already am."

"We have to get out of bed. We're going to be late."

"Yeah. You're right."

Steve let her go. "You first in the shower."

"That's it? Use me, then try to lose me?"

"I never want to lose you." He reached for her.

"Stop that. I have to call Cathy and tell her that she's on her own this morning. You and I will have time for that after school."

"I hope the fact that you are right doesn't make you any more happy than it makes me." He stood.

"Believe me, it doesn't. Now go." She watched Steve leave. *The man looks as good going as he does coming,* she thought as she picked up the phone.

"Big wedding or small? How soon can we get married?" Steve asked as they rode to school.

"That's two different questions. As for the first, I can't afford the kind of wedding the show was going to give us, but that's okay. That's not the important part."

"You tell me what you want and I'll help you get it. Some traditions are best abandoned. This will be your one and only wedding. I want it to be perfect." He leaned over and gave her a quick kiss.

"I'm marrying you. That's what will make it perfect."

"Thank you, but I want you to plan on all of the frills you want."

"I want Cathy as my maid of honor, of course. I don't have any other attendants in mind." She glanced at him and frowned. "How about you? How can you pick just one friend?"

"No problem. James and I have been friends since high school. We made a pact a long time ago that we'd stand up for each other."

"Okay. A small reception, I guess. Maybe cake and punch? The guest list will be too long for more than that. We can't leave anybody at school out. And I have a lot of friends at church." She sighed. "There's a lot to do. We have to find a place and . . ."

"Tell you what. The groom always gives the bride a gift. The reception is on me."

"He does? It is?"

"If not, he should." He squeezed her hand. "Anyway, my gift to you will be taking care of the details."

"You don't have to do that. It's the bride's responsibility."

"That's another of those traditions we'll do away with. I'll get Cathy to help me. Trust me on this. I won't disappoint you."

"I know you won't."

"After school today we go get a marriage license," Steve said as he parked. He walked around and opened her door. "I don't want to take a chance on you changing your mind." He kissed her.

"Never again." Dana took his hand and they walked into school like that.

"I see you got the ring back on," Elaine said.

"You noticed?"

"Chile, I don't miss much, especially when a bling-bling is gone missing. You two set a date?"

"ASAP, as they say." A stillness fell over the office. Dana glanced at each one in turn. "No, I am not pregnant, but why should we wait?"

"I'd say let's make it today, if that was possible," Steve added. "I don't see why a license should be required anyway."

"So the government can get more out of your pocket, of course," two of the other teachers said together. Everybody was still laughing as Dana and Steve went down the hall.

"I know I said I'd make it today, but I think we should wait to get married."

"Change your mind already?"

"You know better." He gave her a quick kiss.

PERFECT WEDDING

"We're going to do it right, so we need time to plan. I think we should wait until school is out." He groaned. "I can't believe that I'm suggesting that we wait six weeks to get married. You won't change your mind, Dana, will you?"

"You know me better than that." She eased his mouth to hers. They were still smiling as they separated to go into their classrooms.

Dana ordered lunch from a nearby restaurant. Her smile widened as she thought of the reason why she hadn't brought one today.

The day dragged past, but it finally ended. Steve drove directly to city hall as if the waiting period to get married were longer than three days. Matching grins showed on their faces and they were still in place when, license tucked safely into Steve's pocket, they reached her house. Soon they were showing each other their love all over again.

The next day Dana and Steve met for lunch. This time it wasn't school that was in their conversation.

"I think you should buy your dress today."

"Today?"

"Why wait until the last minute?"

"Six weeks is not the last minute, but if Cathy is free, I'll go today. Of course, it's going to be hard to find her free from Ken, but I have a better chance of her being available on a Thursday instead of a Friday." She laughed. "She and Ken might beat us to the altar."

"Not unless they already have a license and don't want a big wedding."

"I feel as if I'm in a race."

"No race. Everybody gets to win." Steve grinned. "I need Cathy's number. We have to get the details together."

Dana wrote the number and gave it to him. "You're sure you want to do this without me?"

"Positive. I think, between us, Cathy and I can plan a reception that you can be proud of."

"Okay."

"Also, I have some stuff to do, so I won't see you until tomorrow and then only at school. I signed up for a new basketball contest. We scheduled a meeting for tonight." He frowned. "Tomorrow night, too. Saturday we play in Reading, so we planned to leave Friday. Look, baby. I can probably find somebody to take my place."

"No, don't do that." She placed a hand on his arm. "We have the rest of our lives. Go ahead."

"You sure?"

"I'm sure." She smiled. "Besides, we need time apart so we can get some sleep."

"Yeah, I guess you're right."

Dana called Cathy on her cell phone and made arrangements to meet her at home.

Steve dropped Dana off and she waited for Cathy. They left right away for a bridal shop not far away.

"You know what style you want?" Cathy asked along the way.

"I don't have a clue, but I'll know it when I see it."

Four hours and six shops later, a grinning Dana walked with Cathy back to her car.

"Girl, this must be as hard as shopping for a

PERFECT WEDDING

house. I had no idea there were so many different choices out there," Cathy said.

"But I found the perfect gown."

"Yes, you did. In addition to finding my bridesmaid gown for your wedding, I did a little preliminary shopping for my wedding gown." She reached over and hugged Dana. "Thanks for letting me pick out my dress."

"You're the one who has to wear it. Makes sense to me. I thought the fit of my gown was all right, but I went along with the saleswoman who said it needed a little alteration." Dana fed into the traffic on the Schuylkill Expressway.

"You'll be an advertisement for her shop. They want everybody to think it's perfect."

"But I wanted to show it to Steve."

"Uh-uh. Bad luck. Probably bad vibes, too. The groom doesn't see the wedding dress until his bride comes to him wearing it."

"I am so excited. I can't wait."

"You don't have a choice. Steve has big plans to surprise you."

"You're right." She grinned. "Isn't he sweet?"

"Almost as sweet as Ken."

"I think we have to agree to disagree on that point."

"Agreed." Cathy laughed and Dana joined her.

They were silent as Dana left the expressway and still as she drove up Lincoln Drive. "Okay. Take my mind off me and tell me about you. Made any plans?" she said as she parked.

"Come on in. I'll tell you about it while I find something for us to eat. Wedding gown shopping works up an appetite."

"That plus the fact that we are way past dinnertime."

They laughed as they went to Cathy's apartment.

"Okay. Here it is," Cathy said as they made sandwiches. "Kenny would fly to Vegas tomorrow, but his mother said he'd better not get married where she can't see him. We haven't set a date yet. It will have to be before football season, though."

"I know that's not your idea."

"Not really. It's kind of a necessity."

"You know you have to explain." Dana took her plate to the table and sat.

"Well, when you're working for the organization, you have to go with their schedule." Cathy fixed her with a stare.

"Huh?" Dana's sandwich stopped before it reached her mouth.

"Kenny is taking a job with the Eagles." Cathy's smile stretched across her face. "He'll be part of the coaching staff. He always wanted to coach for a pro team. Now's his chance."

"That is fantastic." Dana reached over and grabbed Cathy's hand.

"Do you know what that means?"

"Tickets for all of the games for your near and dear friends?"

"That too."

"Really? No lie?"

"Would I dare to kid an Eagles fanatic?"

"You know I'm gonna let that slide. Was this a surprise?"

"I knew Ken wanted to coach. I was afraid he'd get a job in another city and I'd have to move."

"Ain't life great? We both found our perfect man."

"Oh yeah."

As they ate, each was thinking about her own wedding.

Chapter 26

Time crept past slower than an arthritic turtle, but the chaos of the end of school was over and Dana's wedding day finally arrived. They had set the date as the first Saturday after the end of the school year. The morning came as a perfect, wonderful Saturday meant for a wedding.

"You are a beautiful, radiant bride," Cathy told Dana. She made a final adjustment of the short veil.

"I didn't think this day would ever come. Six weeks. Six long, long weeks." Dana straightened the lace around her neck. "You don't think this gown is too much, do you?" She stared in the full-length mirror and frowned. "All of this lace. And so many tiny pearls. Do you think any oysters are left intact?"

"Yes, it's too much. Shall we slip out the side door and take it back?"

"You really think it's too much?" Dana frowned

PERFECT WEDDING

and turned sideways. "I didn't get the train the saleswoman was trying to sell me."

"Dana, I'm joking." Cathy released an exaggerated sigh. "Note to self, never tease a woman who is about to get married."

"Yeah, I am. About to get married, I mean." Dana's frown disappeared and a smile took its place.

"Are you ready or are you waiting for Steve to change his mind?"

"Yes, I am and no, I'm not."

"Believe it or not, I understood that." Cathy peeked into the hall and nodded. The music began. She gave Dana a careful hug, smoothed the front of her own dress, and left the room.

I can't believe this is real, Dana thought as she waited for her cue. Then she didn't think of anything except Steve waiting for her.

The pews were full, but Dana didn't notice. Steve, waiting for her at the end of the center aisle, held her full attention. Finally she reached him and took her place beside him. The love shining in his eyes met the same glowing in her own.

They repeated the traditional vows and Dana was glad they hadn't opted for writing their own. There was no way she could have focused on anything except Steve.

Reverend Dent pronounced them husband and wife. He barely gave Steve permission to kiss the bride before they complied. Applause filled the church.

In a daze, Dana stood beside Steve and accepted the congratulations and best wishes of those forming a line.

"Picture time," Cathy said after the line was gone. "Fairmont Park, here we come."

"Okay." Dana and Steve stood with their arms around each other, gazing into each other's eyes.

"We can't do that unless we leave," Cathy prompted.

"Oh. Right." Steve said, but neither he nor Dana moved.

Cathy gestured to Kenny.

"A little help here, please. I can't move them by myself."

She grabbed Dana's hand and led them to the door. Kenny gave Steve a little push.

"This is why the bride and groom ride in a limo. If it was left up to him to drive, they'd never leave the church."

"Absolutely," Kenny agreed as he walked behind them.

They stopped at the car, but Dana and Steve just stood staring at each other.

"Okay, time for the big guns. If you two don't get your pictures taken, then go to the reception. You can't leave on your honeymoon. How's that?"

The couple turned to stare at her. Then they got into the car.

It wasn't long before the photographer finished and they were on their way to the reception.

"I hope you're pleased with what we did," Steve said as the limo parked outside an upscale restaurant.

"Anything will be fine." Dana looked around. "We're having the reception here? What happened to cake and punch at church?"

"My basketball buddy owns this place. He's taking care of us."

PERFECT WEDDING

Steve kissed Dana, then followed her from the car. He took her hand and led her inside.

They got to a private room and he turned her to him. He kissed her quickly. "I love you, baby."

"I love you more."

"We'll see about that later." He kissed her again. "Let's show our friends that we haven't forgotten about them." He opened the door. Dana stood in stunned silence.

Linen-draped tables were placed around the room. Vases of blue and white flowers were centered on each table. The people were mingling, helping themselves to the hors d'oeuvres on several tables scattered throughout the room. Waiters and waitresses circulated, offering hot canapés. Two fountains bubbled punch. Blue and white crepe paper draped the sides of the room, pinned in place every so often by paper wedding bells. A trio on a stage provided soft jazz background music.

"Oh." Dana stood in the doorway, her eyes as wide as a kid's on Christmas morning.

"Is that a pleased 'oh' or a disappointed one?"

"Wow."

"I guessed it's a pleased one." Steve kissed her cheek. "Come on, Mrs. Rollings, let's show our guests that we're here." He put his arm around and urged her into the room. As soon as they were seen, greetings were shouted.

"If my hands weren't full, I'd be leading the applause," Mrs. Wilson yelled.

Dana and Steve made their way to the head table. As Dana walked, she noticed groups of the kids from their classes scattered with the adults.

"Good. You invited the kids."

"I couldn't leave them out."

Then Cathy took charge. "Okay, people. Let's be seated. The reason for us being here has finally arrived." She held up her hand. "I know. I was with them, but I hurried them along as best I could. If not for me, they'd still be back there standing in church staring at each other." Laughter and the rustle of people moving escorted them to their seats.

Happy conversations mixed together as the meal was served. From time to time a glass tinkled and Steve and Dana kissed.

After the traditional dance, the throwing of the bouquet and garter, the cutting of the four-tiered cake, as soon as decency allowed, the newlyweds left.

"You're quiet. Was there something that you didn't like?" Steve asked as they rode away.

"I'm so, so overwhelmed. I was ready for cake and punch. I never expected this much." She shook her head. "It was all so wonderful." She wiped her eyes.

"Hey, none of that," Steve said as he gently moved her hand away. He wiped the tears with the pads of his thumbs, then kissed her. "We can't have a teary bride. The folks at the hotel will think you're unhappy."

"Unhappy? I couldn't be happier. I didn't need the reality show. I just *had* the perfect wedding. Thank you." She brushed her lips against his.

"You can show me your thanks later."

"It's a deal." She looked outside. "Aren't we going to my house to get my things?"

"Cathy took care of packing for you. As we speak, our things are waiting in the bridal suite." He kissed her. "I think we can qualify for that."

"Where are we going?" Dana looked out the window.

"I booked the suite at a hotel near the airport. We have an early flight."

"You never told me where we're going on our honeymoon."

"Does it matter?"

"Not as long as it's with you."

"You better believe that I'll be with you. I'll be with you for the rest of our lives."

"I'll hold you to that."

"I'll tell you where we're going after we check in. That way, if you're disappointed, I can take your mind off your disappointment."

"I know you'd be good at that, but I won't be unhappy with your choice. I told you that anywhere you decided upon would be okay with me. I meant it." She kissed him. "But I want to know as soon as we get to the room. This curiosity is killing me. Only satisfaction can end it."

"I think I can manage the satisfaction part." He kissed her. "I'll also tell you our destination."

They stole kisses during the entire ride to the hotel. They were escorted to their room and finally were alone as husband and wife.

"Okay," Dana said as soon as the door was shut. "Okay. Tell me. Which island are we going to?"

"I guess I won't be able to interest you in anything else until I do." He stared at her. "Actually, it's more like four islands." He waited for it to sink in.

"Four islands?" Her eyes widened. "You didn't."

"If I didn't, those folks sold me some counterfeit tickets." He grinned. "How about it? Are you ready to get leid? That's l-e-i-d, not l-a-i-d."

Dana's eyes filled with tears. "You didn't have to do this. Home would have been all right. I would have been happy with you anywhere."

"I know." He wiped her eyes. "That's what makes me even happier to give you this."

"Oh, Steve."

"Home can wait until we get back in three weeks. Now, are you ready to get laid? That's l-a-i-d."

"Any time, any place, as long as it's with you."

They wrapped themselves in love and each other's arms and put the finishing touches on a perfect wedding.

SIZZLING ROMANCE BY
Rochelle Alers

__HIDEAWAY	1-58314-179-0	$5.99US/$7.99CAN
__PRIVATE PASSIONS	1-58314-151-0	$5.99US/$7.99CAN
__JUST BEFORE DAWN	1-58314-103-0	$5.99US/$7.99CAN
__HARVEST MOON	1-58314-056-5	$4.99US/$6.99CAN
__SUMMER MAGIC	1-58314-012-3	$4.99US/$6.50CAN
__HAPPILY EVER AFTER	0-7860-0064-3	$4.99US/$6.99CAN
__HEAVEN SENT	0-7860-0530-0	$4.99US/$6.50CAN
__HOMECOMING	1-58314-271-1	$6.99US/$9.99CAN
__RENEGADE	1-58314-272-X	$6.99US/$9.99CAN
__NO COMPROMISE	1-58314-270-3	$6.99US/$9.99CAN
__VOWS	0-7860-0463-0	$4.99US/$6.50CAN

Available Wherever Books Are Sold!

Visit our website at **www.arabesque.com.**

Put a Little Romance in Your Life With
Bettye Griffin

__At Long Last Love $4.99US/$6.50CAN
   0-7860-0610-2

__Closer Than Close $6.99US/$9.99CAN
   1-58314-276-2

__From This Day Forward $6.99US/$9.99CAN
   1-58314-275-4

__Love Affair $5.99US/$7.99CAN
   1-58314-138-3

__A Love of Her Own $4.99US/$6.99CAN
   1-58314-053-0

__Prelude to a Kiss $5.99US/$7.99CAN
   1-58314-139-1

Available Wherever Books Are Sold!

Visit our website at **www.kensington.com**.